MICHAEL BORZ

THE BLOOD CODE

BOOK 1

MAGIC DOME BOOKS

The Blood Code
Book #1
Copyright © Michael Borz 2025
Cover Art © Ivan Khivrenko 2025
Cover designer: Vladimir Manyukhin
English translation copyright © Boris Smirnov 2025
Published by Magic Dome Books, 2025
ISBN: 978-80-7702-174-6
All Rights Reserved

Table of Contents:

Chapter 1

THE FIREWOOD CRACKLED SOOTHINGLY, the gusting wind whipping the flames into a merry dance. It would have been a peaceful scene, one to relish and relax to, were it not for one small detail: This was an execution and the executioners were about to burn a man alive... Me, that is.

A panel of twelve high inquisitors had gathered to see the sentence carried out. Half of them were praying for me, while the other half cursed me. The foolishness of it all made me chuckle. They were like a gaggle of stooges, getting in each other's way. Neither their prayers nor their curses would do them any good in the end, yet that didn't keep the judges' expressions from radiating triumph and arrogance. They were convinced that they had defeated me at last.

They were far from right about that, though why bother telling them?

I let them believe as they wished. I neither resisted when they inscribed seals on my body to restrain my powers, nor when they'd condemned me and pronounced my sentence. I always knew that it would end like this and I had made my preparations.

Even if blood magic was unavailable to me at the moment, I still had some power left. The first thing I did was desensitize my nerve endings so my body wouldn't feel the flames' blaze. That way my mind could remain sharp. I had activated blood beacons across a dozen of the nearest planes to draw my soul. I was curious to see if my escape would work. No one had ever attempted such complex blood magic before, but long ago an oracle had issued a prophecy and I believed it would now come true.

"I wonder," I said to my executioners, "are you overconfident or just plain stupid? Do you think my death will ensure your own safety?"

Some of the judges stuttered in their chants, while others gritted their teeth in anger. They didn't like that I wasn't begging for mercy or screaming in agony.

"No, no, don't stop on my account — keep going! The longer I burn, the weaker grow the seals upon the nether plane."

Ah there! A few more of them went silent at my words.

"But my seals on the nether plane are the least of your worries, right? You've never cared about anyone but yourselves. So, once my soul leaves this mortal body, you're all in for a real treat! A death curse from a blood mage will be just a little memento to remember me by."

I mocked them without revealing all my cards. It was delightful to see the fear, to revel in the confusion and doubt on my enemies' faces.

They could all screw themselves — there'd be no happy endings for them after their treachery!

"Don't believe me?" A wicked grin spread across my face. "You should!"

Suddenly the menial stoking the flames closest to me began shaking. The capillaries in his head began to burst and blood began streaming from every orifice.

"Aaa-aah-aaah!" he screamed, collapsing.

"Do you believe me now?" I cackled maniacally. "All of you are already doomed!"

I watched their faces twist in horror — a magnificent sight!

The fire had consumed the lower half of my body but I still wasn't dying. I couldn't feel the pull of the beacons, as if the planes available for my soul had suddenly flickered out of existence. Time was running out. The judges' heads were swelling, blood filling them like overripe plums. Any second now, they would start popping. It was a shame to die of course, but at least I'd get a lovely fireworks display on my way out.

The seal on my left hand holding my powers back began to smolder with black fire. It was gathering the last dregs of my gift, ripping it painfully from my very soul.

Through my agony, I heard an unfamiliar voice.

"Do you want to live?" it said.

"I do!" I wasn't sure whether the voice was a hallucination of my fading mind or a whisper of hope from another plane.

"Then you owe me, and don't you forget it."

At those words the world went dark.

* * *

"Come on out, Komarin! Come on out, you little brat!" a nasty little voice sounded from somewhere nearby. "Your mosquito god won't save you now! I'll end you quickly, in the name of the Rat!"

What is this nonsense? They couldn't even burn me properly and now they have the gall to berate me. Ugh! Memories of the fire, the inquisitors and the twelve failed blood beacons came flooding back amid the pounding in my head. Yet it seemed I had survived somehow...

"Komarrrrin!" the voice echoed across the marshes. "Come out and die like a man! It's all you have left..."

The marshes indeed... It was damp here, the muck squishing underfoot with every step, an omnipresent buzz of insects, moss-covered trunks, mud and turgid water all around. Not that I was complaining. My ass still smarted from the ring of fire and the damp landscape before me now seemed as welcoming as home. Hell, I'd be happy to ribbit like a frog if it meant I could stay here.

The only trouble was that something told me that this murderous voice was intent on killing *me*. Dying twice in one day? Even I didn't deserve that.

My body finally regained sensation — and for the first time in five years, I felt my blood powers, albeit weakly. I looked at my left hand, where that cursed seal still smoldered with black fire, and started in shock: My hand was thin, delicate — Blood save me — was it a girl's hand?! Oh that would be a hilarious turn of events! To verify, I reached down with my other hand. But no, I was still a man — albeit not fully grown yet, but that was only a matter of time.

Next, barely holding back my excitement, I reached out to my blood sense. It responded immediately like a cheap floozy seeing a shiny coin. My senses sharpened. I felt faint heartbeats on the edge of my consciousness. One of my pursuers was about thirty meters away, another was circling around, sixty meters out.

Huh, but this was a nice surprise: I sensed blood nearby, fading, erasing a life. Thick and viscous, it begged to be tasted, to share its final memory. Looking about, I quickly found the man in a long black cloak, dying among the ferns. I couldn't resist the pleasure of sampling the blood from the assassin's gurgling throat.

As soon as I did so, the last half hour of his life flashed before my eyes. It wasn't much, but it was a start. He was part of a squad hunting a boy: deathly-pale and red-eyed, thin as a reed and stubborn. After all, who would flee into a swamp to escape his killers? Still, the kid wasn't entirely hopeless. He did manage to conjure a small summoning circle and even slit his killer's throat to power it. Though he got a dirk in his liver for his trouble — but that was a minor detail now. His blood seemed to have held enough magical affinity to summon help... Or perhaps the local deity had intervened.

One of my pursuers' voices echoed nearby, interrupting my thoughts. I pulled the dirk out of my abdomen and slipped quietly into the swamp water, using a reed to breathe through. I was just in time. The assassin found his companion's body and bent over to check if he was still alive. Couldn't have asked for a better moment. I surfaced and my dirk sliced through his Achilles tendon like paper, tasting fresh blood. The man collapsed like a felled tree. There's no running away with that kind of wound. Not that there'd be any point in running. He'd just die tired. My next strike drove the dirk into his gut. The hunter-turned-prey squealed like a pig in a slaughterhouse. Time to end it. I cut his throat and carved open his chest to get to his heart before his soul could leave his body.

Silently thanking whoever had summoned me to this place, I sliced into the heart.

"Accept this humble offering," I muttered, "a hunter who raised his hand against your follower." A warm breeze of grace came by way of reply from the local deity.

Sampling this one's blood left me a bit disappointed. He was just another hired cutthroat, but at least he had something to tell me. The hit squad were hunting a certain Mikhail Yuryevich Komarin, the sole remaining heir of the maybe not ancient, but nonetheless aristocratic Komarin family. The family had earned its status and title a few centuries ago for its loyal service to the Emperor. For three generations, the family had distinguished itself in the espionage business. But in recent years, they had fallen out of favor, retreated to their family estate in the swamps of the Novgorod region, and kept as low a profile as they could manage. That hadn't saved them however.

One by one, over the course of a decade, Mikhail's grandfather, father, mother, and a couple of uncles died under mysterious, sometimes violent circumstances. And now, on the day when the last heir of the Komarin bloodline came of age, the hunters had come for young Misha.

But I was distracted! What about the third assassin? Hmm. The third one wasn't so simple. He was hopping around the swamp chaotically, like a frog, appearing in one place then vanishing and reappearing in another. This wasn't a good sign. It seemed that his locations were forming one large summoning circle. If only I had a drop of his blood to work with...

"Ask and ye shall receive," a deep, self-important voice sounded in my head. 'Sblood! The local deity had shown up to the party after all.

A mosquito began buzzing near my ear, its high-pitched whine grating on my nerves. I swatted at it absentmindedly, though generally I left such bloodsuckers alone — having been one myself in my previous life.

"Nice try, but she didn't come to feast on you," the local patron deity spoke again. "She's brought you a drop of blood, as you requested."

"Well, aren't you helpful." I smiled, extending the back of my hand. The mosquito landed for just a second before flying away, leaving behind a drop of blood that was instantly absorbed into my skin. Blood to blood. The gift gave me at least some information.

Hmm... Curious. My last pursuer was gifted like me, also dabbling in blood magic, though he mostly dealt in curses. His abilities were about as strong as a village healer's, but he made up for it with his zeal. He was currently conjuring a curse over this poor swamp, but for what? To end the local lineage... To curse these lands... Only to later buy them up for a pittance, along with the noble title they conferred...

A nice little scam, but a mosquito's proboscis would save my lands from this villain.

He was just about to start powering the curse's mana contours and I was happy to help. Focusing on my opponent's blood, I slipped into his consciousness. The connection was weak, superficial due to the holy seal on my hand, but there was no time for regrets. I focused on the task at hand.

Oh, but how shaky he was, his hands all trembling! Who tries to conjure curses with this kind of tremor? Why, he could die... and in this case, he absolutely should. One wrong move and thanks to my efforts, the curse's contour shifted and the mana powering the curse began to flow from its caster, instead of the mysterious nearby mana pool he'd meant to use.

It didn't take long. In a matter of minutes the caster's body had shriveled and desiccated into a mummy.

Scanning the area again with my blood sense, I detected no more heartbeats. The time had come to talk.

Experience told me that soul transfers between planes didn't happen by random chance. They happened when some divine being was really in a tight spot. Now I just needed to figure out who I owed for this second chance that had been given me. I might be a blood mage, dark spawn, blah blah blah, but blood isn't a tool that any amoral bastard can use. The Blood Code wouldn't forgive such things — so I needed to find out the terms of the deal and start negotiating.

"Very perceptive," replied the voice in my head.

"Whom do I have the honor of speaking with?" I decided to be polite. After all, it was a deity who had saved me from the pyre and subdued my seal.

"I am called Aedes," the voice responded, now businesslike, "the Mosquito god of this world. For the last three hundred years, I have watched over the Komarin family, who are now being hunted by certain individuals. And you?"

"Sorry, but didn't you check who you were saving from the fire before transporting me to your plane?" I asked, genuinely surprised.

"It didn't matter to me who you were or what your name was. What mattered was that you had the right abilities, principles and brains for the job. I didn't have time to deal with the rest. Mikhail was about to die."

I liked Aedes' straightforwardness — no pomp, just direct and to the point. Working with someone like this could be enjoyable.

"Are the certain individuals you mentioned entangled in human disputes or divine ones?" I asked, trying to gauge the size of the mess I'd ended up in. Whatever it was, I guess it was better than being roasted to a crisp on a pyre.

"I thought it was a human matter at first, but considering they've wiped out two of my noble lines in the last seven hundred years, I'm not so sure anymore," Aedes replied pensively.

Indeed, two extinguished families was not a good record for a god. It was easy to imagine that with a record like that no family would want to be under this deity's protection. In the divine circles this would entail a blow to his reputation and leave him faithless — and powerless — in the long run. I understood his motives well enough. I'd gone through something similar myself. Now it was clear why Aedes had pulled over my soul from the other plane. He needed not only my skills but also my experience. Well, looks like we'll be fighting together from here on out.

"What do you need from me?"

"Nothing too crazy, really. Just live and enjoy

your life. Have as many kids as you can to continue the lineage and replenish my followers. You know how it works: The more believers I have, the stronger I get," Aedes explained. "And the stronger I am, the more perks you'll get from my protection."

"Sounds good to me," I replied. Then I held up my hand. "What about this seal? It's… um… really cramping my style."

"That's easy. The faster you get me more believers, the faster I'll gain enough strength to dispel that seal. At the moment, I can only weaken its effects. By the way, whose toes did you step on in your former plane to not only get sealed up like this, but to have them pursuing you across the plane boundaries?" my patron asked, curiosity in his voice.

"Oh, basically everyone's toes all at once," I grimaced, recalling the last few years of my life. "There aren't any light-worshiping zealots around here perchance?"

"Ugh! What a distasteful thing to suggest," Aedes started at my question. "No, we don't have darkness and light in this plane. We're all totems here — patron deities of families that we protect. Cross one of them, and they'll hunt you down just as mercilessly as those… holy zealots who are after you. So, try to keep your head down for a while and avoid stepping on any toes. I expended a lot of my power to get you here and then I expended some more to mask your seal, so I've got nothing left to cover you with."

I took his warning to heart. I didn't plan on stirring up a hornet's nest in my new plane. I'd need to figure out the lay of the land here first.

"Can I summon a mosquito whenever I want?" I asked, intrigued by a skill that seemed pretty useful to a blood mage. The possibilities were exhilarating.

"Oh, that? Sure, no problem. You won't be able to manifest a mosquito, but the nearest ones will always respond to your summons, just like they do for me," Aedes replied. "I've got to go now. You can get the ring from your granny."

"My granny? I thought little Misha here was an orphan."

"Misha's not the orphan — *you* are! And you'd better get used to it!" Aedes corrected me. "As for your granny..." His voice filled with admiration. "Well, if she were fifty years younger, I'd court her myself. You'll like her — you won't find a bloodsucker like her anywhere else."

The feeling of the divine presence faded from my mind. I salvaged what I could from the memories of the assassins and then set off to celebrate my new birthday. It was nice to sense that the blood magic was working and Misha's memories were gradually merging with mine. Bless that Aedes! The new knowledge wasn't overwhelming, coming gradually in manageable doses. If I focused on a question, the answer, if there was one, would eventually pop up in my memory as if my own.

* * *

Well, what could I say? My new estate, Hmarevo, was impressive indeed. It wasn't the country cottage with carved shutters I had imagined, but a regular keep with thick walls, corner towers and embrasures for archers. The whole edifice was surrounded by a stockade and a moat of brackish water, possibly fed by the swamp or some nearby stream.

The surprises started as soon as I reached the drawbridge over the moat. Here I encountered two desiccated, bloodless corpses in long black cloaks.

Their tongues had been ripped out and their eyes gouged. I didn't feel sorry for them however. The guys who'd tried to drown me in the swamp had worn cloaks just like these. And that meant that these two had met a fitting end.

As I moved forward, the number of bodies increased. Climbing the porch steps, I already knew what to expect. Walking through the hall into one of the smaller sitting rooms, I met the author of all this carnage. A young, blond beauty in a crimson-black dress was lounging by the fireplace, finishing her meal with an air of majesty. The black cloaked assassin in her grasp wasn't even struggling anymore, just quietly moaning as bloody tears streamed down his face.

"So this is Mikhail's granny, huh?" I thought, enchanted. She was gorgeous, absolutely stunning!

It wasn't hard to figure out that this was the last surviving matron of the Komarin line — not with three portraits of her hanging over the fireplace: one of her as a young maiden, looking just as she did now; another, of a luscious beauty who knew her worth; and the last, of a deadly, mature aristocrat whose gaze would've made the inquisitors from my former life start crossing themselves.

And Aedes was right, she really was quite the bloodsucker! She had drained over a dozen assassins in one go and that was no small feat. She wasn't sipping a drop at a time like a mosquito after all. It seemed clear to me that "Nan" hadn't fed in a while and the present feast had wound back the clock on her physical appearance by many decades.

"Bon appétit, Agatha Petrovna," I offered, with the politeness her age and station merited, though frankly, I wouldn't have minded being polite to her somewhere in the bedroom on silk sheets. After all, she wasn't my real grandmother — just adopted.

She looked up at me and with a dainty gesture wiped the blood from the corners of her mouth before licking her lips in an incredibly seductive way.

"And good health to you, my dear grandson!" she giggled, almost drunkenly. "What's brought you to possess our little Misha?"

I raised an eyebrow in silent curiosity, wishing to hear her guess first.

"No need to be coy. I felt the soul of the last heir of the Komarin bloodline depart this plane. And that means our patron deity managed to swap someone new in at the last moment," Agatha Petrovna said, looking at her barely living "meal" with revulsion before snapping his neck with a gentle flick of her wrist. Her next movement was one I sensed rather than saw. In less than a heartbeat, the vampire appeared before me, baring her extended fangs in a predatory grin. But by then, my dirk was already pressed to her throat, suggesting we exchange pleasantries in a more... cordial way.

Agatha was slightly shorter than me, so I had to make a conscious effort to meet her gaze and not get distracted by her nubile, pointed breasts.

"You are to give me a ring," I said with a charming smile.

"Maybe you're not useless after all," Agatha muttered to herself, reaching boldly into her cleavage and pulling out an ancient adamantine signet ring with a mosquito engraved on it. "Misha would've soiled himself from fear by now."

"No need to be insulting..." I shook my head, defending my body's previous owner. "He did manage to perform a minor summoning and even sent his killer to the afterlife in the process."

"It didn't do him any good," Agatha said, stepping back and twirling the family ring around her finger. "I'll have to keep an eye on you. You need to go to the academy in the nether plane, while I stir things up here a bit."

"I'm afraid that's not happening," I recalled Aedes' warning about the zealots scouring the nether plane for my long-suffering soul. "The nether plane is off-limits to me at the moment."

Agatha raised an eyebrow in surprise, as if perceiving who I really was for the first time — and then lunged into battle. Her claws lengthened, flashing dangerously close to my throat. Parrying her strikes as best I could, I noticed she wasn't fighting at full strength, holding back deliberately. Our sparring session lasted less than five minutes but drained every bit of stamina from my new body. Even with my dueling experience helping me anticipate her attacks, I couldn't always react in time. In short, I was weak.

Nan stopped fighting as suddenly as she had started.

"Fine, since you can't go to the nether plane, I'll send you to the Mosquitoes instead," she said, spinning the ring around her manicured finger. "You'll get this in three months — if you're still alive then, that is."

Her suggestive, malicious smile gave me a bad feeling.

"Who are the Mosquitoes?"

"A private school, founded by your great-grandfather, far from prying eyes and... beyond the reach of the imperial law enforcement agencies," Agatha replied with a warmth and nostalgia that caught me off guard. "Its graduates are trained to be highly sought-after specialists in certain... exclusive circles. Our services are obscenely expensive."

A cult? An assassins' guild? Out loud, I asked something else entirely:

"Aren't you supposed to be preserving the family line? Isn't that your goal?"

"If you become one of the Mosquitoes' graduates, your and our family's odds of survival will increase significantly. The ring would be a hindrance there. The school enforces total anonymity among its pupils, as well as an utter absence of connections to their patron deities."

I pretended to think it over, though a lack of connection to Aedes didn't scare me. My own experience and blood powers would be more than enough, and I could use the time to bulk up physically. Suddenly, I noticed Agatha's expression change. She hastily pulled another ring with a black stone from her finger and tossed it to me. As I caught it instinctively, a multicolored portal bloomed into existence before me.

"Tell them Agatha sent you!" I heard Nan say, as she practically hurled me into the portal. She began to say something else — but a deafening explosion drowned out her words. As the shockwave rushed in our direction, the portal's vortex snapped shut behind me.

Chapter 2

Cobblestones met me as I tumbled out of the portal and crumpled into a roll to soften my fall. In the next instant, an axe blade came down right next to my head, striking a sheet of sparks from the stone floor.

What the...?! Scrabbling, I rolled away again as the axe blade came down once more on the spot where I'd been. A battle was raging all around me: Four warriors were being pressed into an ever tighter circle, each one facing two or three opponents at once. The portal had disgorged me right in the middle of this melee. I didn't even have time to stand up — having to keep rolling and tumbling around like a crazed squirrel over the bloodstained stones.

Hmm, blood eh? That's good though. Fresh blood, not yet clotted. As I rolled, my skin absorbed the substances of other lives, weaving them into an intoxicating cocktail of excitement, adrenaline, despair, desire and even lust — overwhelming my self-control in the process. Red fog blanketed my vision as the bloodlust set in, completely shutting off my mind and leaving me at the mercy of my raw reflexes.

When I came to, I found myself resting on a wooden bunk, battered and bruised. The grim stone walls, the lack of windows and the crude latrine in the corner suggested I was in a solitary cell rather than a healer's tent.

The crimson fog obscured my short term memory. Not a good sign. The last time I'd lost control like this was in my youth, back when I couldn't keep others' blood separate from my own. Could it be that one of the combatants had bloodlust in his blood? Was that what had overwhelmed me so completely? At least Misha's body was still weak or I might have done some real damage to those around me.

My vision was still blurry, but at least this place didn't look like a torture chamber. There was, however, a bald man sitting across from me in a black military uniform without any insignia on it, his image doubling and merging back into itself constantly.

His face was utterly forgettable, the kind you'd never remember even if you saw it multiple times a day. The only noticeable feature to him was a strange tattoo on his neck, partially hidden by his uniform.

"Well, well, welcome back, ya little wiggler," he

hissed in a flat voice. "Who sent you?"

A good question. Judging by Agatha's warning, it wasn't a good idea to throw about any family names around here, so I had only one option.

"Agatha sent me," I said, slipping the black stone ring off my pinkie finger and holding it out to him.

The tattooed man took the ring and turned it over thoughtfully in his hand. No sigil, no divine symbol. Just an ordinary, unremarkable woman's ring.

"Why didn't she bring you herself?"

"She said she was going to 'stir things up a bit' back home," I quoted Mikhail's grandma verbatim, hoping the explosion at the last minute hadn't been her popping after her bloody glut. Adopted or not, she was still family. "She promised to come to my graduation."

"A bold statement," came the whispered reply. "What were you on during that fight?"

"I was dazed, that's all," I replied honestly. "Some imbecile almost cleft my head from my body several times and my vision went red. That's all I remember." That was the truth, although as ever, the devil was in the details.

The bald man stared at me intensely for a minute but didn't press further.

"All right. Get dressed," he said, tossing me a heavy paper bag. Inside I found a full set of clothes, including underwear, field gear, a belt, gloves and a scarf. A pair of high-laced boots was waiting by the bed. "You'll spend the rest of tonight in the barracks and tomorrow we'll see what you're made of in the field."

I didn't need to be asked twice. Covered with nothing but a thin sheet, I was already freezing, so I got dressed in record time, only struggling with my boot laces. The bald man smirked to himself, observing me from the corner of his eye. I could hardly believe at how quickly Misha's body took to the unfamiliar clothes.

We were about to leave when the bald man suddenly turned and demanded, "Show me your left wrist." I didn't resist and complied obediently, feeling a thin chain snap around my wrist. "Never take it off. It alters your appearance."

"Do the others have these too?" I asked, examining the bluish artifact.

"Yes. Anonymity is one of our school's core principles. You're lucky you were covered in blood during the battle and no one got a good look at your face."

I didn't ask any further questions. We left the cellar, which I guessed served as a holding cell and barely paid attention as we made our way to the barracks. My exhaustion and numerous injuries were taking their toll. The brawl had been a free for all — every man for himself — and I had gotten cut up pretty badly. However, thanks to the adrenaline and the blood I'd absorbed, the worst of the wounds had already healed over with scabs. The rest were bearable, mere flesh wounds. Thankfully the locals hadn't skimped on bandages either, making sure I wouldn't give up my ghost to Aedes prematurely.

It was the dead of night outside. Our footsteps crunched on the gravel. The wind carried the scent of pine and resin. Occasionally, the ancient trees creaked, blending with the croaking frogs in the nearby swamp. The forest was old and mighty. Although Mikhail's memories contained some knowledge of this place, I couldn't access them fully just yet.

We arrived at the barracks, a low stone building with a tiled roof. Inside, it was surprisingly cool — not as cold as outside, but enough to make me rethink taking my clothes off. The dim light from the ceiling lamps revealed rows of bunks along the walls in which the local cadets were deep in slumber. Some snored, others groaned quietly in pain. It seemed treatment wasn't a priority here, though Mikhail's memories did flicker with recollections of miracle elixirs and healing mages who could pull someone back from death's door. Apparently, I'd been lucky: If I hadn't healed myself, no one else would have. But that was the nice thing about blood magic. It was incredibly versatile, and I'd never trade it for elemental magic.

The bald man gestured to the nearest empty bunk by the entrance. "Settle in. Reveille is at dawn," he said, and as he left, I barely caught his parting words: "Try and survive your injuries until then."

I took his warning seriously and spent the next four hours before dawn wide awake. I was feeling decent after my blood-fueled blackout, but I couldn't say the same for my bunkmate. The girl next to me was shivering so badly her teeth rattled loud enough to shame a woodpecker.

It was hard to ignore the noise. I had planned to spend those four hours productively, sifting through Mikhail's memories. Since I was already fully dressed, my decision to share my blanket with her was spontaneous. As I covered the girl, she curled up in a ball and I noted her fragile frame and blond hair sticking out from under her blanket. Then I felt something else — a sense of recognition, a vague echo of intuition. Hawthorn. A healing herb for treating wounds. A glance into Mikhail's memories explained what hawthorn had to do with the girl.

It turned out the gods in this plane weren't just animals, birds or insects like Aedes — they could also be plants. Families with plant deities were usually weaker and served as vassals to the stronger clans. My bunkmate came from one such family. The Holy Hawthorn shrub was their patron deity. I probably recognized her blood's signature from what I'd absorbed during the fight.

Interesting. My powers seemed to have gained new capabilities in this plane. Now, it looked like I could remember anyone whose blood I had absorbed and identify their patron deity. If I could detect their powers too, that would be perfect — but even without that, I couldn't complain.

Reaching out with my blood sense, I swept it across the barracks, searching for those whose blood I had already tasted. The result was unexpected. Out of the two dozen cadets, I recognized twelve from the first battle. So much for anonymity.

There were all kinds of patron deities here: birds, fish, flowers and trees. There were even a couple of unclaimed, or rather, godless and totemless individuals. Dark horses, so to speak, with no patrons, all on their own. It seemed that by sending me to the mosquitoes, Agatha had tossed me into a nest of aristocratic offspring. It was like a jar full of scorpions, where only the strongest would survive. And it wasn't just men — there were three girls here too: Hawthorn, Burdock and Frog. Though how they ended up here remained a mystery.

I also noted another cadet for future reference. He had Bear as his totem, and it was his blood, with its hint of bloodlust, that had shattered all my flimsy barriers. At the moment, his snoring was like a warhorn trumpeting through the barracks' void.

I couldn't identify the other eight cadets.

Meanwhile, the girl next to me had stopped shivering and slipped deeper into sleep, and I turned my attention to Mikhail's memories, searching for more information about this place.

His family never talked much about it, but Mikhail knew a few things. For example, this private school had once been a training ground for spies. The main focus of the Mosquitoes had been espionage and undercover operations, not combat.

But after the death of the last career military

officer in the family, the school had become something like a boarding house for the rich, where privileged children were trained by absurdly expensive and highly specialized tutors.

Incidentally, Agatha Petrovna had been one such specialist, training Mikhail personally and drilling into him the principles of blood magic, ritualism and even sacrifice. Mikhail could never understand why he was subjected to such torment when all he ever wanted was to become a seal scribe.

In a way, I felt for him. The heir of the Komarin lineage barely had any aptitude for blood magic, but he was a natural when it came to the art of creating and applying magical seals. And yet, for the sake of his family's survival, he had diligently studied Agatha's teachings, despite barely managing to apply most of what he learned.

I delved eagerly into Misha's memories, trying to assess Agatha's level of arcane skill. It appeared that my new Nan would rank among the top fifty blood mages back in my plane, yet she was still far from being the first among equals.

Overall, the situation suited me perfectly. My pursuers from my former plane had been thrown off my trail, I had time to adjust to this new plane, and all that remained was to take everything these Mosquitoes could offer and figure out how to increase the number of Aedes' followers. I had to remove this damned holy seal from my hand as soon as possible. Having to operate through direct contact with blood made me feel like a naive initiate at the very lowest level of my magic's possibilities. Then again, I didn't even have this much a few days ago. So, praise Aedes! This was a beginning and things could only improve from here on out.

* * *

The clock struck midnight and the offices of the Ministry of Defense fell silent. A single window on the third floor remained lit. A man in his forties sat at his desk, tapping his fingers thoughtfully on the heavy oak surface.

His family's patron deity was the Rat and he even resembled it — he was short, hunched, with sparse whiskers under his longish nose and he had beady, furtive eyes. Like his god, Arkady Ivanovich lived by the principle: "Everything for the rat nest, everything for the brood." His patience, attention to detail and persistence allowed him to gather information bit by bit, creating truly ingenious plans to enrich his family.

The assassins he had sent to the farthest reaches of the vast homeland had gone silent. And it wasn't just the assasins — there was no word from his nephew either. He had charged Anthony with putting an end to the provincial Komarin family, who had managed to claim ownership of two unique estates three hundred years ago. There were millions — possibly even billions — of rubles at stake in those locations, but it all had to be done in such a way that the Mosquito god who ruled that backwater wouldn't get his nose wet.

Arkady chuckled at his own pun. Ten years of subtle manipulation, falsifying documents, expunging records from the archives and slowly eliminating all competitors. But it would all be worth it soon.

At last, his communication amulet buzzed softly. Arkady held it to his ear, listening to the news with an expressionless face, occasionally twitching his whiskers like a true rodent.

"How many bodies? ... You had to blow up the place? ... A mummy? ... What about the other members of the family?" After getting answers to all his questions, Arkady's voice acquired a steely edge. "I'm taking personal control of the investigation. I expect the preliminary report on my desk tomorrow."

He hung up and his thoughts began to race. So, Anthony had paid for his arrogance and ended up a mummy. Arkady felt no pity for his prematurely desiccated relative. The family was large and prolific. One fool more or less didn't matter; there were more waiting in the wings. But there were plenty of benefits to be reaped from his nephew's demise as well — such as being able to assume personal control of this matter, as well as claiming the military pension and medal for a family death in the line of duty.

Still, what had gone so wrong that the second kill squad had been forced to blow up the heavily fortified mansion? What could a feeble boy and an elderly nanny possibly have thrown at them? He'd have to pay a pretty penny to a death mage to verify their demise in the explosion. But it was better to overpay once and secure his rights now, than to rage and rue his arrogance later.

*   *   *

Spider was reviewing the new cadet's personal file. The instructors had been ordered not to interfere in the skirmishes between the cadets. In just five days, aside from the brutal physical training, these so-called aristocrats had managed to establish their own hierarchy. At the top stood one of the bear-totem students, with smaller predators as his lackeys, while all the plant, amphibian, and especially totem-less cadets toiled as their underlings.

The only remaining holdout was the second heir of the healer Hawthorn family. The small girl bared her teeth time and time again, never openly confronting her bullies but refusing to kowtow to them in any sense of the word. The other female cadets, Burdock and Frog, seemed quite content meanwhile, having effectively slept with half their class. Sometimes anonymity served to reveal a pupil's true inclinations, and these weren't always pretty — but that was their families' problem.

Up until last night, Spider had planned to take on Hawthorn as his personal student, protecting her from the advances of the local alpha male. But things turned out even better. Agatha, who hadn't been heard from in a good seven decades now, suddenly sent her own protege to the school. And the boy was anything but ordinary. His fighting style, which he had used to fend off the new recruits along with the instructors when they intervened during yesterday's brawl, was unlike anything Spider had seen before.

It resembled something used by some of the Brazilian fighters — they called it capoeira. A lot of spinning movements, dance-like steps, sweeps and adroit redirection of the opponent's inertia. But the most significant difference? Blood! The boy had practically bathed in it. Spider counted at least ten serious hits on him and nearly two dozen glancing blows. And every time, the newcomer seemed to dive into the fresh blood on the cobblestones, either healing himself or fueling his battle trance.

This alone suggested that the boy was the last scion of the Komarin family, hidden from the world for the last ten years to protect him from the increasingly frequent assassination attempts. And that in turn meant that not only had Agatha protected him, but that she had raised a true Komarin in spirit. Of course, he wasn't fully developed yet, but the blood... the blood answered his call, and that was a crucial development out here so close to the anomalies.

They, the trained scouts and the last blood-bound bannermen of the Komarin family, had no choice but to wait and see whom Aedes would appoint to lead the family. All they could do until then was keep the school running. Though, to be honest, even that hadn't been a great success.

All their requests for funding to the Ministry of Defense were met with boilerplate responses like "There's no money in the current budget, but keep trying," "Your inquiry is important to us but not a priority for the military," and the masterpiece: "Due to the prolonged lack of confirmation for the necessity of state personnel at designated secret facilities, funding will be cut. We recommend returning to active service to receive the necessary provisions."

Spider spat at the mere recollection of this humiliation. They already *were* in active service, and if the Ministry was overrun with rats, he and his men weren't about to become like them. Honor and duty still meant something to the Komarin family. They would hold their ground here at the edge of the anomalies for as long as they had to.

Chapter 3

By and by, I dozed off — only to be awoken by an unceremonious poke in my ribs and a voice hissing: "Get up before they really lay into you."

Hmm, the voice was Hawthorn's. She could've stayed quiet and looked on as the entire barracks pummeled me to a pulp, but she decided to warn me in time. So gratitude wasn't beyond her. The surprising thing though was that Burdock and Frog were sneaking up to my bunk on tiptoe, along with the rest of the "welcoming party." Bear was already barricading the door with a bar to make sure I couldn't escape.

For whatever reason, the familiar tingle of excitement was beginning to rise within me. I must've soaked in their blood pretty well if its effects hadn't worn off overnight. The 19 on 1 odds didn't sit well with me, though. I needed to even the playing field without giving myself away. Using my blood sense I reached out to the blood of the offenders who were familiar to me and did the least energy-consuming thing I could. Ladies first!

"Uh-oh! Oh no! Mommy! I've gotta go! Move! Get out of the way!" the girls erupted in squeals, timidly at first but soon giving way to curses and cries. Clutching their burbling stomachs, Burdock and Frog bolted for the latrines, shoving everyone out of their way.

Any notion of subtlety went out the window now. One after another, the rest of the instigators rushed in the same direction, while the remaining eight stood uncertainly, glancing between my sleepy form and the bathroom's door — which re-sounded with the cannon blasts of their compan-ions' bodily failures.

There wasn't enough room for Bear and a few other cadets in the toilets, so in a frantic effort to find an open stall, they tore down the door along with the bar that had been propping it shut.

"I warned them not to overeat at dinner," Haw-thorn chimed in again, unintentionally covering up my sabotage of my classmates' intestinal tracts. "These newfangled healing elixirs don't mix well with a full stomach."

It was hard not to smile at the sight of the re-maining eight cadets, nervously shifting from foot to foot, reckoning up what they had eaten the night before and calculating their chances of join-ing the ranks of the penitents.

In the end, they decided not to tempt fate and returned to their bunks.

"Thanks!" I mouthed to Hawthorn, catching a glimpse of her blue eyes peeking out from under the blankets. She just snorted and burrowed deeper into her warm nest. I wondered if I was seeing the girl's real appearance or an illusion cast by the artifact. I leaned toward the former option — blood never did respond well to illusion magic.

Fifteen minutes later, we heard the shouts and curses of the instructors. The gist of their tirades was clear enough: They were furious over the cadets' lack of self-control at dinner and were now forcing them to clean up the mess they had made all over the school grounds.

Everyone had to do their part. The girls were tasked with cleaning the barracks, while the boys had to clean the rest of the school, which had been thoroughly bespattered by the stricken cadets. Two hours later, public opinion had shifted and now everyone wanted to throttle the ones who had caused the mess. The perpetrators cast ever more suspicious glances my way, but no one made a move. Sore backsides and churning stomachs had a way of stifling any desire to fight. But as it turned out, not even a burning rear end could suppress the instinct to reproduce.

The school itself resembled a mid-sized mansion or estate, hidden deep within an ancient forest. The stone walls with their towers were taller than those at Hmarevo, but it was clear both estates had been built based on the same blueprint. What surprised me, though, was that despite being surrounded by a forest, not a single mosquito responded to my call. Either any calls to the local deities were truly blocked here, or I couldn't summon a mosquito without the ring.

Unexpectedly, I happened to overhear the answer to this question. After we finished cleaning, we headed to the dining hall, where trays of bland rice porridge, boiled eggs, and cups of brown broth sat steaming on the roughly hewn mess tables. The cadets eyed their breakfasts warily.

"Oak bark broth is so last century," Hawthorn muttered to herself as she sat down on a bench by the wall. "But at least it'll stop the diarrhea, if the magic won't."

"What'd you say, you little brat?!" Bear immediately growled, settling in next to the blonde and pressing her against the wall with his massive frame.

"Why is he so persistent?" I thought as I picked up my breakfast tray. As much as I wanted to eat, it looked like I was going to have to step in.

"This is a demon school and it runs on demonic rules! 'You have to be able to defend yourself without magic, using only what's at hand,'" Hawthorn mimicked one of the instructors before turning to Bear. "Why don't you back off before I give you a permanent case of incontinence?"

It seemed this wasn't the first confrontation between them, yet judging by Bear's reply, the warning didn't have the intended effect on him:

"Quit playing hard to get, like you're some untouchable princess! The others don't mind sneaking off to play, but there aren't enough to go around, and I'm not standing in line," he growled, lifting her jacket with one hand and pawing at her body. "It's a win-win: You get to blow off your stress from excess magic use and I get to enjoy myself — somatically!"

I slowly edged toward the alpha male, closing the distance for a strike. As a man, I could understand Bear. Hawthorn was quite the looker — petite, with a narrow waist, a modest chest and long, slender legs — but I definitely didn't approve of his methods. He was about to force the girl, and she wouldn't even know what he looked like, thanks to the school's insistence on anonymity. I was starting to like this place less and less. Where the hell were the instructors?

"What makes you think I even wield magic? Maybe I'm one of the unblessed," the blonde tried to stall, futilely pulling his hand from under her jacket.

"That just means you have no reason to resist when I'm doing you such a favor!" Bear tried to press his entire body against her.

"Do me a favor instead!" I grinned bloodthirstily and, taking advantage of his confusion, hit him square in the throat with my wooden tray. Bear suddenly lost interest in his little game, clutching his throat and struggling to breathe. Hawthorn didn't miss a beat either, clapping her hands over his ears from where she sat.

"You idiot! Do you really think I can't figure out who you are?" she hissed right in his ear, making sure everyone could hear. "One more move like that, and outside the school, you'll end up a eunuch — even if you're the Krechet heir!"

The girl was already at the doorway when an instructor's booming voice suddenly filled the room, as if he had materialized out of thin air:

"Breakfast is over! Move it, wigglers! Out to the training yard on the double and familiarize yourselves with your equipment! Move it! Move it! Move it!"

Amazingly, none of the cadets objected. They jogged out to the yard, leaving behind their unfinished breakfasts, disrupted by our little spectacle. We lined up quickly. Despite the delays the morning's cleanup had caused, field training was still very much the order of the day.

Large backpacks lay at our feet. Hawthorn's pack was so tall it nearly reached to her chin.

"You will now unpack and repack your backpacks, planning for a week-long hike," the instructor barked.

I couldn't help but smirk. Mikhail's memories told me that Agatha often sent him on trips through swamps under the guise of these so-called "hikes." Needless to say they were far from scenic. At the time, Mikhail thought his Nan was tormenting him for the sake of it, but now it was clear she'd been preparing him for his time with the Mosquitoes all along.

I unpacked my bag on autopilot. Mikhail's muscle memory worked beautifully, and I silently thanked Agatha for it. The items appeared before me and were sorted based on necessity for the woody, swampy terrain. I was now almost certain that our route would take us through marshlands. I sorted the all-season tent, insulating mat, small digging tool, camouflage cloaks, personal first aid kit, tarps for shelter, individual rations for seven days, and waterproof bags into a pile of indispensable items.

I also placed the fingerless gloves, face cloths, ropes, water purification systems, a mug, a flask, and even thermal tablets for heating food and boiling water in the useful pile. Bringing extra sets of clothes and waterproof-windproof gear was also a good idea. I noticed the instructor occasionally casting curious glances at my work. Hawthorn, too, subtly shifted out of line to peek at what I was doing. The girl wasn't dumb and quickly adjusted her inventory.

After waiting for her to finish, I swiftly packed everything into a small hiking backpack, which had been cleverly hidden at the bottom of the larger one. After some thought, I also decided to bring the larger pack, having first rolled it up as tightly as I could. I had a feeling it could double as a stretcher in a pinch.

Who could know that I already sensed trouble brewing on the horizon. Meanwhile, the instructor launched into his briefing:

"You lot are used to feeling invincible when you use your magic and your family's powers. But our goal is to show you that you're capable of much more. None of you truly know your limits yet. With our instruction, you will not only reach them but surpass them. The first stage will be an eight-hour march, accompanied by instructors, to the starting point. The second stage will involve an individual route prepared for each of you. At the final checkpoint, an instructor will be waiting with a map for the third stage. And lastly," the instructor paused for effect and then added, glaring at Bear pointedly, "remember to stay alert, vigilant, and keep in mind that anonymity does not absolve you of honorable conduct. This concludes your briefing! About face! Left, left, left-right-left! Follow the guide at a light jog. Now, march!"

And off we went, running through the shadowy forest. The layer of pine needles was springy beneath our feet. The air was so crisp and fresh it felt like you could drown in it, like drinking water straight from a spring. Birds chirped, and the breeze rustled the treetops. It seemed perfect — at first.

Humping half a backpack was naturally better than lugging a full one, but half an hour in, our tongues were practically long enough to wrap around our necks like scarves. The air was burning our lungs.

Frog and Burdock had given up even earlier, whining and demanding their current boyfriends carry their nearly empty backpacks. That's when they learned their first lesson: together in bed, but apart in life. As they began to realize this harsh reality, their anger helped keep them going, although they fell back to the tail end of our column.

While we trudged monotonously behind the instructor, he ran ahead, mocking us with a full pack loaded with snowshoes, a helmet, winter clothes, and a whole backpack full of items needed only for different climates.

I kept my eyes on my feet, trying not to lose sight of the instructor's back. Mikhail's training was holding up, but the various cuts I'd gotten in yesterday's brawl stung and burned with the sweat streaming down my body. The pain was unbearable, and I would've given anything just to wash off the salt and change my clothes, yet our forced march went on and on.

I moved to the middle of the group, joining the others there. Hawthorn was running too, teeth clenched, clearly struggling. But unlike the ragged gasping of most of the cadets, her breathing was steady. Her face was pale, while the rest of us looked like overripe tomatoes. Even Mikhail's body, despite the training, was holding up worse than hers.

Seeing this I began to suspect in earnest that she was a healer. Even though her magic had no effect on the others in the school, she could surely use it on herself — and she seemed to be doing just that.

"I guess I'm not the only one nature gave perks to," I thought, with a touch of envy.

Speaking of perks, four hours in, the instructor called for a break. We collapsed right where we stood. The only thing that revived me was the sight of a forest lake just ahead, shimmering in the midday sun. My wounds still ached and itched, so I dragged myself to the water's edge and began stripping off my clothes. The cool water beckoned soothingly after four hours of running. Oddly, the other cadets followed my example. The noise and chaos were unimaginable. Youth is tough to kill, no matter the hardship.

Carefully folding my clothes, I began unwrapping the strips of once-white fabric I had been using as makeshift bandages. The noise around me suddenly fell silent and I noticed that all the cadets stood rooted at the water's edge. It didn't take long to figure out why — they were examining their reflections in the water.

Looking down, I saw myself — but not quite. Mikhail's body remained the same — tall, skinny, around six foot one, with dark hair and a decently masculine face. But my eyes — the eyes from my past life — were still there. They say eyes are the windows to the soul, and I guess that's true. They were bloodshot and exhausted, and the look of them suggested that they had witnessed too much.

I was covered with numerous wounds which my sweating had inflamed. It looked like someone had tried to slice me up like a cabbage but didn't quite succeed. Carefully, I began rinsing the bandages. I'd wrap them around my body again once they dried.

After wringing out the bandages, I laid them over my clothes and finally waded into the lake. The groan that escaped me was practically euphoric. I gritted my teeth to keep from crying out as the cool water soothed my wounds. The burning stopped, and I was able to swim a few laps in the lake without too much pain.

Bear was splashing nearby, giving me strange looks. I didn't have the time or energy to figure out what they meant, so I swam back to the shore, hoping to dry off before putting my field gear back on.

A surprise awaited me. Tucked in and neatly hidden beneath the bandages were some hawthorn leaves.

I looked around, but the girl from the Hawthorn family was nowhere to be seen. Mikhail's memories reminded me that the leaves needed to be washed and rubbed a little to release their juices before being applied to my wounds. I did my best, though my past life had trained me more in dismemberment than healing. So, I re-wrapped my wounds as best I could. At least the dirty, sweaty uniform would go over the bandages.

We endured the next two hours thanks to the thought that "whatever doesn't kill you makes you stronger."

Optimism is vital, but even it runs out eventually. By the end of the sixth hour, the girls had fallen significantly behind. So much so that I gave up and turned back. Sure, Burdock and Frog had wanted to beat me up, but I suspected that was more out of herd instinct. What really piqued my interest was why Hawthorn had fallen behind. She had seemed to be doing better than most. I found them around a bend, near a tall rocky outcrop covered in moss and young trees. Frog was vomiting violently, while Hawthorn held her hair and Burdock offered water to wash her face and rinse her mouth.

"What's wrong? Is it the food?" I asked Hawthorn, hoping for an answer. She shook her head.

"It hurts! Oh Frog goddess, it hurts so much! Help me!" Frog doubled over again, her skin taking on a greenish hue like an actual frog's, and her veins bulging.

"She said that she could sense frogs dying somewhere nearby," Hawthorn mumbled, almost apologetically at the absurdity of it.

Blood Almighty!

I guessed that it was impossible not to sense the mass deaths of your patron deity's creatures. And if you were cut off from divine support and sustenance, you could quite literally croak along with the frogs.

"Where?! Show me!" I nearly growled to the weakened girl. She weakly waved her hand toward a rocky outcrop some distance away. Well, at least I had a direction.

I quickly cast my blood sense as far as I could in the indicated direction. Searching for frogs was like filtering through a sieve — frogs are not as easy to locate as people. But there, at the edge of my perception, was a cluster of tiny blood droplets, fading rapidly, like candles being snuffed out in the wind. If I had to guess, it was a swamp — and what better place for frogs to live? Someone or something really was exterminating the entire frog colony located there.

"I'll go get the instructor!" As I ran to catch up with the main group, I sensed something large and powerful had appeared right in the middle of Frog's domain and was now annihilating it.

It took me five minutes to catch up with the main column. Sprinting ahead, I reached the instructor and blurted out:

"Permission to speak! One of the cadets is suffering from extreme exhaustion due to a magical energy drain."

"Halt cadets! Take a fifteen-minute break."

While the others collapsed to rest, the instructor pulled me aside.

"What proof do you have? How do I know you aren't trying to derail the exercise?" The instructor's gaze was intense, as if he suspected me of being a saboteur.

"The girl didn't think twice about casting off her anonymity," I replied with the most compelling reason I had. "Someone is slaughtering all the frogs nearby and she's overwhelmed. She's got neither magic nor her deity to aid her."

"Where?" The instructor took me more seriously now.

"To the southwest of here. There's a huge swamp there..."

The instructor pulled a flat, magical amulet from his pocket, activated it, and spoke in a tense, quiet voice: "We have an emergency. Code yellow. Location: Village of Little Quagmire. Evacuate the Swamp Maiden beyond the boundary. Grid coordinates: 1-6."

With that, the conversation ended, but I remained fixated on the strange device. From Mikhail's memories, I recognized the it to be a comulet, a rare and expensive technomagical device for long distance communication. Interesting. In my home plane, we used to communicate the old-fashioned way, via blood spirits. Whether you were kissing a beautiful woman or dissecting a creature, you had to answer the call. It was a sort of blood-based social network, where you couldn't get lost or disappear no matter where you were. The longer you lived, the bigger your contact list grew. Some had the misfortune of dying — sometimes with my help — but more were always added. All in all, it was quite convenient. For a blood mage, at least.

Every respectable blood mage had their own blood index, which contained the blood codes of all their friends and enemies, political and spiritual leaders, aristocratic families, and just useful and important people. I used to be "the one" simply because no one had my blood. Talent, skill, and my ability to cover my tracks helped with that. I once broke my own rule for someone dear to me... and the bastards killed her, setting my own blood against me.

My thoughts were interrupted by a shrill ringing coming from the comulet.

"Damn it! Roger that! Code red! I'm taking her to grid coordinates 1-8 and returning to the incubator. How many? Got it! I'll be right there once I deliver the wigglers!"

After that, the instructor ordered us to retrieve Frog, lay her green-tinged body on a stretcher and jog to the extraction point, taking turns carrying her. The girl was barely breathing, her body shaking violently. The instructor pulled a syringe from his personal kit and injected her with a clear serum, causing her to immediately go limp.

The other cadets tensed, and some began muttering quietly, crowding around the instructor.

"Calm down! It's medicine! It should stop the magic drain. We've detected a breach of the nether plane nearby," he waited for us to grasp the gravity of his words before continuing. "I'm evacuating you back to the school. Stay there until reinforcements arrive. No heroics. Get the injured to the infirmary."

His clipped, urgent commands were a clear indication that the situation was very bad.

We started running again. This time, the tension was thick in the air. Without their family powers, most of the cadets were as helpless as blind kittens, and now there was a breach on top of it all. Plenty to worry about. Mikhail had only theoretical knowledge of breaches in this plane, so I didn't dwell on it. What troubled me was something else.

The farther we ran, the more anxious I felt. Something like a magnet was calling me back toward that cursed swamp where the frogs had perished en masse. There was no logical explanation for it, but I ran like the others, taking my turns carrying Frog on the stretcher.

We reached the evacuation point in half an hour and arrived at the school minutes later. For the first time, I saw a portal scroll at work. The instructor pulled a sealed scroll from his coat and broke the seal. Within seconds, the portal vortex opened, much like the one Agatha had cast with her ring.

The instructor stepped through first, ensuring it was safe, and then waved the rest of us through. Two totem-less cadets grabbed the stretcher with Frog and rushed her to the infirmary.

The rest of us stood hesitantly in the court-yard.

"Should we summon our family bloodbound?" Bear suggested uncertainly. So, it seemed he wasn't entirely without human feelings, or maybe he was just worried about his own safety. "We're not exactly commoners here..."

The comulet crackled to life again.

We all froze, straining to hear the message. There were shouts and curses amid the static and the sound of explosions. The staccato of automatic rifle fire drowned out the conversation. The instructor said nothing, his frown growing deeper. After a long pause, he lowered the comulet, his knuckles white with tension. It seemed he had made up his mind at last.

"All of you are of legal age and fully responsible for your decisions," he growled through gritted teeth. "Your families' bloodbound shall not set foot here. Nor shall there be any aid from your family gods. None at all. There are only government troops here and they're dying, defending that there village of Little Quagmire. It's so remote, even portal coordinates don't always work properly. Reinforcements from the Ministry of Defense will take at least half an hour to arrive, if we're lucky. We have to hold on until then. So, if any of you have personal attack or defense spells without any bloodline magic mixed in… There are three hundred civilians there, mostly women, children and elders…"

He trailed off, letting us imagine for ourselves what would happen to those people without help for the next half-hour.

"I'm a seal scribe," I volunteered first, drawn to the breach, "but I only know what to do in theory. I'll give it a shot."

"I have bloodlust," Bear muttered quietly to my surprise. "But I'll need a healer afterward… or I might die without even noticing."

"I can heal," Hawthorn replied through gritted teeth. "But I can only handle about ten serious wounds before I'll need someone to revive me. And there's probably already plenty of injured down there…" She glanced apologetically at the boy she had threatened to castrate earlier in the day.

Two more cadets stepped forward, neither of whom I'd drawn blood from. One had the ability to harden his skin to stone, and the other could shoot poisoned darts, like a porcupine. The rest averted their eyes and kept silent.

"Volunteers, step forward! The rest are dismissed! Report to barracks."

Little Quagmire was perched on the edge of a deep ravine and the Mosquito instructors were holding the line from the ridge. They were fighting in sync: One group was firing their rifles, occasionally tossing grenades that sent shrapnel flying. Mikhail had trained in throwing similar explosives since childhood, hitting targets over fifty meters away. The second group was using AoE spells, alternating between flame squalls and hail storms. From time to time, the ravine's floor erupted with stone spikes, as if trying to impale some unseen enemy like a butterfly on a pin. The only problem was, the smoke, fire, and stinking swamp below obscured any view of whatever enemy it was they were fighting.

"You've lost your mind!" a voice rasped behind me. It was the bald man who had interrogated me last night. His voice was barely audible over the cacophony of battle. "Why the hell did you bring the wigglers here?"

"They volunteered. Maybe if Orlov realizes that there's a major breach here, he'll hurry up for once! We've been neglected for so long it can't get any worse. Besides, this one — " the instructor pointed at me, " — is a seal scribe, albeit a novice."

Spider flashed a warning glance at me, as if to say, "Don't stick your neck in a noose!" But what he actually asked was something else:

"Who here has weapons training?"

"Me," Bear responded crisply, like a soldier. "I'm proficient with anything that shoots, cuts, stabs or explodes."

Why the hell was someone with his level of training sent here? I wondered briefly before another thought occurred to me. Why did he act like a complete idiot with hormones in all the wrong places? Or had I overlooked something about his relationship with Hawthorn?

"Guys, get ready," Spider rasped, nodding at Bear.

Bear saluted in silence.

"Alright, I get him, but what about the girl?" The bald man shook his head in frustration but was interrupted by our battle-hardened blonde.

"Anyone critically injured here? I'm a healer. I can help."

There was no turning down an offer like that. Spider seemed to forget all about me and Bear, while the nearby fighters handed Bear a rifle and some magazines.

"Who are we fighting?" I asked, if only to seem professional. To be honest, I wasn't afraid — if anything, a wild exhilaration was bubbling in my veins, combined with nostalgia. I felt like I was back home.

The powers inside me surged, demanding release. The binding seal on my hand strained like an overfilled dam ready to burst at any moment. I found myself rocking on my heels, itching to dive off the cliff and into the chaos below. I was being pulled toward the invisible plane rift, like a magnet. My blood sense was in overdrive, scanning the battle-torn hill, the villagers hiding in cellars, the wounded in the makeshift infirmary, and Hawthorn darting between the injured with superhuman speed. Already resigned to not hearing an answer, I caught a response from one of the Mosquito mages who had been casting hail storms.

"Down there in the swamp..." he began, but didn't finish, as a purple tentacle shot from the smoke, wrapping around him and dragging him into the rift even as he screamed and fired wildly.

"Just like the old days back home!" a crazy thought flickered in my mind. "My purple darling! Oh, how much fun we used to have! But this can't be happening here and now, right?"

I shoved two fingers into my mouth and whistled sharply. The tentacle froze mid-swing, dropped its slightly crumpled prey to the ground, and then, much more gently, wrapped itself around me.

Without hesitation, I bit into the tentacle. The blood from the otherworldly creature was absorbed into me instantly, and after a few minutes, I finally heard a familiar voice in my mind:

"Where have you been? We've been looking for you!"

CHAPTER 4

His Excellency Count Daniel Andreyevich Orlov spent his rare hours of repose at his estate, admiring the training of his prized possession — a three-year-old stallion named Buran. A bay with perfect proportions and slender legs, the horse was magnificent from ears to tail. It was well known that the Minister of Defense was an avid horse breeder and equestrian, but few knew that Daniel Andreyevich had managed to create an entirely new horse breed — the Orlov Trotter.

Buran was destined to become the main stud and the nation's pride at the upcoming World Horse Breeding Exhibition, soon to be held in Saint Petersburg. There had been so much effort expended, so many experiments conducted, and all that work had not been in vain!

"Your Excellency," the head groom interrupted the count's admiration of his stallion, "Buran needs a mate. There are a few candidates, but you understand…"

The count understood — the emperor had already claimed the first foal as a gift for one of his children.

"We will wait and see, Tikhon. There is still time!"

Yes, Buran had time, but as for the count… Emperor Krechet often reproached him, saying it would be better if Count Orlov devoted the same enthusiasm to starting a family as breeding horses, but Daniel Andreyevich never found the time. There were all kinds of affairs and responsibilities to see to. When you run the military department of one of the world's leading powers, you'd be lucky to find a few hours for rest, let alone find the time to start a family.

That was what made moments like these all the more precious. As he admired his work, the count didn't immediately notice the warmth emanating from the ancient departmental artifact, which had been hanging uselessly around his neck for the last fifty years. Being a military man with a sense of duty, Daniel Andreyevich had strictly followed the instructions of the previous Minister of War of the Russian Empire. He had been told that the pendant was of national, if not global, importance, so it must have been true.

At first, the count had tried to investigate it, but then an endless stream of urgent matters had distracted him, pulling him away from the mystery around his neck. The only thing he remembered about the artifact was that it was supposed to signal a particularly powerful breach from the nether plane. However, the artifact had not done a thing during the other ruptures in Moscow or other cities. And even the previous minister had happily reported that there had been no such major breaches during his tenure.

This is why Daniel Andreyevich now became seriously alarmed. The amulet, shaped like a teardrop, kept heating up, to the point where he was forced to abruptly rip it off from around his neck and drop it to the ground — where it now glowed red-hot.

Dialing the number of his personal secretary, the Minister of Defense barked into his comulet:

"Get me the reports on all ongoing breaches, ASAP! Turn the entire place upside down if you have to — there's a global level breach happening somewhere! I'll be there in five minutes!"

The call ended, and the count rushed past the servants to his office to retrieve a portal scroll. It wasn't the aristocratic way to travel, but it was quick and practical.

It occurred to him that he really should get into the habit carrying a few such scrolls with him so he wouldn't have to run around like a madman. The sight of a Defense Minister running, whether in peacetime or wartime, invariably caused panic, even if the servants were bound by an oath of loyalty to remain silent.

* * *

"Tilda, you have no idea how glad I am to see you!" I hugged the octopus-girl I was so close to in my past life, wondering how she had ended up here. "You better stop causing trouble! I hope you haven't killed anyone yet..."

Matilda blushed deeply, her skin turning a dark shade of violet verging on black.

"I tried to be careful, but it was so hard to break through... and those...," she said with the voice of a very vengeful woman. "Well, they just keep shooting at me!"

She was gently carrying me toward either the portal or the breach she had come through. As the gunfire wasn't stopping, Tilda had to wrap me in her tentacles, practically forming a protective cocoon around me. That's my girl, my bodyguard.

"How did you find me?"

"Don't you think I could locate a part of my own self in the River of Time? You shared your soul and blood with me when you saved me as a child."

"Hmm, I figured it was our blood link," I muttered under my breath, but she heard.

"Oh, go on with your blood tricks! You've often missed the forest for the trees, so I'm not surprised," snorted the violet beauty — well, beauty by octopus standards, I guess. "I could never have found you by blood alone, though I tried, no sense in denying it. Just wasted my time. But, oh, did I make a splash," Tilda said dreamily and with pleasure. "Our friends caused such a ruckus when you disappeared! All the seals on the nether plane broke and everyone you used to hunt showed up out of their deep respect for you — to pay a visit to the twelve estates of your zealot executioners. Why we tore those places apart!"

Tilda thumped her tentacles in excitement, as if applauding. I could imagine how it looked from the outside. Fifteen-meter-long tentacles rising from a portal, through the smoke. These thoughts reminded me of something else.

"Darling," I told her, "the local emperor's army is expected to arrive in half an hour to help seal this breach. So we need to wrap up our little chat."

I bit into my wrist and generously smeared my blood on one of Tilda's tentacles. She huffed in irritation.

"What's with the weakling act? You've barely got any magic left, and even your blood tricks seem pathetic now."

"What can I say? For the first time in my life, those zealots managed to inscribe a seal on me properly," I shrugged philosophically, already resigned to the temporary situation. "At least with local blood, I'll always be able to send you an invitation. No need to disturb the River of Time."

"Don't forget to send one! Or I'll die old, forgotten and useless!" The octopus-girl dramatically wiped an inky tear from her eye. What an actress!

"By the way, what's the time difference between us?" I asked, suddenly realizing it might be important. Matilda hadn't changed much since our last meeting, but it was worth clarifying, just in case.

"I spent a year and a half searching for your roasted corpse," replied my friend — and one of the most dangerous creatures from our nether plane — completely seriously.

Talk about synchronization: a day and a half here equaled a year and a half back home. For Matilda, time meant nothing, of course. We'd known each other for almost two hundred years, but the difference was still worth keeping in mind.

"All right, Tilda, let's wrap up this unofficial visit. I'll try to arrange a second one in a few days. I've got a bad feeling there's some trouble's on its way here."

I was more serious than ever. While chatting with my old friend, I kept scanning the area around us. And sure enough, just off to the side of Little Quagmire, a detachment of the emperor's men had appeared out of nowhere. Less than an hour had passed. If this had been a real breach and not just a friendly visit, there wouldn't have been anything left of the local defenders — just blood puddles already soaking into the ground. Clearly, they didn't care much about the local populace. But there was no use jumping to conclusions at the moment. First, we had to wrap up this show.

"Got enough strength to close the rift?" the octopus asked doubtfully, lowering me onto the scorched, barren ground that had once been a vast swamp.

"Well, I'll give it a try. Seems I've got a similar ability 'round here — an innate one. Might as well test it out."

"Don't go getting yourself killed in the next couple of days," Matilda snorted, slithering back into the breach. "Last time I left you alone for a bit, when I came back, there was nothing but a kebab left in the middle of the town square!"

"I love you too," I sent a playful kiss to the octopus and focused on Mikhail's memories. I had to close the rift. Now, how was that kind of thing done here..?

* * *

"What's the purpose of you lot sitting here if you can't locate a breach of such a magnitude?!" Count Orlov was furious. Half an hour had passed since his minister's pendant had turned red-hot, and they still hadn't pinpointed the breach. If this was an invasion, a whole district could've been overrun by now!

His personal secretary shrank into himself, bracing himself against the boss's fury.

Count Orlov could be fierce and harsh when the situation called for it and now was one of those times. Without giving any specifics, he had the entire ministry in an uproar, demanding they find what might as well have been a foreign invasion.

Arkady Ivanovich had scoured every department, gathered all reports on breaches within the empire, even checked with his shadow informants, but there was nothing supernatural to report.

Every territory seemed to be accounted for and under control. And, as often happens, the first warning that something was indeed amiss came from the most unexpected source.

A nondescript young man in a black uniform without insignia hesitantly entered the minister's office.

"Your Excellency, may I have a word?" he asked. He smelled of sweat and smoke and looked as if he'd been dragged through a swamp before arriving.

"Permission granted, son," replied the Minister of Defense wearily, involuntarily recalling how his own career had started in the field. Those were the best years of his service, when it was clear who was a friend and who was a foe, and he personally had far more respect for soldiers like this than for the bureaucratic rats holed up in his ministry.

"A soldier from special unit 'Mosquito' has arrived with a request for operational support, in accordance with the direct order of the late Emperor Alexei Krechet."

"Bring me the archivist, now!" the minister barked loudly enough to rattle the windows. Then in a calmer, softer tone, he addressed the soldier, "Where? How long ago? And why am I only now hearing about a special unit codenamed 'Mosquito'?"

"Near Lakhdenpokhya, Karelia, half an hour ago. I don't know how to answer your second question, Your Excellency!" the soldier responded crisply. "But, if I may, you should have...," he hesitated, glancing at the crowd of people in the office, but continued, "a departmental artifact. It should have signaled."

The count glanced at his mentalist, waiting for confirmation that the messenger was telling the truth. His mere mention of the artifact was enough for Count Orlov, but it didn't hurt to be cautious. Waiting for the archivist made no sense now.

"How many reinforcements do you need?" the minister asked. "Will a company be enough?"

"No, Your Excellency. A regular company would be useless here. We need special forces with active personal abilities. No bloodline magic."

There were indeed such soldiers in the service of the Ministry of Defense. They were affectionately called the Eagles, but how could the Mosquito unit have known about them? Pressing the alarm button in the highly classified division that reported directly to him, Daniel Andreyevich Orlov thought that maybe it was high time he deployed directly to the field himself. This situation was too extraordinary — not only had the Ministry of Defense missed a breach, but it seemed to have lost track of a special unit within its own ranks. That was a complete disaster. Something like this could lead to more than courts-martial — for this, heads could roll.

*　*　*

The Eagles were clearly in no rush. If the monster hadn't calmed down after snagging Agatha's protégé, the Mosquito unit would've been wiped out by now. The rifle fire and grenades did about as much to the octopus as pebbles to an elephant — they barely irritated it. Magic wasn't doing much damage either. The massive tentacles with suction cups kept emerging from the smoke again and again. What were the Mosquitoes supposed to do, hit it with artillery? But there was no artillery. There was nothing but a few dozen bloodbound bannermen here from an almost extinct lineage.

Spider had ordered them to cease fire when he saw the creature weave a cocoon of tentacles and begin retreating to the rift. He understood that the monster was retreating of its own volition.

"You're not even going to try to rescue him?" asked the healer from the Hawthorn clan quietly. "He...," she faltered, unsure how to express her internal turmoil, "he managed to trade himself for one of your men."

"Not an option," Spider cut her off. "We couldn't even save our own. Right now, martial law applies, and the priority is to protect the larger group of civilians."

He wasn't about to lead his people into a suicide attack. He had almost three hundred civilians behind him, and there was no assurance that the newcomer was indeed the last Komarin. Spider consoled himself with the thought that if the newcomer were truly in danger and a true Komarin, their blood oath would have twisted them all into knots, forcing them to rush blindly to the bloodline's sole inheritor. The fact that this hadn't happened wasn't much of a justification, but it was all he had.

The Hawthorn healer stomped her foot in frustration but didn't back down.

"Look! Over there..." the girl squeaked in a trembling voice and hid behind Spider's back.

Spider had to turn a full 180 degrees to see the arrival of reinforcements. It was a terrifying sight, even to the seasoned reconnaissance veterans. Three infantry fighting vehicles, armed with huge cannons and bristling with machine guns along the sides, were moving silently through the village. The caliber of the auto-cannons inspired a sacred fear — they was clearly designed to fire 30 mm rounds. And those machine guns... The combined power of those three IFVs could have taken down that giant octopus from a safe distance.

How much did this operation cost? And the next logical question was who was commanding this detachment? The answer came quickly. The lead IFV's hatch swung open and out popped the Mosquito messenger followed by one of the empire's most recognizable faces — Defense Minister Count Orlov himself. Dressed in his field uniform, he still looked like a battle-hardened wolf, though he had spent more than fifty years defending his homeland not on the battlefield but in the offices.

At the sight of Count Orlov, the entire Mosquito unit snapped to stiff attention.

"Greetings, soldiers!"

"Greetings, Your Excellency, Defense Minister!" two dozen throats rejoined. Soldiers remained soldiers, even in retirement.

"Who's the CO here? I want a sitrep this instant!"

"There's been a breach at the designated classified site, sir! The breaching creature is tentatively classified as a Level 6 or Level 7 denizen of the nether plane. We held our positions to protect three hundred civilians until reinforcements arrived. There have been no casualties among our service personnel. Fifteen civilians have been killed and there are several more severely wounded. They require immediate evacuation. There are also some volunteers among the service personnel who have not yet taken the oath and are therefore not bound by non-disclosure vows." Having concluded his report, Spider carefully awaited the minister's reaction while keeping an eye on the arriving soldiers, who were fanning out to cordon off the swamp.

"Isolate the volunteers and administer the non-disclosure oath," Orlov commanded. "Evacuate the wounded to the regimental hospital. Move the civilians beyond artillery range."

The count's orders made perfect sense, yet they also caused Spider some alarm. If artillery opened fire, his new cadet wouldn't stand a chance of surviving.

"Wait, Uncle Daniel, don't use artillery!" The girl from the Hawthorn clan poked her head out from behind Spider's shoulder. "The octopus has one of our cadets. And besides, it's stopped fighting."

"The creature is no longer attacking?" Orlov

asked, puzzled.

"Affirmative, Your Excellency! The octopus has been completely calm since it snatched the Mosquito cadet."

Count Orlov scrutinized the girl closely and then asked with surprise in his voice, "Svetlana, is that you?"

"Yes," the cadet answered, lowering her head, and then added quietly, "Just don't tell my father, please."

"Your father's going rip my head off," Orlov said colorfully, but then changed his orders as requested.

The smoke didn't dissipate. The peat bogs were still smoldering, forcing the reinforcements to put on gas masks and call in mages to try and clear the smoke to get a better view of the breach.

When at last they succeeded, the sight was something to behold: In the middle of the smoldering swamp knelt a young man in a black uniform with blood-red threads emanating from his wrists and weaving a containment seal over the rift. The octopus was gone; all that remained was the deathly pale mage and the shimmering red surface reflecting the setting sun's rays. The rift shrank, growing smaller and smaller, pulling toward the center until it closed with a hiss.

In the next instant, the boy collapsed to the ground.

*   *   *

Oh, how wrong was I in my arrogance. It turned out that a seal scribe here and a seal scribe in my home plane were two entirely different things, with nothing in common aside from the name. In my past life, I could negotiate with or subdue the nether plane creatures using blood magic and then we could seal the breaches together. I would contribute my blood from the human side and they would add theirs from the nether plane. Doing so created a kind of blood pact, a peace treaty and non-aggression pact between the two planes.

But in this world, a seal scribe had to stabilize and detach the breach from the portal mage who'd cast it. It was a high-paying skill and Misha had hoped to make a good living with it. And yet, that knowledge was of no use in helping me close this damned portal.

Leaving an open rift between two planes invited chaos, wars, and genocide — not to mention the twelve inquisitors I had cursed before I died — to cross at will. I wasn't ready to face them yet. Once the seal on my hand was broken however, it would be a different story...

I shook my head, pushing away the sweet thoughts of revenge. This wasn't the time or place.

So, I'd have to do this the old-fashioned way. I was pitifully weak, but I'd have to make do with what I had.

The rift lay upon the surface of the swamp, instead of hanging in the air like in Mikhail's memories. The first thing I needed was a decent amount of blood, and I had to bite long and deep and even in several places along my arm to get enough of it. Then at last I could move on to the creative part of this job.

Have you ever taken an exam on a subject you barely understood, having merely skimmed the textbook half an hour before? That's what I was doing right now… creative work indeed.

And I couldn't just repeat what I knew from my former life — the power levels and metaphysics in this place were different — so I had to improvise, relying more on intuition than on the what Mikhail had memorized and the rituals I had perfected. My blood, obeying my commands, formed a thin film in an intricate pattern over the portal's surface.

Matilda hadn't held back when she'd come through and now I was paying for it. I'd already used about a liter and a half of blood, and the rift was still resisting. On top of that, I had to weave not only the closing sutures into the seal but leave a gap big enough for the octopus. In effect, this spell required a multi-functional identification system — friend or foe — while the ring of the imperial soldiers closed in around the swamp. At least they'd stopped shooting and throwing grenades my way.

The smoke gradually cleared, and soon everyone could see the scarlet blotch, nearly a hundred square meters wide and me — the idiot self-taught mage, pale to the point of turning blue. Finally, I felt the portal was fully covered by a shroud of my blood.

The fabric of the plane was slowly pulling together into a rough seam, like a wartime surgeon using stitches to suture a deep wound, unconcerned with aesthetics.

At that moment, through some special vision, pulsing from the lack of blood inside me and the abundance of it outside, I saw the breach Matilda had torn shrink. Meter by meter, centimeter by centimeter. Just let it work. My blood ran out, my strength drained with it, and the portal gradually sealed shut, closing with a sharp zip. I don't know what happened after that because I passed out.

CHAPTER 5

"DIDN'T I TELL YOU not to stick your neck out need-lessly?" Aedes sighed wearily as he appeared before my mind's eye.

Oh Blood Almighty! Would you look at this monster...

An enormous six-legged mosquito hovered before me, almost five meters tall, with mesh wings and two serrated mandibles on, well... his face, I guess. He was floating in the swirling nothingness — what a sight. Impressive!

"You did say that," I replied once my shock wore off.

"So how come you're lying here half-dead?"

"Well, I'm not dead yet," I shrugged philosoph-ically, hearing quiet cursing behind my back. "At least I sealed the breach."

"What kind of creature was that? Its level set our troops scurrying..."

"She is from another world," I replied honestly, "specifically, from my home plane."

"You don't say!" Aedes exclaimed. "You've got uglies like that where you come from?"

"Tilda isn't exactly ugly. She's my friend," I defended my beauty. "She's so determined, she even managed to locate me through the River of Time."

"Ehh…" Aedes paused, stunned. "Have you ever tried, you know, with human girls? You might be pleasantly surprised."

"Pfft!" I burst out laughing at his tactfully unspoken implication. "She's not that kind of friend! I think you call them pets or familiars, something like that. Tilda is one of those from my past life — so she found me and decided to drop in for a visit."

Aedes fell silent for a long time, twittering his mesh wings.

"And how many more of these 'friends' do you have?" His voice now contained a hint of caution mixed with curiosity.

"There were only two like her… one was killed."

"And what about the others, the ones not like her?"

"The others are busy in my past world, tormenting my executioners."

Aedes floated in the weightlessness, swaying gently as if on a wave. I would've guessed he was in deep thought, but reading the facial expressions of a mosquito was a bit difficult.

"All right, to hell with the disguise. I'll need to keep a close eye on you, and without the ring, I have no idea what's happening with you."

Before me appeared the ring I had seen before, engraved with a mosquito on its crest. Only now its appearance had changed. There was a clear tube running along the inside, filled with a red liquid. I stared curiously at the upgrade, waiting for an explanation.

"What are you looking at?" the god grumbled, nudging the ring toward me. "That's a drop of my blood. Consider it your last chance, if things get really bad. I can revive you, but I can do it only once, so don't get carried away."

The ring slid onto my finger perfectly, melding with my skin and becoming almost invisible.

I whistled inwardly, impressed by the honor bestowed upon me. I had divine blood! Oh, Aedes, how much I could've accomplished with this back in my old world! So many experiments, so many possibilities! Why, I could've even tried to bring *her* back from the River of Time!

"I don't know who you're thinking about or what the River of Time is, but this only works on you and Mikhail's blood," Aedes quickly brought me back down to earth. "You are Mikhail Komarin. Forget the past!"

I mentally agreed with my patron, but I had too good a memory to forget those responsible for her death — and mine! The time to dwell on that had not come yet, however.

* * *

I woke up in a hospital bed but didn't rush to open my eyes. Through half-closed eyelids, I watched Hawthorn scurrying around me, looking over her shoulder nervously.

"'We did everything we could!'" she mocked someone angrily. "'His energy channels are scorched!' Ugh! Stupid field medics! I'll show you how it's done!"

She spat on the floor. Then, cracking her knuckles as if preparing for a fight, the healer conjured a greenish, sparkling orb between her hands. It was like a ball of lightning — small at first but gradually growing in size.

Her mention of my energy channels concerned me and I began checking my physical condition. In some ways, the local healers were right. My energy channels did resemble a tangled ball of frayed threads instead of the smooth pathways running alongside my blood vessels as they should have been. But I didn't detect any irreversible damage. A bit more blood, and I could fix everything in a couple of days, even strengthening the weak points along the way.

Meanwhile, the orb in Hawthorn's hands had grown to the size of a human head, and the girl decided to begin the treatment. Her eyes glowed with a soft green light as a thin tendril of energy detached from the orb and flowed into my solar plexus. My first reaction, and all subsequent ones, could be described in one word — "delicious." Using my inner blood sense, I observed as the healer untangled, reinforced, and in some places even fused my energy channels together. Blood would've done this instinctively, using the circulatory system as a model, but here I saw the masterful work of a healer. Impressive!

After two hours, the orb between the girl's hands had thinned and disappeared. She was drenched in sweat, but there was a triumphant smile on her face.

"Well, there goes their idea of magical disability! He'll be up and running again in no time!" She was about to leave when she noticed the ring on my finger. "Oh! This is unexpected. But at least I know who you belong to now. I have a feeling you're going to drain a lot of blood from everyone!"

Smiling at her own joke, Hawthorn left. But my day — or evening — of visits wasn't over yet. I felt great, thanks to one blond beauty, so I didn't bother pretending to be asleep anymore.

Half an hour later, a man in military uniform entered the room. He was the kind of grizzled veteran the soldiers would often call their "Pops" because he was like a father to them. His age and years of office work were beginning to tell in his appearance. Sifting through Mikhail's memories, I was more than a little surprised. Not every breach warranted a personal visit from the defense minister himself.

"Greetings, Your Excellency!" I spoke first, as was proper for someone of lower rank and standing.

"And good health to you, son. How are you feeling?" asked Count Orlov, settling into the government-issue hospital chair, which groaned under his weight.

"Like I've just died and gotten a second chance — I just want to live so badly!" I joked, not lying in the slightest. That's exactly how it felt. After Hawthorn's treatment, all my instincts had grown keener. I wanted to eat, drink, and, well, I wouldn't have minded a little female company either.

Orlov glanced at his ring and then smiled at me, more relaxed now. So, he has an artifact that detects lies — good to know. I wonder what else he has?

It was as if the count read my thoughts, because he pulled a small red pyramid from his pocket and placed it on the bedside table.

"No one can eavesdrop on us now," he commented. "I'll ask you some questions, and you try to answer briefly or with a simple yes or no. Your fate depends on it."

I nodded, accepting the rules of the game — this felt like a rather gentle interrogation. I doubted he could surprise me after the three years I'd spent in the zealots' torture chambers, but who knows? I focused on Misha's memories, sensing that most of the questions would be about his life, not mine.

"Name?"

"Baron Mikhail Yuryevich Komarin," I said, showing him the family seal on my finger.

"Age?"

"Eighteen years old."

"What were you doing in the classified zone?"

"It's my land by birthright and by decree of His Imperial Majesty Alexei Krechet."

"You did not answer my question!" The minister pressed, not taking his eyes off his ring, which emitted a steady gray glow.

"I was sent there for special training before entering the Academy."

"And? What else?" the minister insisted.

"I was escaping an assassination attempt."

Orlov lifted his eyes from the ring, astonished to hear a young man say something like this, but the ring glowed pure white, confirming the truth of my statement.

"Who is your father?"

"Baronet Yuri Mikhailovich Komarin, retired officer of the Mosquito special unit. He died ten years ago due to an accident."

"Mother?"

"Maria Vasilievna Komarin, née Vinogradov. Deceased eight years ago. Accident."

"Brothers, sisters?"

"None that I'm aware of."

"Uncles, aunts?"

"My uncles were Sergei Mikhailovich Komarin and Dmitry Mikhailovich Komarin, retired officers from special unit Mosquito. Deceased six years ago and four years ago, respectively. Both due to accidents."

The minister was openly frowning now, his eyes flashing with frustration.

"Who raised you?"

"My grandfather, Baron Mikhail Yuryevich Komarin, retired officer, commander of the Mosquito
special unit. Deceased two years ago. Accident."

"Who else?"

Of course, that didn't add up — how could I
have lived two years as a complete orphan without
a guardian when the rest of my family was plagued
by such accidents?

"My grandfather's second wife, Baroness Agatha Petrovna Komarin. Retired officer of the Mosquito special unit. Presumed deceased following
an explosion on the day of my eighteenth birthday,
right after she saved me from an assassination attempt."

Orlov's eye began to twitch. Odd, usually it's
the person being interrogated who suffers a nervous tic, not the one conducting it.

"How did you seal the breach?"

"I wish I knew, sir! It just happened, intui-
tively."

The minister looked like he wanted to say
something, but the ring flared white, acknowledging my total honesty.

"What happened to the creature?"

"It went back home."

"It left on its own, just like that?"

"Yes!" The ring blazed white, and the minister
grimaced. It was the most convenient answer for a
truth-check.

"Why didn't it attack you?"

"Oh, it touched me plenty, but I guess I didn't

taste good," I said with a straight face, though my eyes sparkled with amusement.

Orlov, who had been leaning forward during the interrogation, now leaned back in his chair, exhaling. It seemed the questioning had been harder on him than on me.

"Why didn't your family come to me directly for help?" The tone of the question was different — this was clearly regret sounding in his voice.

Now, that was a good question, one I would have loved to ask the Komarin family myself. Misha's memories, as with all the previous questions about the family, provided the answer.

"They did! We were denied personal audiences three times. I can provide the responses to our official requests. The Motherland did not require our services for three hundred years — not since the last breach. But now that a new one's opened, here you are, the defense minister himself."

I was pushing things a bit. But that was the sentiment of the entire Komarin family, who lived in isolation, guarding two anomalies, dying at the hands of mysterious assassins, and yet, even in disgrace, still loyally serving their Motherland.

Orlov's face twisted at my words. He looked genuinely ashamed. And until today, he hadn't even known the Komarins existed or about their problems. But now he was taking it personally. Amazing! A politician with a conscience. Or maybe he was just that good of an actor. Though it didn't seem like an act.

"Well, son," Orlov finally spoke, looking up

from the ring but leaving his hand where I could clearly see it, "I'm taking personal control of the investigation into the attempts on your family's life. I'll also see to it that funding is restored to the Mosquito special unit." His ring glowed white, confirming his sincerity. "For closing a breach of this level, you're entitled to a reward. I'll be sure to add enough compensation to restore your family estate."

On the one hand, I didn't want to be indebted to Orlov, but on the other, he and his ministry owed the Komarins a great deal over the past years. We had upheld our end of the deal, fulfilling our duty under all circumstances, keeping the oath they had sworn to the Emperor.

So, without hesitation, I accepted the offer. Now, I just had to figure out how much ministerial generosity and conscience were worth. Oh, and I almost forgot — it was time to rebuild my personal library. I sent a mental summons to the local mosquitoes and to my surprise, received a chorus of replies. Well, this was turning into quite the celebration. I chose three of the swiftest females and commanded them to collect Orlov's blood. For his part, the minister didn't hurry to go.

"And another thing — based on what we've seen, are you a seal scribe?"

"Yes," I cautiously confirmed the count's hunch.

"What level?"

"Level 2 currently with a maximum of Level 5."

This news seemed to surprise Orlov quite a bit.

Misha's grandfather had a very particular view of education. He hadn't wanted me to attend the Imperial Academy, believing he could teach me everything I needed with the help of tutors. So Misha had earned his second level the hard way. His first level he'd easily attained by traveling with his grandfather's mage friends, but it was Agatha who had trained him up to Level 2 — through blood magic and ritual practice. And given Mikhail's natural inclination for blood magic, it would've been easier to pound a square peg into a round hole than to achieve that second level. But Misha's... I mean, my grandfather insisted that both abilities be developed equally, without leaning too heavily in one direction.

"With that kind of potential, you should be in the Academy," Orlov cast a fishing line, trying to hook me with bait like a naive fish.

"Yes, Your Excellency! And proudly die during the first semester — in an accident!" I couldn't hold back my sarcasm, snapping a salute. "No. Until I find out who tried to destroy my family, I'm not stepping into the limelight. Besides, we Komarins have our own school, and it's just as good as the Imperial Academy. It is staffed with people loyal to my bloodline."

The last sentence didn't go unnoticed.

"You think..."

"It's not my place to think, but the imperial authorities abandoned my family to its fate for ten long years! And we were under the Emperor's protection after all. If this investigation digs deep enough, it could easily uncover something that suggests treason."

The minister fell into deep thought — so deep he didn't even notice my mosquitoes take three drops of his blood. Now, I just needed to decide where to start building my new blood library.

* * *

It had been a long time since Arkady Ivanovich had prepared so meticulously for his superior's return. Every trace had been wiped clean, the scapegoat — previously fattened up for just such an occasion — had been found and eliminated. The embezzler and bribe-taker, Khomyakov, suddenly turned out to be guilty of concealing information vital to the state. His confession listed such a litany of sins it was almost enviable. He had wept, begged on his knees, pleading not to be sent to the torture chambers, willing to sign anything if only he were allowed to end it all with a mere bullet to the head. To avoid any trouble with the death mages, they even managed to cremate the body — entirely by accident, of course.

A man in a black cloak and wide-brimmed hat, obscuring his face, entered the office without knocking. Without asking for permission, he sat down in a chair and propped his mud-splattered boots — still caked with swamp muck — on the desk, which was piled with papers of national importance.

"What the hell are you doing here, you idiot?"

Arkady Ivanovich knocked the man's feet off the desk, frantically checking the documents for damage. "You could've just called! One call!"

"Oh, no!" the man drawled sarcastically, rummaging through a nearby cabinet for alcohol. Finding a bottle of exquisite twelve-year-old Armenian brandy, he uncorked it and swigged sacrilegiously straight from the bottle. "I've decided to change the terms of our deal, unilaterally!"

"Who do you think you're mouthing off to, you rat? Have you forgotten who feeds you?" Outwardly, Arkady Ivanovich was calm as a rock, but inside, he was already imagining the satisfying crunch of the man's neck between his fingers. The temptation was so strong, he almost gave in for a moment, but alas, a personal death mage was far too valuable to waste on a momentary murderous impulse.

"How could I forget my dear old father?" The bottle was already a third empty. "But I had a little chat with a cousin recently and learned some very interesting things!"

"Which cousin?"

"The recently deceased one," the death mage's grin stretched across his face, flashing all thirty-two teeth. He winked at his father and added, "After our chat though, he won't be saying anything to anyone else!"

"Well?"

Arkady Ivanovich was losing his patience. What his own son — the bastard child of a peasant girl — was telling him wasn't particularly impressive. Anthony had known very little, so there wasn't much he could reveal.

"Well?" The "son" took a hefty swig of brandy. "If I manage to finish what you've started, I want to join the family as your legitimate heir."

"How do I know they're not already dead?"

"Hum... How indeed?"

Arkady Ivanovich's comulet rang, drawing his attention.

"Yes, Your Excellency!"

"Pull up all the documents on special unit 'Mosquito,' including the financial reports," the minister's voice was thoughtful and occasionally interrupted by static. "And don't forget to send me a copy of the Emperor's decree!"

"It's already done, Your Excellency. New information has come to light. A report is awaiting you on your desk."

"That's what I like to hear! I appreciate it!" his superior praised him. "And draft an order to disburse a bonus to the Mosquito seal scribe for sealing a major breach. We need to reward this boy properly."

"Whose name shall I draft it for?"

"The name is Baron Mikhail Yuryevich Komarin."

"Understood, Count Orlov!"

The call ended, but the silence in the office was immediately broken by the insolent voice of the death mage:

"So, is it a deal... or shall I pay the minister a visit?"

CHAPTER 6

BEFORE RETURNING TO THE CAPITAL, Daniel Andreyevich managed to have a brief conversation with Svetlana. The shabby little hospital yard with its five pine trees and a bench in the shade didn't offer much privacy, but there was no other choice.

"Tell me, you little rascal, at what point did Madam Duplessis' finishing school for aristocratic girls turn into a survival training school for the Ministry of Defense's special forces?" Orlov tried his best to sound stern, hoping to appeal to the conscience of his old friend's daughter. It was a pointless effort, but he had to at least try.

"Uncle Daniel," the blond nuisance sniffled, practically crying into his chest as she hugged him tightly, "please don't tell my parents, pleeease!" She resorted to the most effective method of female manipulation, her blue eyes brimming with tears. "They'll either send me back to learn etiquette, or make me take dance classes, or drag me to salons and parties with all those suitors, and that's the last thing I want to do! Why does Slava get to study combat medicine and I don't? Why does he get special training and I don't? Why…"

"Because you're a girl! You're supposed to get married and have children, not crawl through swamps with a rifle and helmet!" Orlov stroked his friend's daughter's head, knowing full well his words would only fire her up.

"And who said that? What kind of outdated nonsense is that? Uncle Daniel, what makes me any worse than Slava?" Svetlana let go of the count, her face flushed, nearly steaming with indignation. Forgetting all caution, she blurted out, "Today I stabilized a dozen wounded! Everyone was saved! I patched up that seal scribe from the swamps in two hours, while your field medics were ready to declare him a magical cripple! So how am I worse? Eleven people saved in one day! And all my parents ever tell me is 'You need to get engaged!'"

Orlov just shook his head. She was a troublesome girl, through and through. But, having no children of his own, he loved Svetlana more than anyone. She was more like him than her calm, level-headed father, who was the chief physician to the imperial family.

"Oh, Svetlana, your father will wring my neck if he finds out I knew about this and didn't send you home," Orlov already knew he'd give in to this dragonfly's persistence. Especially since her words carried weight — eleven lives worth of weight. He'd also have to talk to her father, Count Hawthorn, to make sure he didn't push the girl too hard into marriage. If she rebelled, they'd be searching for her across all of Mother Russia.

"Uncle Daniel, we won't tell him!" The girl winked mischievously and quickly added, "and anyway, everything turned out fine in the end!"

The minister just shook his head. Ah, youth, with its near-invincible belief in immortality. He'd been like that once, too. The memory alone made him sigh heavily.

"You'll deal with your father yourself. I'll keep quiet, but at least take a look at the suitors. Maybe one will strike your fancy."

"Yeah right! I've met those suitors and seen how they act away from their parents' eyes," Svetlana grimaced as if she'd just caught a whiff of a latrine. "Uncle, they'll screw anything that moves, and if it doesn't move, they'll shake it awake and screw it too!"

"Svetlana! Where are your manners?" Orlov coughed, trying to hide his laughter. "No one's going to force you to do anything. You know that. If you find someone you like, I'll personally put in a good word for you. So, if I were you, I'd take my destiny into my own hands."

The girl fell silent, frowning in deep thought. Her displeasure was obvious, but she didn't argue. Clearly, his advice had resonated with her.

"I'll think about it, Uncle Daniel. I promise!"

"There's a good girl!" Orlov hugged her and

spun her around like he had when she was little. She laughed heartily, but didn't protest. "Want me to drop you off back at your school?"

"Our instructors are waiting for us. We'll use portal scrolls to return," Svetlana smiled.

"Those Mosquito kids are well taken care of," the Defense Minister mused aloud.

"I think it's more of a necessity, due to the anomaly."

"Oh, Svetlana, anomalies are classified top secret!" Orlov grabbed his head in disbelief. "You do know that breaking a magical oath can mean death, right?"

"Don't take me for a fool. I might be a blonde, but that has nothing to do with intelligence," the girl grinned brightly, a mischievous glint in her eyes. "This excuse might just be better than a family secret!"

"Someone's in for some happiness…"

"They sure are," muttered Hawthorn under her breath, "as long as they behave themselves. If not, widowhood is just around the corner!"

"Svetlana!" Count Orlov coughed again, trying to hide his laughter. What a healer.

"All right, all right, I'll be quiet!"

*　*　*

Two armored monsters — six-meter-long infantry fighting vehicles painted in camouflage and bearing Mosquito emblems — were waiting for me in the parking lot of the military hospital. I'd never seen such marvels of engineering before, though Mikhail's memories were filled with journeys in nothing but these IFVs.

As my late grandfather used to say, "Even Emperor Krechet himself couldn't pry us out of this tin can!" But Grandpa had been dead for two years now, which only proved one thing: for every tin can, there's a pry bar long enough to open it.

A dozen of the same instructors who had been with me before stood by the convoy, and this time, upon seeing me, they synchronously slammed their fists against their chests in a salute. I hesitated a moment before returning the gesture, which made the ring on my finger glow red. The instructors' eyes widened in shock, but they quickly regained their composure.

Without further discussion, one of the IFV's doors swung open, and I climbed inside.

The interior of the armored vehicle was divided into two sections. The troop compartment where the soldiers sat was combined with a medical bay, judging by the integrated medical-magical equipment. In a separate area, there was a command section with plush leather seats, a minibar tucked into one corner, complete with an ashtray and even a stationary communications amulet.

This armored vehicle wasn't cheap — it was a mobile command post. While Spider and I made ourselves comfortable in the luxury section, the soldiers took their seats in the troop compartment, eyeing me as if I were some sort of resurrected deity. Sure, I looked good, but something told me their awe had nothing to do with my appearance.

"Your Lordship, it's good to see you in good health!" Spider's voice caught my attention.

"Likewise. Were there many casualties from the breach?" I asked, trying to gauge the damage caused by Tilda's cameo.

"No losses among the Mosquito forces. That creature choked out a few of them but didn't kill them. Fifteen civilians, however, were lost."

"Such a shame about the civilians. We'll need to allocate compensation to their families," I said, leaning back in my seat and studying Spider.

"A petition has already been submitted to the Ministry, but I fear it'll get lost in the system, as usual."

"Not this time. If necessary, we'll compensate them with our own funds. Money's no longer an issue."

Finances had been a sore subject for the past few years. On one hand, our family had more wealth than we could spend, but on the other, the Komarins kept that fact quiet.

The mere fact that our personal bannermen had been meticulously recruited from the ranks of common-born servants, with their education funded at various academies, said a lot. Not every noble family could afford to pay for even a few off-spring to attend. Aristocratic privileges usually allowed for free education. The Komarins, however, had trained nearly six hundred of their servants through various means.

Cutting-edge technology and weapons were

purchased from the Ministry of Defense for our special unit's needs. Sometimes, equipment was imported from abroad at exorbitant prices. But things had started falling apart ten years ago. Loopholes were closed, access to key officials was cut off and, on top of it all, there were the "accidents." It all pointed to someone who saw us as a thorn in their side — someone who knew exactly how vast our resources were and how we moved funds through the system, often disguised as government financing.

The current dire situation was due to a legal loophole. We had money, but only the direct heir, upon reaching adulthood, could access it — meaning me! Until that moment, I'd been given a stipend that, while not modest, was far from enough to cover the needs of our family's bannermen. Even Agatha Petrovna, who'd married into the family, received an allowance smaller than mine, as she had no children with my grandfather. In hindsight, she was probably brought into the family to avoid suspicion.

These previously fragmented facts had recently come together. Hawthorn's treatment had an unexpected side effect, so to speak. I no longer felt the divide between myself and Misha. We had finally merged into one individual. And I had plenty to think about.

The vehicle picked up speed slowly, steadily accelerating. For a while, we drove on paved roads, but soon we turned onto dirt paths. Spider averted his gaze, clearly uncomfortable, until I broke the silence.

"Why didn't you leave with the others or transfer to another branch of the armed service?"

I watched Spider's expression carefully. Funny — our roles had reversed. In the cell, he had scrutinized me intensely, but now I had the initiative. The only difference was that I already knew the answer. I just wanted to hear his version of it.

"Mikhail Yuryevich, we are your bloodbound. Loyal until death. And the money... We managed as best we could. We even started those training courses with Agatha Petrovna's permission, just to make ends meet," Spider spoke directly, not avoiding my gaze, not fawning or groveling. He did not have a guilty conscience and I knew this not by deducing it from his expression — but from a sample of his blood that my mosquitoes had already brought me. Just as they had from every other soldier in the armored vehicles. It's always better to check everyone at once rather than regret missing a traitor in your own ranks later.

Every single one of them was a loyal bannerman of the Komarins and part of my grandfather's personal guard — bloodbound, as they called themselves. Indeed, using my gift, I could see the red threads of our blood link stretching from me to the soldiers, flecked with gold — a sign that their oath was given voluntarily and sincerely. Another new ability had surfaced, allowing me to see their magical affinities. The soldiers' magical cores looked like whirlpools of water, icicles, fiery tornadoes, and other fascinating elements. It turned out my grandfather had recruited quite the extraordinary force. If only I had more like them... But all in good time. After ten years of assassination attempts, our guard had been severely thinned out.

"Your Lordship, may I ask a question?"

"Go ahead."

"Why didn't you tell us who you were right away?"

"And what would that have changed? I didn't have the ring. I planned to undergo training on equal footing with the others, without any special treatment."

"But how?" Spider pointed at the family ring, confused. "Where did it come from?"

"Our patron deity rewarded me for closing the breach, just as he did my ancestor long ago."

"For the glory of Aedes!" Spider replied instantly.

"For the glory," I echoed automatically, though my thoughts were elsewhere.

Oddly enough, beyond the family lands, the binding seal on my hand felt much weaker. While scanning my bloodbound soldiers, I unconsciously extended my blood sense to its maximum, trying to cover the second vehicle. The range of my ability had increased dramatically. Besides my own soldiers, I sensed an ambush three kilometers ahead on the forest road.

"Slow down," I ordered, trying to buy time. The driver of our vehicle reacted instantly, without asking questions. And, likewise, the mosquitoes in the woodlands around us responded to my request immediately. My small, personal army of scouts. Thank you, Aedes! This was one of the best abilities he could have bestowed upon me.

The scouts worked fast. Once I had blood samples, I was shocked.

First of all, the ambushers were all common-born. Secondly, they were preparing something big. And by "big," I didn't mean icicles or fireballs. No, they were preparing something cataclysmic — on the level of an inferno or a storm of chain lightning. Three teams of five mages were conjuring lethal spells. Above each group, I saw hazy symbols of the elemental magic they wielded — fire, earth and air.

Guessing what they intended to hit us with was impossible. Well, not entirely impossible, but not with just a few drops of blood. And curiously, there were no water mages. Oh well, I'd deal with that later. But no, here come the water mages! They'd cut us off from behind, closing the trap. I had to make a decision on how to proceed as quickly as possible.

I trusted my ten bannermen, of course, but I had no desire to get caught in the crossfire of four elemental mages at once. A crazy idea popped into my head — why not fake my own death? That way, I could see which vultures would come to circle us first. After all, they'd been working toward their goal for ten years. Why not lure them in with a tempting piece of bait?

I focused on the threads leading to my soldiers. Let's see how much the family ring simplifies working with those bound to my bloodline.

"This is Baron Komarin speaking," I announced. "There's an assassination attempt being prepared against us. Theoretically, we have zero chances. Four powerful squads of elemental mages are working on something deadly up ahead. I propose we do as follows..."

* * *

Marcus was nervous. This was their first contract of such scale. When he, an ex-commander of a border unit, suggested that his comrades form a mercenary group, they'd been skeptical. However, the pension for retired soldiers wasn't much, and the one thing they were good at was fighting.

Over time, Marcus cobbled together four teams of elemental mages from his former comrades. They offered clients mixed squads or specialized hit teams tailored to specific elements. All in all, business was booming.

Marcus made sure to rotate his team members to avoid dissatisfaction, but all the groups had never worked together before. Four squads — it was practically a mini-army. But Marcus felt deep down that the right opportunity would come, and so it did. It was but a single contract, but what a contract! They had to ensure success and there was no room for failure. The payout was more than enough to cover all their moral, material, and other costs. In simpler terms, if they had earned this much in the regular army, they might never have retired.

The surprises began immediately. Instead of expensive but cumbersome civilian vehicles, two military-grade armored monsters appeared on the forest road. They resembled machines Marcus had seen in the most secure areas of the imperial border. It was clear the vehicles' munitions had been removed, but that didn't mean the soldiers inside weren't armed themselves.

So their ambush had to be adjusted on the fly. Blowing up the armored vehicles with regular spells wasn't going to work — they were likely built to withstand magic of at least Level 3 or 4. The mercenaries decided it wasn't worth the risk.

This setup had been created for a rare and exceptional situation, and it seemed that moment had arrived. Each team was preparing a devastating AoE spell that could decide a medieval war in their favor. Together, they guaranteed certain death.

Marcus gave the order to prepare backup charges, just in case they had to hold the spell longer than expected. The contract accounted for the use of additional resources, so the mercenaries spared no expense, working meticulously.

"Earth!" Marcus's word set the ambush into motion.

As soon as the armored vehicles crossed the designated line, the earth beneath them split open, and the vehicles plunged five meters into the ground.

"Water!" Marcus barked. "Air!"

At his command, the water mages created two water spheres around the armored vehicles, and the air mages vacuumed the oxygen out of them. For safety, they held them in this watery void for almost half an hour.

During that time, the fire and earth mages were on edge, expecting a last-ditch, suicidal attack from their targets. But there were no signs of life, which both relieved and unsettled them. It didn't make sense. A cornered rat fights back more viciously, but apparently, there were no rats here.

"Earth! Fire!" Marcus gave the order to move to the final stage, waiting longer than necessary just to be sure. "Water, stand by for protection!"

The earth mages raised layers of stone to the surface, and the fire mages melted them, creating hermetically sealed sarcophagi, the final resting place for their unfortunate victims. Granite encased the armored vehicles, trapping them in solid rock.

The water mages, meanwhile, maintained a five-meter protective shell to shield the forest from accidental fires.

Marcus's heart ached as he watched the armored vehicles disappear into the flames. They were worth a fortune. What was remarkable was that even after all the spells, the vehicles were barely damaged. But the order had been clear — everyone inside the vehicles bearing the Mosquito emblem had to be eliminated.

Some vague memory scratched at the back of Marcus's mind, something about the Mosquito emblem. A shadow of recognition, but it didn't fully form into a memory.

The armored vehicles vanished, buried under layers of cooling stone. The walls of the chasm closed, as if a localized apocalypse hadn't occurred there just thirty minutes ago.

"Zhiva, Trava, you're up."

The slender twin girls got to work. While Trava restored the landscape, healing the vegetation at the edges of the road, Marcus quietly pulled Zhiva aside and asked the question that preoccupied him most:

"How many were there, and when did they die?"

"There were eleven occupants. Six soldiers in the first vehicle, five in the second. They struggled to the end. I stopped sensing any life as soon as the vehicles sank into the molten stone."

"Could the stone have interfered with your sense?" Marcus was being cautious. He couldn't afford to fail such a serious contract.

"No, I can detect living beings up to a kilometer underground, even worms," Zhiva gritted her teeth. She hated when anyone doubted her professionalism. "There are no living beings down there now."

Marcus nodded and was about to ask another question when someone interrupted him:

"Marcus, a word."

The men stepped aside, not disturbing Trava as she continued her work.

"I'm not sure if this is important, but you need

to know," said the earth mage, a bearded, stocky man, looking a bit shaken. "I remembered something. About twenty years ago, the Ministry of Defense had a special program for gifted commonborn mages. They were trained in academies and then recruited into a top-secret special unit. Their emblem was a mosquito."

Chapter 7

My bloodbound were shaking me with all their might, trying to bring me to my senses. Splashing water on me and slapping my face didn't help much, but Spider wasn't the commander of the old guard for nothing. After a few minutes, they forced my mouth open and poured in some truly invigorating liquid — a mix of two parts of single-malt whiskey and one part fresh blood. I took two greedy gulps and finally started coming around.

"How are you feeling?"

"Where are we?" I ignored the question, more worried about how far we'd traveled and how soon we could expect company.

"We are on the shore of Lake Ladoga. We got teleported about a hundred kilometers," Spider reported, stammering slightly as he kept squeezing blood from his own palm into a second glass, adding less alcohol this time.

"Baron, you're a monster!" exclaimed the second squad's commander with admiration in his voice. "In the name of Aedes, I was sure we were done for... yet you managed to get us out of that trap — and you even brought the IFVs!"

To be fair, I hadn't intended to bring along the infantry fighting vehicles. It just happened somehow, which was probably why I'd overexerted myself just a bit.

Transporting a dozen men using the blood bond is one thing, but dragging along two 25-ton armored vehicles is another. There's no blood in them, obviously.

My head was finally clearing, and I was beginning to understand the magnitude of the stunt I'd just pulled off.

"What the hell, gentlemen?" was all I could say. "Who links armored vehicles through a blood bond? Come on, own up, you perverts!"

There were chuckles from the group.

"Agatha Petrovna upgraded these IFVs," Spider explained this unexpected detail. "Originally, macros powered their defensive and offensive systems, but the baroness, Aedes rest her soul, created a duplicate circuit linked to mage blood, so the mages could control them in real-time, boosting attack or defense as needed. It's what kept us alive." The commander shook his head, sealing the cut with a plaster before tucking his hand back into his glove.

"I must say, those mercenaries did a professional job," commented the instructor, Beetle, who'd run the forced march with us. "Four AoE spells at once would've torn our standard defenses apart. Without upgrades, the armor would've held off a Level 3 spell from a mage — or a very weak Level 4 one. But four elemental mages channeling their attacks together? We were goners."

As I sipped from the second glass, I took a look around. The Mosquitoes had already dug into the forest, thrown camo nets over the IFVs, and even reconnoitered the nearest village. The whole time, I'd been out cold. That was no good.

To our assassins, we were dead as dead can be. If it hadn't been for Agatha and her experiments, we'd be eleven corpses buried under a forest road now.

"What's next, Mikhail Yurievich?" Spider asked the pressing question. "If the state declares you deceased, our lands could pass on to someone with the right connections in six months' time."

"You've got the right idea! Your job is to go back and finish training the recruits. My job will be to track down anyone who thinks they'll benefit from picking up our crumbs." Spider looked ready to object, but I cut him off. "No objections. I need you at the school. Ministry officials will start showing up there after we've disappeared. Keep an eye on everyone. And don't forget — you all need to wear disguise artifacts from now on. Meanwhile, I'll stir up trouble in this wasps' nest. My grandfather and I had a plan for this."

I deliberately mentioned my grandfather. The old baron was an experienced intrigant who always had several backup plans for every contingence, including life and death. The ruse he'd planned for this particular occasion was already working.

"What about communications?" Spider persisted. "Our comulets don't work over such distances. We won't be able to come help you!"

"Well, we always have the blood link. Aren't I a blood mage?" I replied. "But without orders, don't even think about offering help. The game we're about to play will be a risky one."

* * *

That evening, I reached the cultural capital of my new homeland. A kind-hearted local gave me a ride to the nearest town, where I hired a coach to take me to Saint Petersburg. There was of course the option of taking the locomotive, but since I was still officially missing, I figured I had better not show my face in crowded places.

Portal scrolls are a great thing, really, albeit expensive. However, they wouldn't have worked for the place I needed to get to.

I hadn't lied about my grandfather having a plan. Just before Mikhail's sixteenth birthday, after the fifth attempt on his life, Baron Komarin shared some information with his grandson, which was now coming in handy.

I wonder if it's customary here to offer gratitude to the deceased. Does it help them in any way?

"It does," my patron deity mused in response to my silent question. "It makes their reincarnation more likely."

Then, Mikhail Yurievich Komarin, alias Grandpa, alias Old Baron, I wish you a speedy rebirth. I never met you, but judging by your actions when you were still alive, I already like you.

The rickety coach dropped me at the very edge of Saint Petersburg, in a rough part of town run by the so-called Sparrow Gang — a nest of banditry and depravity, which according to Grandpa, nevertheless boasted more honesty and justice than any aristocratic salon in the city center.

The carriage door swung open and the terrified face of the driver appeared before me.

"Sir, I'm sorry, but I cannot go any further. I value my life too dearly."

The guy had gone pale, visibly terrified of entering the rough district and, understandably, afraid for his life.

"Thank you, my good man. This is as far as I need to go."

I slipped out of the carriage like a shadow. My dark clothing, which bore no insignia, blended perfectly into the twilight of the deserted streets. Bottles, scraps of newspaper, half-rotten crates… animal bones and perhaps not just animal bones.

The local mosquitoes swiftly fanned out in search of any lurking locals while I cranked up my blood sense to full and took off.

After about thirty minutes and two bodies later, I reached my destination. No pangs of conscience — the two bodies belonged to some cutthroats who tried to take my life. I took theirs instead. Two scumbags now lay peacefully at the bottom of a rubbish-filled, dried-up canal. As for me, rest was something I could only dream of.

It was an annoying random encounter too. I couldn't even drink from them. Both of those bastards carried such a bouquet of diseases, it would've been safer to drink from a puddle than to taste their blood. If it weren't for the damned holy seal on my hand, I could cleanse their blood of impurities. Yet, with my powers still limited, I had to be cautious.

I knocked quietly on a nondescript door with peeling paint — and a small window slid open.

"What do you want?" a surly voice barked through clenched teeth.

"A Bloody Mary and a handful of grapes."

The window snapped shut, and after a minute, the door opened to let me in. There were signs of decay everywhere — long, narrow hallways covered in cobwebs, empty, grimy walls with cleaner rectangles where paintings had once hung, magical lamps, some lit, some not, either in a bid to save energy or hide the disrepair.

Madam Ju-Ju's brothel had gone to seed a bit since the first and only time Mikhail had been here. The local girls had made him a man, while his Grandpa introduced him to one of his hiding places.

The madam's office still held traces of its former luxury. Massive oak furniture, a few reproductions of famous painters and an exquisite fan collection covering an entire wall — this was all that remained of what had once been one of Saint Petersburg's finest brothels.

The madam greeted me personally. Petite, shapely, with bright red lips and a mole above her upper lip, she looked no more than thirty but was at least sixty. I had to force myself to keep my gaze on her face, though her figure, hugged by a tight, sheer dress, would've made many envious.

"Madam, you're as captivating and timeless as ever!" I half-bowed, kissing her delicate hand sheathed in a long black glove.

"Young man, I hardly recognize you. You were so shy when we met and now, you've changed so much." Her crystal voice echoed sweetly through her office.

Ah! Madam was testing Misha's mettle. Not everyone could withstand the natural allure of this truly stunning woman, a magnificent former spy.

"Madam, I'd gladly succumb to your charms, but if I did, Grandfather might return from the dead to see his no-good grandson. Let's not disturb his rest!" I shot her a cheeky wink. "But if your intentions are sincere, I promise not to disgrace the family name."

For the first time, Madam flashed me a genuine smile.

"A fool, yet so much like your grandfather!" The former spy settled into her chair, nodding for me to take the one opposite. "Would you like some refreshment?"

"What do you have to offer?"

"Asians, mixed-race beauties, noble girls and not-so-noble ones, gifted ones and even a couple of virgins," Madam listed with a smile, watching my intrigued reaction.

Her offer was certainly a pleasant surprise, though I'd already caught a sense of her selection on my way to her office. My winged scouts had already brought me a sampling of the blood of everyone in the brothel, Madam included. Of all the girls, only one caught my interest — and not for physical reasons.

"The Asian girl with dark hair and cherry-colored eyes, a hopeless addict," I announced my choice, noting Madam Ju-Ju's frown. "I would like to take her with me. If a ransom is required, I'll pay — in money or favors."

"She's not worth it, Misha..." Madam stammered. "She's beyond saving. I tried; even my healers have given up."

"With all due respect, Madam, if she's a dead asset to you, she's valuable to me," I said, tapping my fingers on the armrest as I awaited delivery of one of the most talented illusion mages I'd encountered. "I want her," I declared slowly, pausing to emphasize each word as I held Madam Ju-Ju's gaze.

Discovering such a treasure so close to Grandfather's stash was nothing short of a miracle. Coincidences like this didn't happen by chance. Either Lady Fortune had a soft spot for me or I was simply one hell of a lucky son of a gun.

"Fine, you may have her! But you'll go broke buying her the junk she needs to stay alive. My whole brothel practically works to fund her habit."

I just smirked. Madam was downplaying things — this whole brothel was still running thanks to that girl's talents. She somehow managed to bring all her clients' wildest fantasies to life. At the very least, she earned her keep in doses.

And Madam couldn't refuse me. Hard to refuse when you owe someone a life debt.

Five minutes later, the girl was brought in. Emaciated, with hollow cheeks and dark circles under her eyes, she looked like a ghost. Her white kimono did nothing for her frail appearance.

She couldn't even stand on her own. As soon as they released her, she collapsed into the chair next to mine, breathing heavily. Beads of sweat dotted her face as she curled into herself.

I lifted the sleeve of her kimono. Just as I'd thought — her veins were punctured from wrist to armpit. No matter; we'd make her better again. Not for free, of course, but I wasn't going to let a talent like hers perish from addiction.

I left Madam Ju-Ju's brothel, having first emptied Grandfather's stash, with the girl hoisted over my shoulder.

In my pocket were keys to a safehouse and forged documents identifying me as one Gavrila Petrovich Vinogradov, a distant nephew of late Misha's late mother. Grandfather had done well. The papers, the residence, the bank account — it was all prepared well in advance. But the most valuable item was his letter, with some of his thoughts on recent events. I would use his ideas and analysis to form my plan of action.

The coach driver only grunted when he saw the girl. There was plenty of things to see in the territory of the Sparrow Gangs, but there was one golden rule: "The less you know, the longer you live."

Giving him the address of my safehouse, I let my thoughts drift as we set out. I needed to speak to my patron deity.

"Aedes, can you hear me?" I said mentally.

"I hear you!" My patron's irritated voice came through. "Is it urgent?"

"What's your standing with your Asian counterparts?"

"Hum?" Aedes replied with more interest. "We're not exactly friendly, but we're not at war either. What happened?"

"I just happened across the heiress to the Kitsune clan — the cherry-eyed fox deity is her patron. The girl's a hopeless addict with one foot in the grave. I can save her, but it'll take time and resources."

"So what do you want from me?"

"I'm offering you an opportunity, some aces to hold up your sleeve. I'm more than sure you have some political conflicts in which any ally could be valuable."

There was silence for a few moments, but then Aedes finally responded.

"You're not just bringing up allies for no reason, are you? What are you really after?"

"I need permission to temporarily mask your patron ring with an illusion. I'd like to take on the guise of a member of the Vinogradov family, so I can find out who's targeting our own family."

"Are you out of your mind?!" Aedes exploded. "I dragged you here from another plane, rescued you from a pyre, accepted you into my family clan and now you're planning to bolt off to the Vinogradovs?"

I waited out his first — and even second — wave of anger. Anger was good. He hadn't refused outright, so there was a chance he'd see things my way. After a few minutes, when his torrent of invective directed at me finally exhausted itself, I clarified:

"I'm not taking off your ring and I'm not abandoning the Komarin family. I just want to apply an illusion to myself!"

"Will you look at him! Apply an illusion to a divine artifact! This isn't a matter of befuddling some yokels at the country fair! You realize that to use another family symbol, you'd need permission from Muscadine, the patron god of the Vinogradovs? That grouch has been in a foul mood for a century. He barely has any clan left and now you want to come waltzing in claiming the Vinogradov blood on your mother's side?"

"All I ask is that you set up a parley. Please! We'll work it out! And I swear I won't switch clans. I would have to contravene the Code otherwise."

Aedes mumbled something incoherent about

humans not knowing their limits and making a god run errands like a secretary, but his anger had abated and his voice was now more filled with irritation and a hint of curiosity. I was asking him to form alliances with other gods, even if only temporary, and that hadn't happened in a long while.

The more he observed my soul, the more convinced he became that his spontaneous choice hadn't been so bad. The recent oath only strengthened his divinity. He could tell that as long as he held on for a while longer, things could actually start turning around for him.

*   *   *

Arkady Ivanovich was finally celebrating his long-sought triumph. The sweet sensation intoxicated him more than a bottle of vodka on an empty stomach. However, despite the feeling of exhilaration welling up within him, outwardly, Arkady Ivanovich remained as calm as an iceberg off the Icelandic coast. Ten years of work and careful planning were about to pay off. Just six more months and the Rat clan would acquire vast new territories and riches.

He especially relished the expression on that young pup's face — the death mage who aspired to become the principal Rat heir but ended up cleaning up after the assassins. Witnesses were unnecessary, and it wasn't even about the money. The price could have been steeper, but Arkady Ivanovich liked to cover all his bases. Who knew if some soldier might suddenly remember his honor or, heaven forbid, his conscience? Professional ethics still mattered. This way, by arranging the disappearance of the Komarin heir as well as a well-trained unit of ex-soldiers, he could later claim that the whole thing was a conflict of interest and pin the deaths on the assassins while concealing the role of the one pulling the strings.

On his way to see Count Orlov, Arkady Ivanovich had no idea how the old warrior would take the news.

The Minister of Defense stood by the window, sipping brandy — at one in the afternoon. Even Arkady Ivanovich's famous restraint slipped; his eyebrows crawled up his forehead in mute surprise.

"I read your report about the Komarins. Excellent work!" The minister finished his glass in one gulp. "Since you're so involved, I'd like you to see this matter through. I realize this isn't exactly your area of expertise, but, forgive me, there's no one else I trust to handle this." The count turned from the window, returning thoughtfully to his chair. "I want you to got to Hmarevo, supervise the investigation and oversee the estate's restoration. There's been much too many assassination attempts against one clan. My men will take control for now, and we'll decide the rest as we go."

The personal secretary bowed, clicking his heels. He was beaming to himself. Orlov was unwittingly sending him to settle into his new domain. He'd need to find some clues that would lead to a dead end or another scapegoat — in order to justify a longer stay, but so far, everything was aligning unbelievably well.

And Orlov didn't even know there was no one left to save. The Komarin bloodline was gone. It had been — and now it was no more.

Chapter 8

THE SAFEHOUSE TURNED OUT to be a cozy two-story manor with a garden and a small dock on one of the myriad canals that crisscross Saint Petersburg. I liked the location, which came with the bonus of an escape route via the canal. The manor itself was not too grand, but far from modest — and therefore perfect for blending into high society, where the correct appearance was often worth more than how much money you had. And since my new alias, Gavrila Vinogradov, had aristocratic blood but no title, social status was something I had to consider carefully.

To my surprise, we were expected. To unlock the house, I had to dip the key in blood before inserting it into the lock and turning it — a clever invention of Agatha Petrovna. She really had been an amazing woman when it came to blood magic. I was beginning to realize I'd underestimated her potential as one of the top fifty in my world's ranks. She was still scoring points, and something told me there'd be more surprises from her to come.

After this "friend-or-foe" check, I stepped inside my new residence. We were greeted by a tall, reed-thin butler, a plump, gray-haired housekeeper and a pair of maids with such unremarkable faces that "plain as a mouse" didn't do them justice.

"Welcome, Gavrila Petrovich! Your bedroom has been prepared for you and the guest rooms are ready as well! We are ready to serve you a late dinner if you wish. The baths are drawn and heated."

Now that's what I call service!

"Thank you! This young lady isn't well. Assist her with food and hygiene, and let me know when she's ready for... her treatment," I said with a grimace, already picturing what this treatment would entail, but there was no choice. I needed her in reasonably decent shape, so I'd have to bear it. "I will have my dinner in the study, please."

The maids took the girl by her arms and carried her upstairs, while I followed the butler to the study.

Not bad. The room was furnished with fine wood, a marble fireplace, a thick carpet, bookshelves, and a stand with ceremonial weapons. Simple and tasteful. Fit for hosting guests.

The butler brought me my dinner: broth, sliced meats, medium-rare beef and a salad.

"Gavrila Petrovich, after the treatment session... Will you require a top-up?"

I hesitated for only a moment before nodding, scanning the servants with my gift. All blood-bound, all Komarin faithful, all sworn to oaths of service. The plain maids, as it turned out, were also quite powerful Level 5 mages. They had no elemental affinities, but I'd figure that out later. The butler was a Level 4 fire mage and the housekeeper was a healer of the same level.

Grandpa, you genius! What a team he'd put together. How much did this all cost? Not for the first time, I wondered about the sources of my new family's wealth.

"Minerals," came Aedes' voice as he appeared in human form, settling into an armchair by the fireplace. He looked like a dandy, in a black suit, with a cane and a crimson neck scarf. His face was indistinct with sunglasses in an adamantine frames perched on his nose, obscuring his eyes.

"I'm honored to welcome my patron god to my humble residence," I bowed my head in greeting and sat down in the armchair next to him.

He acknowledged my greeting with a graceful nod.

"Minerals are the primary source of your wealth," he went on. "After the first cross-dimensional breach was sealed, geologists discovered that the very nature of the affected area had changed. I didn't delve into the details, but the metals we extracted were sold directly to the defense industry for armor. Some mega-energetic agglomerates — what you call macros — were also unearthed and those ended up in the private stores of the wealthiest clans by means of secret auctions. So, the Komarins made good money but true to their word, they kept a low profile and did their duty guarding the anomalies. For three hundred years, your family administered its domain with a steady hand, while the world all around them rotted."

"Thank you for the information. It's invaluable, especially given the recent breach. I'll have my bannermen seal off any access to the breach site."

Aedes grew quiet, gazing distantly at the fire. I didn't rush him. If a god decided to honor me with his attention, he had his reasons — and I wasn't wrong.

"How long will the treatment take?" he finally asked, cutting to the heart of the matter.

"At most, six months. With my current powers, I can only manage one session a month."

"That's too long."

"There are three possible outcomes: 'alive,' 'healthy' and 'gifted.' If I go as fast as I can, I can only guarantee two out of three," I replied with a shrug, fully understanding I wouldn't choose that option even if ordered. In the worst case, I'd have to go back to my home plane to heal her, but I couldn't make that journey as long as my hand remained sealed.

"She has four months; then the Kitsune clan will cut her off from its blood link with a ritual. It seems that a cadet branch of the family is stirring things up, looking to install their own heir in her place."

"What about Kitsune herself? Can't she just handle the troublemakers?" I was genuinely puzzled now. Gods, after all, had the power to bless and curse. They could do practically anything, so why not put upstart followers in their place? My skepticism must have been clear and Aedes' face soured as if he'd bitten into a lemon.

"If only it were that simple. Our kind has... well, restrictions on interfering with the lives of our believers. Just imagine what would happen if all the gods decided to grant their bloodbound superpowers. A war would follow, wiping out entire families and ultimately weakening the gods. The same applies to curses or overt displays of power. Kitsune could curse or banish Akira — the upstart I mentioned — but that would cost her a chunk of her followers and, in turn, her power. We gods always have to maintain a balance in which the mortals and gods remain separate."

I understood what he was saying, and yet Aedes had pulled me from another plane. There seemed no clearer example of gods meddling with mortals to me. I didn't even want to guess how much of his power the maneuver had cost him.

"I know what you're thinking, but yours was a special case. An emergency impelled me to take drastic measures. Don't ever mention that you're from another plane around here. Not even to your wife on her deathbed. There could be consequences. In our world, people don't just dislike plane-hoppers like you — they destroy them on principle."

The conversation had taken an enlightening turn. I hadn't planned to broadcast my foreign origins, but I hadn't expected outright persecution either.

"Back to the matter at hand, Kitsune would be very grateful if you could manage to heal Teimei sooner," Aedes removed his glasses, revealing enormous compound eyes. "And here's a small gift to aid you in Teimei's recovery."

"How unexpected." I took the glasses and tried them on. The world transformed instantly, first going dark, then bursting into vibrant colors. Looking at Aedes, I barely kept myself from recoiling in shock:

He was Energy — pure, searing! It twisted, shifted in shape and intensity. I wanted to reach out, drink it in, submerge myself in it. I'd never seen so many shades of blood in my long existence. It was entrancing, captivating and I had to force myself to look away.

"Well done!" my patron praised my self-control. "Few can resist the temptation. You'll figure out the artifact — there are some surprises hidden in it. Kitsune was generous on behalf of her heir. Imagine her gratitude if you heal her in time."

I wasn't so optimistic about my chances, so I changed the subject.

"Any luck arranging a meeting with Muscadine?"

"I passed along your request but received no response."

I thanked Aedes sincerely. Without him, I'd

have had no chance of reaching another god, much less gaining a bonus artifact like these spectacles. I'd have to test them a bit to find out what surprises they had in store.

Lost in thought, I realized my family totem had vanished without a farewell. It was just as well. He'd already gone above and beyond for my requests.

Remembering what Aedes had said, I contacted Spider through our blood link. My conversation with the Mosquito commander was brief: I ordered him to keep everyone away from the breach site until I gave the go-ahead. As long as I remained missing in action, no one — not even the Ministry of Defense — could claim my lands. I had a fair suspicion that the swamp, post-breach, had become a priceless source of family wealth. Then I asked Spider how things were going with the recruits, or the "wrigglers" as the Mosquitoes called them.

"Hawthorn has Bear on the run. The girls have formed an alliance, so the guys have become incels. On the upside, the breach really boosted their motivation regarding the training," Spider reported succinctly. "Hawthorn also asked about you. I had to tell her that the Ministry called you up for training as a promising seal mage. She didn't believe it, but she didn't ask more questions."

Smart girl — if she knows when to hold her tongue, she might make a good personal healer. But that's far in the future. For now, I needed to tend to Kitsune's heir, Teimei. Without her help and Muscadine's permission, I could only act remotely. And if I really wanted to provoke my enemies, I had plenty of work ahead of me.

*　*　*

It seemed the maids had misunderstood how to prepare Teimei for treatment. She smelled of delicate floral perfume and wore something sheer and white — barely "clothing," in the loosest sense. And "loose" was not what I could say about my pants at the sight of her.

Despite her frail appearance, Teimei was well-proportioned, reminding me of bamboo — stiff, resilient and deadly.

Her dark hair fanned out on the pillow as groans slipped from her lips, not of pleasure or desire, but of pain from her withdrawals. I knew I could help with that, but I had to get her to a stable state first.

Shaking all unprofessional thoughts from my head, I scanned her with my blood sense. In her energy schema, black patches stained her arms and even her inner thighs. From these, tendrils extended out through her body, clinging to her vital organs and lymph nodes. The main energy channels looked like sausages that had been gnawed by starving dogs.

This was bad. No wonder the healers couldn't help. The energy they invested in her would simply leak out of her like out of a sieve. I'd have to stanch the loss of life force from her before working on her energy contours.

Teimei shivered violently, her body coated in sweat that plastered the thin fabric to her skin. It was quite an alluring sight. But those who get distracted can't work with blood. So I set to work.

I'd always thought of blood as an almost divine essence, like a kind of demiurge. Blood had its own peculiar perspective and only helped those who shared its views, which didn't necessarily align with good or evil. Motive and cause mattered more to blood than any moral considerations.

This ritual would make Teimei a servant to my will, even a puppet, but it would hold her on the edge of death. A double standard.

Just as Agatha Petrovna had created a duplicate control contour in the armored car linked to the Mosquitoes' blood offerings, I would do something similar with Teimei, anchoring her to me. It'd drain me heavily, needing nearly a basin of blood to sustain, but if I could endure the first month, the bond would become easier to bear afterward.

I grabbed a letter opener from the study — a razor-sharp tool, perfect for my purpose. After removing her robe, I began the ancient, simple ritual. It required me to carve matching runes on both of us, establishing a crude but powerful barrier against the poison saturating her system. Not only did I encase each of her organs in my blood and will, but I had to take direct control over their functions.

I'd be monitoring her decayed, energy-drained

body for a month. Every failure would feel like my own pain, but the suffering would be well worth it.

Blood magic might lack flash but never effectiveness. The next three hours were more like a farmer plowing a field than a grand mage performing miracles with a flick of the wand.

With each rune I carved on myself, I carved an identical one on Teimei. Our blood mingled, almost reacting chemically. The poison had all but replaced her own blood so that only faint traces remained of her once-powerful magic and ancient lineage. It seemed that she was alive out of sheer stubbornness and the power she had been born with. I couldn't determine exactly what that was, but that wasn't the goal right now.

Rune by rune, I took control over the body of Kitsune's heiress. But as I worked, I realized Misha's strength wasn't enough for the duplicate circuit.

"Bring me strong, fresh blood," I ordered the butler through the blood link. Moments later, he entered silently with two goblets.

I scanned their contents and was surprised to find one contained fresh blood from a maid, and the other the same, mixed with local herbs and powders.

"What are the additives in the second goblet?" I asked, not out of curiosity, but because my hands were already trembling from exertion. Two-thirds of my vital organs were twisting from the pain Teimei felt and my blood sense was spurring me to drink from the goblets as soon as I could.

"Ingredients from the family estates: herbs, pollen, ground-up macros."

No wonder it felt so nourishing. This blood contained components altered by otherworldly influence, possibly even from my world. Without a second thought, I downed both goblets — first the pure blood, then the cocktail. Euphoria surged through me, the pain washed away in a wave, leaving only a slight ache and tingling at the sites of the freshly-carved runes.

I'd have to investigate the local alchemy a little closer if it could have an effect like this.

After that, the rest of the ritual went smoother. The runes formed a complex pattern on our skins, linking me to Teimei. I carved the last rune on her forehead. It took some work, but it came out beautifully. On my own body, however, I carved it into the nape of my neck, hiding it under my hair. Who knows what the locals might think of someone with a blood rune on their forehead.

When I finished the ritual, I collapsed onto the bed, which was large enough to fit a harem. The blood infusion still gave me strength, but it was fading quickly due to the constant drain from Teimei. I'd have to find a steady source of sustenance, or I'd drain my maids dry. And with that, I drifted off into a doze — only to be woken at the best part of a dream involving a healthy, grateful Teimei.

"This one?" an unfamiliar irritated voice asked.

"This one," Aedes sighed.

"A complete lunatic," the first voice remarked,

with a trace of admiration.

"Not just that, but persistent and lucky!" my patron added, with what sounded suspiciously like pride.

"Lucky? In what way?" the unknown voice replied skeptically.

"Remember Kitsune's seven-tailed heir who vanished so mysteriously?"

"Vaguely."

"He found her. He's treating her now."

Their voices trailed off as a warm sensation scanned over me.

"Clumsy, but determined!" the stranger mused. "Such people either destroy their clans or elevate them for centuries."

It seemed that Muscadine had agreed to my proposal for a parley. I forced myself to shake off the remnants of the pleasant dream and opened my eyes to the divine nowhere.

I'd been braced for Aedes in his true form, but I hadn't expected a towering humanoid figure made of grapevines. I'd been thinking maybe a talking bush or something.

"What bush?" the deity snarled instantly, sending a dozen vines in my direction, sharp enough to skewer me. "Are you mad?"

"Oh! That's incredible — I want that!" I was genuinely thrilled by Muscadine's reaction. "Could I have two patron gods?"

"Have you lost your mind?!" Both gods' voices snapped in unison, utterly unrefined. Silence followed. They clearly didn't appreciate my little joke.

"Forgive me. I'm tired and not fully awake yet. It was a poor joke, I admit it!" I said quickly. "Oh Great Muscadine, blessed be your vines, I have a business proposition for you."

The gods looked at me with clear irritation, but one needed me to restore his clan, while the other seemed intrigued in what I could offer him. In any case, neither tried to crush me, so it was time to get to the pith of my proposal. I really did have something to offer Muscadine.

"I'm asking your permission to temporarily cloak the Komarin family ring with the illusion of your patronage. In exchange, I will find you a strong, capable heir who will restore the Vinogradov lineage to its former glory."

CHAPTER 9

THE NEXT MORNING FOUND ME GROGGY AND SPENT. I'd spent half the night negotiating with Muscadine. Somewhere around the midpoint, Aedes left, announcing that he had more pressing matters to attend to, but not before reminding me of my oath. At this, Muscadine let out a grating vine-like creak of frustration, clearly disappointed at missing his chance to poach me into his clan. After that, our negotiations only intensified.

In the end, we agreed that Muscadine would not only grant me permission to cloak my family ring with an illusory Vinogradov sigil, but he'd also provide me with an artifact infused with ancestral Muscadine magic as proof of my identity. In exchange, I promised to secure a new heir for his family within one year — one way or another.

The idea of asking for an artifact came to me from Kitsune's gift. If one goddess was willing to spare no expense for her heir, perhaps Muscadine might do the same. He did, though his generosity had its limits: The artifact he gave me only held enough magic for three uses, so I'd have to ration it carefully.

When the butler — who was also my valet — came to wake me, he was speechless with shock. Not only was there now a ring with a grapevine motif on my finger, but a tiny grape-cluster amethyst earring sparkled in my ear. The poor man's mouth opened and closed like a fish tossed ashore, his face reddening as if he were on the verge of apoplexy.

"It's not what you're thinking," I murmured through the blood link as testament to my continued affiliation with the Komarin clan. "My disguise here must be convincing."

Instead of reassuring him, this statement only deepened his shock. For a second, I thought he might keel over. He could grasp transferring from one clan to another, but a divine-level disguise was another matter entirely.

"Gavrila Petrovich," he croaked after a long silence, "your grandfather would be proud! Where shall I serve you your breakfast?"

"In my study. And bring me the morning papers. It's time to reacquaint myself with the Saint Petersburg beau monde."

The butler had almost reached the door when I called him back.

"I'm certain my grandfather never introduced us. But I'd like to know my people by name."

"My name is Arseny, Your Excellency," he replied, deliberately addressing me by my honorific and breaking with the cover story but acknowledging my authority. "The housekeeper is Maria, and the maids are Vera and Nadia."

I nodded in acknowledgment.

"Arseny, assuming we have a carriage in the household, order the coachman to paint the Vinogradov crest on it. I'll also need a personal comulet and calling cards with my number."

"Consider it done, sir," the butler replied, smiling into his mustache. "Do you have any preferences for the card's design?"

"Blood-red with golden grape leaves. And no name, just the number."

Arseny mulled this over. "I believe we can have it ready for you this evening, sir."

Fifteen minutes later, refreshed from a bath and finally dressed in a light indoor suit rather than the Komarin field uniform, I sat in the study, sipping coffee and perusing the papers.

The Imperial Gazette treated me to news about the final rounds of the freshman tournament at the Imperial Academy — which meant that in this world, the youth were pitted against each other from the very outset. Then again, this could be the best way to select the most talented prospects.

I considered that I too would probably have to enroll in the academy, as per the local custom. Better to do it while the seal still dampened my powers; otherwise, I feared what their local artifacts might make of my skill in blood magic.

It would be possible to skip this step, as my grandfather had planned for Mikhail, yet there's no better place to make the connections you'll need later on in life than in the foremost school in the land. Money won't solve everything and relying on Count Orlov for protection was beneath me. The Komarins had already lived in secrecy, conducting affairs solely with the Ministry of Defense. Had they had influential friends and business partners, perhaps they'd have found a way out without having to involve me.

The Social Bulletin offered a goldmine of intel relevant to my interests. After reading about who'd gotten into drunken brawls with whom, who'd been caught in compromising positions, and whose parties had been the wildest, I formed a plan for my outing that evening.

The front page bore an announcement of an upcoming International Flower Exposition and Florist Competition, to be inaugurated in a week by Their Imperial Highnesses Princess Maria and Prince Andrey, the children of the Emperor.

That was a must. If I planned to reenter society, I might as well do it in high style. I even had an idea for how to make a splash at the international florist competition.

But for now, I'd toss my first grenade into the wasps' nest. I quickly wrote two notes and summoned Arseny to the study. The butler appeared almost immediately, as if he'd been expecting orders.

"Arseny, find a boy who's quick on his feet and

have him discreetly pay for ads in the imperial papers. Have *The Imperial Gazette* publish an announcement in the next issue on behalf of the Ministry of Defense, and have the same appear in *The Social Bulletin* a bit later on behalf of the Heraldic Service." I grinned imagining the reaction my little prank would cause. "And I'll also need some pristine white roses to experiment on. Ten dozen should do."

*   *   *

The stress was making Marcus's hands shake. Only three days had passed since his last assignment and already four of his former comrades were unreachable. He'd ordered them to lie low, but not so low as to ignore even their own commander's calls.

Zhiva burst in without knocking. Despite being over fifty, she was as slight and dark-haired as the girl he'd met in the service thirty years ago.

"Marcus, it's a death mage!" she squeaked in a shaky voice. Her body trembled like an aspen leaf and she seemed to jump at every sound. "We're all done for!"

"Calm down, Zhiva! What are you trying to tell me?" The commander tried to reassure the lone life mage in their team, offering her a glass of water, but she covered her face with her hands and broke into bitter sobs, broken by fragmented phrases:

"We've been set up!... He'll come for all of us!... They're covering their tracks... We're already dead!... I saw it with my own two eyes! We have get out of here... I'm so afraid!... They're all dead, Marcus! All four!"

Marcus latched onto that last part. Exactly that many team members had stopped responding to his calls.

"How do you know this, Zhiva? What happened to them?" The mage's sobs only grew worse, so Marcus took the most straightforward approach. He quickly poured whiskey into a glass and handed it to her. "Drink this. Now!"

She took a few gulps, coughing as she caught her breath. Her sobs began to ease.

"Now, start from the beginning."

"It's all because of those damned Komarins!"

* * *

Overcoming Teimei's drug addiction in one fell swoop was impossible, so I had to gradually reduce the dosage. All day, I monitored her condition, quietly relieved that, at the very least, it wasn't getting worse.

But by evening, everything had changed. Wild convulsions wracked the girl as if she'd been possessed by demons from the nether plane. And I was right there with her. The runes weren't working properly. While they gave me the willpower to control and resist the chemistry in Teimei's body, unfortunately, Mikhail's blood was not strong enough. This meant I would have to dive into an entirely unfamiliar type of magic to tear the girl from death's grip.

Draining the third cup of blood from Nadia and Vera, I already knew this would only delay the problem, not solve it. So the idea of finding myself a pool of blood, once figurative, was beginning to take on a very literal meaning.

"Arseny, I need fresh animal blood — preferably pig's — and more supplements from our ancestral lands."

"How much?" Arseny replied through the blood link. My butler's composure and determination were impressive. If something was needed, then it was needed.

"Fill the basin two-thirds full."

"It will be ready in an hour," came the mental reply after a brief pause.

An hour later, I was sitting up to my neck in warm blood, holding an unconscious Teimei close to my chest. The abundance of blood caused a sense of exhilaration to bubble within me, tinged with a professional anger. In my previous life, I could have treated her affliction in one session, but here, with my limited powers, I had to reinvent the wheel — and wade into unfamiliar magical territories. Not only had I painted myself and her in runes, like some traditional handicraft, but now I also had to heal her. Healing wasn't my thing! I was as much of a healer as a headsman is a surgeon, but when life is at stake, one has no choice but to learn.

I carefully opened a vein on my arm to enhance my control. Sure, I could have worked only with animal blood, but I wouldn't have been able to finesse it like Hawthorn could, so I made it easier on myself. That's me — ever the opportunist.

Activating my gift, I studied the results of the previous ritual, disappointed. I had hardly achieved anything with my artistic endeavors. The only real change was that Teimei's internal organs had lightened from black to graphite-gray. But by cutting off the poison's nourishment from her organs, I had unwittingly redirected that filth to her already shredded magical centers and energy channels, triggering today's crisis.

Now, I had to deal with the consequences of my own shortsightedness. Well, it was customary to pay for mistakes in blood, and that's exactly what I was going to do now.

Having drained nearly a liter of my own blood, I leaned back, slipping into a meditative trance. My task now was to feel Teimei's auxiliary contour as if it were my own body and command the blood to repair the internal damage to her channels. Unlike Hawthorn, I wasn't about to micromanage it; I let the blood restore her mana channels in a manner akin to the circulatory system. For lack of anything better, it would have to do.

Magically speaking, watching the struggle between the poison, my blood, and the herbal supplements was fascinating. I felt almost like a spectator at a gladiator bout. Step by step, my "soldiers" pushed the invaders out of Teimei's body, liberating channel after channel, node after node, core after core. It was so mesmerizing that I didn't notice when I passed out.

I woke up to a tickling sensation. I was lying on soft green grass, notably, naked. There hadn't been any point in getting into the tub clothed, hence my current state of undress. Who could have known I'd be summoned as a guest? A tiny cherry-red fox was nudging my ear with her nose, barking and growling adorably.

"So, this is what you look like, Teimei of the Cherry Kitsune clan." I scratched the fox behind her ear and smiled at the magical representation of my patient. The fox in turn melted into a blissful grin and even purred a little.

"And this is what you look like, stranger from another world!" a whisper echoed in my thoughts. "How did you reach me? No one has been able to for the past five years. Even my Mother Goddess cannot hear me."

The fox's melancholy voice was at odds with her playful demeanor as she darted back and forth across the meadow.

"Blood magic is vastly underestimated in this world," I shrugged.

"As is illusion magic," Teimei chuckled. "But if you're here, it means you need something. What do you want?"

"I won't lie. I need your help. That's why I'm trying to heal you now. You won't like my methods I'm afraid," I paused, searching for the right words, but eventually gave up. Call it what you will, slavery is still slavery.

"You think I enjoyed bringing the fantasies of

perverts to life in a brothel?" The little fox sat down before me, tilting her head to one side. "Compared to what I've had to endure over the last five years, your fantasies are the very model of virtue."

I didn't even flinch at her remark. I'd already suspected this was a conjured dream and Teimei had just confirmed my suspicion.

"So, what about your methods?" the fox brought me back to the topic at hand.

"I've enslaved you," I admitted. "Your body, magical nodes, and mana channels are being restored through a duplicate contour using my will and my blood. If it works, you'll owe me your life."

"Will it work?" Teimei asked with doubt. "There's hardly anything left to restore. I shouldn't have survived this long on that filth."

"Only Aedes knows," I confessed honestly, "It's not just drugs. It's some wild mix of curse, parasite and alchemy. At first, I tried to restore your vital organs and systems, but all I managed was to push that filth onto the remnants of your energy channels and magical nodes. So, I had to load myself with blood to try to counterbalance it all and not die from the unforgettable experience of treating you. But I fear even that won't be enough."

"It won't. But what if we help each other? I have an idea..."

* * *

She has an idea. But of course… I was caught between wild laughter and the thrill of excitement. If Teimei's scheme worked, I was in for an unforgettable spectacle tonight. I just hoped I wouldn't end up part of it by accident.

It was well past midnight when my carriage pulled up in front of Count Vidrin's mansion. I had already identified this as one of the places where breaking into high society would be easiest. More than a third of the scandalous articles in the gossip columns began or ended with a reference to this mansion. But even I would never have thought of doing what Teimei proposed.

The carriage stopped at the front entrance. The revelry was in full swing. Music, bursts of laughter, and half-dressed ballerinas running into the garden to escape lecherous aristocrats confirmed that we had arrived at the right address. The coachman opened the door, allowing me to step out with the girl in my arms. The black silk kimono, obtained by Arseny for the occasion, accentuated Teimei's aristocratic pallor and her fragile figure. I made a show of walking unsteadily from too much drink, my dazed gaze completing my guise of a tipsy nobleman.

At the mansion's entrance, a shriveled old man with a penetrating look blocked our path.

"Sir, may I ask who you are here to see and why?"

"Us?" I drawled in mock confusion and then

slurred without waiting for an answer, "We've got a gift! The Count ordered something exotic! Here!" I pushed the Asian girl up to the butler's nose, making him flinch.

"Go right ahead, sir!" he rasped, seeing us off with his eyes before turning to a squealing pair of ballerinas who'd been cheerfully dancing the can-can on the edge of a fountain — and who as if on cue, toppled into it. Things were lively here indeed even without us — and with us, they would be livelier still...

I resolutely made my way through the crowd of inebriated nobles. We were met with whistles, exclamations, and crude remarks; some even tried to get in line. Moreover, a part of the guests, seeing such an exotic "gift," joined our strange procession, anticipating its "unwrapping." I, however, was looking for the man of the hour.

Count Pyotr Semyonovich Vidrin had been mourning his failed engagement with the daughter of his business partner, Duke Kasatkin, for a month now. The young bride-to-be was wealthy, sure, but she wasn't easy on the eyes, so Vidrin didn't feel to bad about the break-up and had been "drowning his sorrows" for a month now in the company of friends and courtesans.

It was unlikely that one could find a happier jilted groom in all of Saint Petersburg than Pyotr Semyonovich. I'd seen Duchess Kasatkina's portrait in the newspaper just yesterday — if I'd been given such a "blessing," I'd have been "mourning" for a month too, if not longer. With such a wife, even polygamy wouldn't be any consolation, since the law required equal respect and, thus, equal satisfaction for all spouses. All in all, I understood the count, which is why tonight could really be a "gift" for him. Teimei had promised to do her utmost.

Finally reaching the ballroom, I found Pyotr Semyonovich in the company of two half-dressed young women — one was openly comforting him under the table, while the other offered her ample bosom, a C-cup at least, as a shoulder to cry on.

The count responded to our appearance by turning his flushed face and downing a shot of vodka from his elbow. Lacking a proper chaser, Pyotr Semyonovich made do with his companion's cleavage. Perfect!

I stopped before Vidrin and with a flourish, yanked the tablecloth along with all its contents off the table. In their stead, the polished oak tabletop received Teimei. The poor count sobered up slightly at the sight of such a "gift."

"Pyotr Semyonovich, allow me to introduce myself — I am Gavrila Petrovich Vinogradov!" I bowed dramatically. "I've heard of your grief, and thus I couldn't help but concern myself with a consolatory gift. This is for you!" Like a magician, I deftly pulled on the thin silk belt, which until now had fastened the kimono to Teimei's body.

In the deafening silence, only the sound of rustling fabric and the guests swallowing their drool could be heard.

The humble word "orgy" didn't even begin to

describe what happened next in Count Pyotr Se-myonovich Vidrin's mansion. Everyone joined in — aristocrats, courtesans, even the servants. It was the first time I'd seen illusion magic used at such scale. And Teimei herself remained lying on the table, untouched and invisible to everyone but me, even as she conjured and radiated an aura of pure sex.

The moans of pleasure grew louder, partners switched like gloves, and people used whatever implements for sexual satisfaction they could get their hands on. At one point, I even noticed the old butler, with a blissful smile, mounting a plump actress. Indeed, I had brought true happiness to this humble abode.

No less than two hours had passed since our arrival when the Kitsune heiress began to recover. Her cheeks flushed, her eyes sparkled with the energy she had drained from the gifted nobles around her. With an incredibly sensual movement, she sat up on the table, parting her thighs just slightly, and beckoned to me with her finger. Her promising tongue slid across her upper lip. Hypnotized, I moved toward Teimei, fully aware that my desire was nothing but an illusion yet unable to resist her invitation. Only a single step separated me from the Asian illusionist when a polite cough sounded behind me, followed by an all-too-familiar voice:

"Well, you certainly know how to throw a party! I think I'll hang around this plane a little longer, if you don't mind!"

Chapter 10

I turned around slowly, expecting to see Vidrin's mansion half-destroyed by an interdimensional rift with Tilda protruding out of it to check out the commotion.

But instead, at the entrance to the ballroom stood a stunning naked beauty with pearlescent skin and violet hair cascading down to below her waist.

"Tilda, if I'd known you looked like this, I might have married you in a past life." I gazed at my friend, who had abandoned her habitual octopus form for this beautiful, human one, with genuine admiration.

"Oh, come on! Back then, you were interested in someone else, and I decided not to add fuel to your already complicated relationships."

While we exchanged pleasantries, Teimei grew annoyed. Apparently, she wasn't used to having her pleasure spoiled. Sliding fluidly off the tabletop, she appeared in front of Tilda in an instant and decided to go all in — without any hesitation, the Kitsune heiress passionately kissed the interloper.

"Hmm," my friend mused thoughtfully as soon as the Asian girl pulled away. "If you have no plans for this lady, I'd like to have some fun with her!"

Teimei's face took on such a stunned expression that I couldn't hold back my laughter, for which I received an angry glare.

"Who is this... dyed hag?" the Asian girl hissed like an angry cat. "And why doesn't my magic work on her?"

"Dyed? This is my natural color!" Matilda playfully twirled a violet lock around her finger, then demonstratively changed her hair to black and slightly lengthened her nails. Teimei's eyes grew as wide as saucers, yet Tilda was only beginning to tease the young fox girl.

"Let's not fight, ladies!" I intervened in the brewing quarrel. "We really should get out of here before we become the subjects of public gossip."

"It's always like this!" Tilda pouted. "No sooner do I arrive, than the party ends! Why do we have to leave in the middle of all the fun?"

"Let her stay," the Asian girl snorted. "I'll give her such a ride that the best brothels in the world will envy her!"

"All right, both of you — out you go!" I commanded the two feisty vixens. "We'll talk at home!"

To my surprise, the girls obeyed and headed

for the exit in silence — surely somewhere a pig had taken wing! We picked up our coachman along the way, pulling him off some maid.

The lad gawked around in bewilderment, I guess having witnessing such rampant and wide-spread debauchery for the first time.

We got into the carriage without conversation, but I deemed it necessary to provide some clarification.

"First of all, Tilda, this is Teimei, heiress of the Cherry Kitsune. She lives with me under a life debt. Once she works it off, she'll return home," I explained. "Teimei is an illusionist with the ability to induce sexual fantasies and even bring some of them to life, through which she gains a heap of energy from everyone she ensnares."

Tilda nodded, taking in the information. All her feigned hurt and sarcasm evaporated like dew in the sun. When necessary, she could be extremely focused and serious.

"Now you," I pointed a finger at Teimei. "I thought we agreed that you wouldn't use your magic on me. Is this how you keep your promises?"

The Kitsune lowered her head, hiding her eyes and saying nothing in reply.

"It wasn't magic, don't be hard on the girl!" Tilda laughed. "She lost her head from gorging on mana. That kind of thing happens. And you need to get yourself a lover, or you'll start confusing magic with ordinary lust."

Teimei blushed sweetly, confirming Tilda's point.

So that's how it was. It was the fox girl's personal initiative, and I had misunderstood everything. I won't deny it was pleasant! But somehow we never manage to finish what we start, either in dreams or reality. Someone always interrupts.

"Teimei, this is Tilda, my friend and..." I hesitated, trying to find a way to explain the nature of our relationship, and finally settled on a more or less suitable word, "bodyguard! As you've noticed, her magic is peculiar. She can also shapeshift into an animal. I won't say which, but she could swallow your little fox without choking. So it's best not to anger her."

Teimei nodded and turned to look out the carriage window, still keeping her head down.

Well then, I'll inform Teimei about moving on to the second part of the plan to find the killers of my family tomorrow. For now, after casting a glance at these two such different women connected to me by chance and my own whim, I decided that they needed some better clothes. Seeing the naked Tilda and the kimono-wrapped Teimei was undeniably pleasant, but I'm not made of iron. My young body craved love and affection, especially from such beauties, so I decided to rid myself of unnecessary temptation. Still, the idea of getting a mistress definitely appealed to me.

* * *

Arseny didn't even bat an eye upon seeing the new member of our company. A rock-solid stoic! It seemed that Tilda also appreciated my butler's composure and sangfroid. After accommodating the ladies for the night in the guest rooms, Arseny appeared in my study in response to my summons through the blood link.

"Gavrila Petrovich, the newspaper ads have been submitted; they'll appear in tomorrow's and Friday's editions. The crest on the carriage has been updated. Here is your comulet and calling cards," Arseny handed me the magical communication device and a beautiful cigarette case, masterfully repurposed as a cardholder. "The roses are have been delivered and are currently in the cellar. The ladies have been settled. I have sent a light supper to their quarters."

Oh Aedes! If only I'd had such support in my past life! I guess I'd earned enough karma back then to be granted such happiness in this one.

"Thank you, Arseny," I took a satisfying sip of the scalding hot, strong coffee. The rest of the night I would have to spend sleepless, and my conscience wouldn't allow me to draw blood from Nadya and Vera for sustenance. So I had to perk up the old-fashioned way. "Do we have a map of the city? I need to understand where the Ministry of Defense and the Heraldic Service are located."

"If I may?" Waiting for my nod, Arseny walked

behind me and took a small oval and azure stone from the shelf. "This is a detailed and scalable map of the city. You need only insert it into the reader and think of the place you wish to look up."

The reader turned out to be a crystal egg that opened into two halves. Placing the stone inside and closing the lid, I thought of the Ministry of Defense building.

A hologram of the city appeared above the table, divided into sectors, one of which glowed green. After a couple of seconds, it zoomed in, and one of the clusters of building was highlighted. How convenient!

In the same way, I thought about the Heraldic Service. Now understanding where everything was located, I could personally pay a visit to the head of the Heraldic Service, Count Zubrov. It was time to fulfill the promise I'd made to Muscadine. I would try the local methods first, and if they didn't help, I would resort to my own.

"Arseny, please find a dressmaker for our ladies. It's unbecoming for them to be without outfits," I tried to estimate what Teimei and Tilda might need. "For now, order a couple of home dresses and one formal outfit for each. And don't forget the accessories: hats, shoes, a handbag and matching lingerie."

I hadn't even finished speaking when a request came through the blood link from the housekeeper Maria.

"Gavrila Petrovich, the young ladies are asking for more wine and snacks, they're celebrating some kind of 'double breakthrough.' Shall I fulfill their request?" The housekeeper was clearly embarrassed to ask my permission in the middle of the night but saw no other option.

So the two furies had already hit it off, and the night hadn't even ended yet. Well, what could I say…

"Send it over, Maria!" I laughed, imagining Teimei's state in the morning. Tilda would be just fine; she could outdrink a dragon, let alone a small, fragile Asian girl. But the Kitsune heiress would regret her morning hangover quite a bit.

Maybe I should crash their girls' night? The idea was tempting in that it could very well end in sex, whether real or illusory. On the other hand, I decided to give the girls a chance to get to know each other better, and I headed to the cellar to tinker with the roses. Something told me that it would take more than ordinary tricks to impress the emperor's daughter. I'd have to think of something more spectacular.

Nevertheless, I still dropped by the girls' quarters before dawn. Surprisingly, they were both equally wasted, which didn't prevent Teimei from casting an illusion on me of such quality that I was amazed. Even Tilda was startled sober when she saw whose guise had been placed on me. And the fox girl had simply taken my true otherworldly appearance, which she had seen in the green meadow. Hiccuping drunkenly, she confessed that only this image remained in her memory, so it was either that or she could turn me into Tilda. The choice was obvious, but now I had to get used to seeing my true reflection in the mirror again.

* * *

The Minister of Defense had spent the night at work and awoke to a suspicious clamor on the street outside his windows.

Since his personal secretary had left on assignment, Count Orlov didn't hesitate to go down to the first floor to find out what was happening and why an agitated crowd had gathered outside the Ministry of Defense building.

The office staff were running around like scalded cats. Yelling, swearing, and arguing resounded throughout the massive compound. As he entered the Department for Civilian Affairs, Daniel Andreyevich caught the tail end of the speech the department head had been making:

"Find me the prankster and launch him so deep into the nether plane that he'll never again forget what it means to joke with the Ministry of Defense!"

"And what shall we do with the crowd?" one of the subordinates squeaked, tucking his head into his shoulders.

"Disperse them! With water cannon and chain lightning, whatever you want!" barked the department head, leading Count Orlov to consider that it was time to seriously address personnel policy.

"If the Ministry of Defense uses force against its own citizens, we'll be the ones sent to the nether plane!"

Everyone in the office whipped around upon hearing the minister's formidable voice. Now it was the turn of the head of the Department for Citizen Affairs to seek safety in his shoulders. It was well known that if Count Orlov was bellowing with rage, there was nothing to be afraid of. However, if the minister spoke calmly, as he did now, a mass of barely restrained menace was accumulating behind his words, and if the levy broke...

"Now, what is the matter?" the minister addressed the intimidated clerk.

"Your Excellency, *The Imperial Gazette* published this public notice this morning. The crowd outside began to assemble a half-hour ago." The young man handed the minister a somewhat crumpled newspaper. The front page bore a public notice that read as follows: "The Ministry of Defense announces a reward for any information on the whereabouts and condition of Baron Mikhail Yuryevich Komarin, MIA. The reward will be paid upon provision of verifiable evidence of his current condition."

The notice had a lone mosquito printed in its corner.

Daniel Andreyevich was used to thinking quickly in critical situations. If not for the mosquito symbol, he might have taken this notice as some prank. In light of the constant attempts on the Komarin family scions, however, the printed symbol struck him as a sure sign that there was more to this.

"Assign two mentalists to this case. Interview anyone who comes forward. I will personally guarantee bounties of ten to fifty thousand rubles to anyone who provides useful information. The mages are to report to me personally and no one else." The count surveyed his staff with a weary look and, taking the newspaper, returned to his office. He needed to think.

* * *

Early in the morning, a young man who introduced himself as Gavrila Petrovich Vinogradov appeared at the offices of the Heraldic Service for an appointment with Count Zubrov, the head of the service.

The young man had put up a tidy sum to secure a direct consultation with the count, whose name was Nikita Illarionovich. The gist of the matter boiled down to the fact that this young Mr. Vinogradov needed a specialist from the Heraldic Service to certify his blood relations as well as his hereditary magical abilities. Such specialists were called sniffers or headhunters. Their services were used so seldom that few even knew they existed.

"Gavrila Petrovich, forgive my curiosity, but how did you become aware that the Heraldic Service might even offer such a service?" Count Zubrov removed his tinted glasses and looked attentively at the young Vinogradov. Where had he come from? If Nikita Illarionovich's memory served him, the princely Vinogradov family had been in decline for several generations and lacked any heirs with strong hereditary powers. The family's cadet branches were impoverished, merging steadily with other families and having no access to the family's main assets. Now, suddenly, this offshoot had appeared out of nowhere. Muscadine's magic in him was sufficient to claim the inheritance of the princely title, but he was in no hurry to do so. Moreover, he now wanted to sift through all the heirs with the help of the sniffers to find someone even stronger.

"My aunt — may Muscadine and Aedes rest her soul — was married to a man who employed the services of your specialists. I understood that this was not an inexpensive request and satisfied only upon your personal recommendation, so I came to you." The young nobleman pulled out a letter from his jacket pocket, sealed with the Komarin family crest. "This is addressed to you."

With a slight feeling of sadness, Nikita Illarionovich examined the sweeping and familiar handwriting of his old friend, who had fought to the end to ensure his family's survival. Breaking the seal, the count skimmed over the sparse lines, which asked him to assist the lad from the Vinogradov family as an old favor. Count Zubrov was particularly struck by one phrase, which, indeed, was the pith of this recommendation:

"He could claim the princely title on the strength of his inherited powers alone, but he, like me, cares about the family, and so he will be looking for the strongest candidate to lead it. Help him, as you once helped me!"

"Well then," Count Zubrov raised his eyes from the letter to the petitioner, "our service will help with your problem. But the search may take some time."

"As it happens, I took the liberty of somewhat accelerating and simplifying this process," the young Vinogradov replied with a polite smile. "An notice will appear in the Friday issue of *The Imperial Gazette* from your department, inviting all blood members of the Vinogradov family to appear before the Heraldic Service." Zubrov shuddered at the thought of the crowds that would flood the local offices of his service. Such initiative was worse than sabotage, but Vinogradov went on, "I did this so that your people can create a registry of all the volunteers, determine the strength of their powers, and use that to search for the lost offshoots of my family. In extreme cases, if there are any questions, you may announce that additional instructions to the will of the last Prince Vinogradov have come to light."

"But he died almost a hundred years ago!" Count Zubrov protested.

"Exactly. If in a hundred years the family hasn't been able to determine the line of succession, we'll help them!" the young Vinogradov winked with a crooked smile, but then, growing serious, he asked, "Nikita Illarionovich, I know the rules. Do you want payment in money or as a favor?"

Count Zubrov examined the young man sitting

in front of him. Something wasn't adding up on an intuitive level. The Vinogradovs knew how to weave words like young vines. Gavrila Petrovich was doing the same, but behind this external charm, the count thought he could detect the predatory grin of a seasoned predator. In this, Vinogradov reminded him of the now-deceased Baron Komarin. One thing Zubrov knew for sure: it was better to have such people as friends. Money didn't solve everything in this world.

"A return favor will do, Gavrila Petrovich! How shall I contact you once we have the results?"

"You only need call me," Vinogradov placed a calling card on the table. It was embossed with an ornament of grape leaves and a comulet code. In the next second, the young man's face became distant. The mask of imperturbability and recklessness slipped off him, revealing anxiety and displeasure. Zubrov didn't understand the reason for the change, but his visitor's face was growing darker and darker. His eyes were filling with blood — yet not in the pupils, as they would normally, but the irises. They shimmered red, like ripe cherries in the light. Nikita Illarionovich couldn't possibly know that this change had been brought about by extreme anger in his visitor, who had just been informed of an intrusion into his ancestral lands.

After a couple of moments of silence, Vinogradov came to. Taking out an old mechanical pocket watch on a chain, he thoughtfully looked at the time and began to gather his things.

"Thank you, Nikita Illarionovich, for your time, and I look forward to our future work together."

The men shook hands, and Vinogradov swiftly left the Heraldic Service offices.

Chapter 11

DAMN IT ALL! How could I forget about Hmarevo? It was already too late to do anything by the time Spider got through to me and let me know than none other than Count Orlov's personal secretary had appeared at my estate. Frankly, I didn't care about ranks — even if the visitor had been the defense minister himself. Hmarevo was my territory and anyone showing up without my permission was more alarming than a red banner to a bull. The uninvited visitor was a nagging thought in my mind and I knew I needed to go there urgently. I trusted my intuition, and now, with my altered appearance and under Muscadine's cover, the desire to see the guests became simply irresistible.

There was still a little less than a week left until the florists' competition. My nightly experiments with the roses had already yielded some preliminary results, but... it still wasn't quite right. Mikhail's mother, being a southerner, missed the warmth and lush greenery, so Hmarevo had its own winter garden and a small greenhouse where Maria recharged her spirits. This gave me a perfect pretext to visit my estate in my new guise.

"Arseny, I want you to submit an application to enter the International Flower Expo and Florist Competition. I will be submitting a new variety of rose that I have called 'A Surprise for the Princess,'" I instructed my bloodbound valet. "I'm leaving for a couple of days. Keep an eye on the ladies. Don't let them out into the city without me unless they're disguised with an illusion."

"I will do as ordered, Your Excellency!"

"You could have told me in person," Tilda grumbled somewhere in the back of my mind.

Damn it!

"Tilda, can you hear us all this time?" I clarified the extent of my friend's abilities.

"No, only what directly concerns me," she replied somewhat guiltily. "I understand boundaries. I won't eavesdrop if it bothers you."

Boundaries — that's good. Very good. Matilda was smart and always knew how to maintain the distance in a friendly relationship. If during the first two hundred years we still treated each other like brother and sister, over time we naturally drifted apart.

She disappeared more and more often into the nether plane, appearing when I needed help closing breaches. Piecing together some facts from my past life, I think I began to understand why she distanced herself from me in recent years.

"Tilda," I called carefully through our blood link.

"There's nothing to talk about," my friend cut me off and shut down.

"I have to go now, but we'll discuss this when I return," I promised mentally. Maybe I shouldn't have; after all, no one likes it when someone pries into their soul. But, Great Blood, how blind I had been. It seems I had to die and be reborn in order to understand the obvious. I guess death is good for clearing the mind.

* * *

Svetlana Hawthorn was running a forced march exactly like the one their class had started running before the breach that had killed the frogs.

This time, the situation was different. Everyone packed their backpacks thoughtfully. Sveta tried to assemble the same kit she had seen Mikhail Komarin carry, suspecting it included everything necessary for the trial that faced her.

Running beside her were Frog and Burdock. The girls gritted their teeth and silently kept up with the pace Sveta set. This week had changed them for the better. On one hand, the girls, having broken free of their families, had decided that anonymity would let them indulge in a wild lifestyle. On the other hand, they did not expect that the guys would simply use them without any extra sentiment. Now, their anger and a resurgent sense of self-worth were fueling their growth.

Sveta herself had finally rid herself of Medvedev's annoying attention. After taking the oath of secrecy, her wannabe fiancé kept well away from her. And no wonder — he had realized that he had tried to coerce the daughter of the imperial healer and was even being considered by her as a potential suitor... Now Medvedev did everything to make up for his former behavior, for which he had been soundly thrashed. He didn't even seem to care how his former cronies now felt about him.

To be fair, the rest of the class was behaving more quietly too. There were fewer squabbles. At long last, everyone was doing what they had come here for. And the instructors in turn, were pushing them all to the limits of their endurance.

The only thing that worried Sveta was Komarin's disappearance. Everyone had returned, except for Misha. Some of the instructors also scrambled their former appearances with illusion artificats. However, for a good healer, such tricks were always in vain, since any good healer remembered her patients not by their faces but by the peculiarities of their mana structure.

For example, Instructor Spider, who had now taken on a new alias, "Instructor Black," had an old injury to the mana channel under his left collarbone. Most likely, at some point, a new channel had been created in order to heal him in the field, yet the combat healer performing the operation had been sloppy and the scars remained at the mana-blood boundary. Sveta could identify all ten instructors by little details like this, despite their altered appearances and new aliases. She could have just as easily identified all her classmates if she had met them out in high society.

Despite all this, the only one who concerned Sveta was Komarin and his absence.

A week later, her father asked Sveta if she could accompany Her Imperial Highness Princess Maria on a social outing.

It wasn't the first time and Sveta would rather have endured another forced march than have to fend off annoying suitors, keep Maria out of trouble and listen to her complaints about how dull she was.

And yet, this one time, Sveta was glad to go out into society, as it would allow her to contact Uncle Daniel and find out where they had sent Komarin. She didn't believe what Instructor Black aka Spider had told her. It was easy for a healer to determine when she was being lied to. All that remained was to confirm her own assumptions.

If she was honest with herself, Sveta was interested in a guy for the first time. Komarin's calmness, composure, decisive actions and unexpected selflessness had all won her over.

It's one thing when all the suitors see you as a stepping stone to get closer to the imperial throne and quite another when they help you simply because they can, without expecting anything in return. Given the aristocratic station she had been born into, true romance was likely out of the question for her, but she did want to make a good friend.

Now pushing all superfluous thoughts out of her head, Sveta steadied her breathing, increased her blood flow, and picked up the pace, catching up with the main group. Affections aside, no one had canceled the hard slog that still stretched interminably before her.

* * *

I used portal scrolls to reach Hmarevo. But I didn't jump directly to the estate, instead, first traveling to a small village of the same name. There, I rented a horse and set off to visit my adopted home. Approaching the estate, I was stopped by operatives from the Eagles special unit, whom I had seen before. They acted strictly according to protocol, asked about the purpose of my visit, checked my ring, and let me pass. After that, however, things got confusing.

Construction crews in unfamiliar uniforms were bustling about my manor, which had been half destroyed in the explosion that killed Agatha. Amid the chaos stood a short, thin man with deep-set, button eyes.

A narrow, long nose and a habit of twisting his lips gave him the semblance of a rodent. As I arrived, he was issuing orders in a clear, authoritative voice.

The local mosquitoes, my lovely helpers, had already brought me his blood sample. There was, of course, too little of it — a mere drop — but the overall impression was mixed.

The man seemed to care about restoring the estate, doing everything precisely, within the budget allocated by the Ministry of Defense — nothing to complain about. And yet a vague feeling that something was off bothered me. This... rodent... seemed to look upon my estate as if it were his personal property. One could, of course, attribute this to honest diligence. Maybe he was merely going about his assignment as if it concerned him personally, but somehow I didn't think so.

As if sensing my intense gaze, the manager turned around and his eyebrows converged over the bridge of his nose in a sign of extreme displeasure.

"Who are you, and how did you get onto restricted territory?" His dry tone and the threatening notes in his voice would surely frighten many — but not me.

"And a good day to you!" I couldn't resist ribbing him for his lack of manners. "My name is Gavrila Petrovich Vinogradov; I am Baron Mikhail Yuryevich Komarin's maternal cousin. I came to congratulate him on his birthday! And who are you? How come you are giving orders on another family's lands? I don't see a mosquito ring on you."

The man froze with an inscrutable expression. He slowly looked me up and down, lingering on the family signet ring and the earring in my ear.

"I am Baron Arkady Ivanovich Krysin, personal secretary to Minister of Defense Count Orlov. In the rightful estate's owner absence, I have been tasked to oversee restoration work on this facility entrusted to me."

So that's who this guy is — the defense minister's personal secretary himself. Of course, I could blindly believe that he's here solely out of duty, but... Somewhere in the ministry, a rat has been digging under our family for years and has remained unpunished. Accordingly, Baron Krysin, whose name and appearance bore the redolence of a rodent, certainly shouldn't be discounted.

"Pleasure to meet you, Baron!" I extended my hand for a handshake, which Krysin ignored. Alrighty then. "Could you tell me where I might find my cousin?"

"Unfortunately, he is currently undergoing training at a private boarding school. He will be unavailable for any personal meetings for the next few months."

Yes indeed! Undergoing training — that's why you'll be surprised tomorrow when they declare me missing.

"That's very unfortunate," I said, unfazed. "We had agreed that I would come by to pick up a few buds of Maria Vasilievna's roses. My aunt was a passionate collector of flowers and loved breeding them. I admit, I have a similar passion." I flashed a charming smile, playing the role of an amiable ninny. "Since Mikhail is away, I suppose I won't linger. I'll visit my aunt's winter garden and rest up a little. After all, the journey out here isn't a short one."

For the first time, Krysin's face betrayed some

shades of emotion, the main one being vexation. Nevertheless, he quickly regained his impassive composure.

"Why naturally, Gavrila Petrovich! I won't keep you," he said politely. "And please refrain from disclosing what you've seen here. After all, this facility is now under close departmental supervision."

"Of course, I understand completely!" I assured Krysin and headed into the manor. Everywhere I went, I encountered construction workers and engineers. Some of them were consulting old blueprints of the building, trying to recreate its original appearance. It all looked like a full-scale, professional restoration job, but for some reason, the mere presence of strangers on my land infuriated me.

I guess it made me sensitive because I felt a chill in my bones as I crossed the ruined threshold of my ancestral home. Trying not to show it, I proceeded to the guest wing, which was more intact compared to the main building.

It seemed to me that every room, every corridor enveloped me in warmth as soon as I stepped inside. It was an unusual impression; I don't remember such an effect when I first entered the house a week ago. Is it possible that the ring provides an additional connection to my ancestral lands in this plane? Or have I completely merged with Mikhail's body at last..?

I wandered through the rooms, trying not to attract attention. I was irresistibly drawn to one place and it wasn't the master's quarters — quite the opposite. Deciding to check my suspicions later, I went to the winter garden to play out my cover story faithfully.

In fact, my adopted mom's greenhouse was surprisingly compact but contained such specimens of flowers that even the imperial gardener would envy her. And it was all because Maria Vinogradova used ingredients from other worlds to do her plant breeding. It was for just such otherworldly flowers that I had now come here.

As I dug around the delicate soil, I felt the presence of Krysin's people close to me. They were keeping an eye on me. Although they surveilled me professionally and from a distance, it was hard not to feel the two constant shadows that had latched onto me after my conversation with the secretary. It was also encouraging that, besides all these strangers, a dozen Komarin bloodbound servants were responding to my blood sense. Tracing these connections, I found people of different ages, magical abilities, and genders. Not all of them felt like fighters, but knowing the foresight of the old baron, they were undoubtedly people I could trust. And so it turned out. The Komarin bloodbound continued to serve the family to the best of their modest strengths and abilities.

Closer to evening, I finally settled on a couple of rose buds from which I planned to create a gift for Her Imperial Highness Maria Petrovna Krechet... And then, I unexpectedly received an invitation from Krysin to have dinner with him.

Well, what can I say? I spent the meal's first

course in a fog. There was a feeling that my consciousness was observing Misha's personality from the outside. It's hard to explain and even harder to describe. Misha's memory generated memories one after another, many from his childhood when his large friendly family sat at that very dining table. Memories of all of them joking together in a blend of dark and military humor. It was funny to me, an otherworlder, but sad for Misha. Too many dear and close people had disappeared from his memories one after another. The laughter had vanished from the rooms of this house, replaced by anxiety and fears. It was frankly an awful experience to relive this with my new host.

All that time, Krysin was trying to engage me in polite conversation, yet I responded only sporadically due to my distraction.

I managed to focus on the conversation at hand only when I accidentally caught an angry glint in the eyes of a maidservant attending to us. The elderly woman in a white cap and apron gave Krysin such a hateful look that it gave me chills. A sense of danger washed over me, forcing me to concentrate on the conversation at hand.

"Forgive me, Arkady Ivanovich, I was lost in thought! I remembered how ten years ago we sat here at the same table with my aunt's family," I sighed sorrowfully, not dissimulating at all. "And now, only Mikhail and I are left alive from that once happy family."

Krysin frowned, nodded understandingly, and

finally repeated his question:

"I was merely inquiring, out of ignorance, about your relationship to your aunt, Maria Vasilievna."

"Oh it was not that close of a relationship. I was her second cousin." My sorrowful smile could have made an hangman's heart melt. "But I often came here to visit because we both shared a passion for plant breeding — a gift from the Muscadine family blood."

Krysin kept nodding and asking prying questions about my family affairs and life plans. Somehow, he unobtrusively shifted to my family regalia. He was particularly interested in the signet ring and the earring in my ear, which a hundred years ago marked the family's principal heir.

At this point, I considered dodging his inquiries, but unexpectedly Muscadine himself came to my rescue.

"Tell him you wear these divine artifacts while fulfilling the will of the last legitimate head of the family."

I repeated my adopted deity's response verbatim, to which Krysin showed genuine surprise:

"Is that possible? To voluntarily relinquish one's primacy in a noble lineage?"

"See, even experienced people are questioning you," Muscadine snorted in my head, still cherishing the idea of getting me into the family.

"It's all Muscadine's will. I dare not oppose it," I spread my hands and mentally replied to Muscadine: "Why do you need an oath-breaker in your family? I'll find you strong blood! I'm already look-ing!"

But Krysin wouldn't let up. Apparently, the situation I described had jarred him out of his customary worldview.

"Well, at least were you offered compensation for fulfilling the will?"

"Yes, Arkady Ivanovich, I won't deceive you. A reward was promised, but not of a material nature," I thought about the loaned artifacts and the divine cover. Such perks from a god are precious and can't be measured in money.

"Too bad, I feel very sorry for you!" Krysin muttered and waved for the next course of our meal. When it came, the waiter also brought a dusty bottle of wine bearing the Vinogradov family crest. "In honor of your visit, I asked them to honor the guest."

The bottle was quickly uncorked. Special glasses were brought for the vintage wine. The elderly maid was practically seething with anger and hatred as she poured the wine into the glasses. And I couldn't ask her directly why as she simply wouldn't understand who was asking.

While I hesitated, watching the maid, Arkady Ivanovich raised his glass and proclaimed a toast:

"To the revival of the once glorious Vinogradov and Komarin families! May they flourish in the glory of their gods! To Muscadine and Aedes!"

Our glasses produced a melodious crystal clink, and Krysin was the first to sip the antique wine.

But as soon as I brought the glass to my lips, Arkady Ivanovich clutched his throat, began to choke, and turned purple before my eyes.

CHAPTER 12

"I NEED A DOCTOR! NOW!" I yelled, catching Krysin even as he wavered and collapsed. I relayed my call through the blood link as well, and no sooner had I done so than the maidservant tending to us jumped as if she'd been struck with a jolt of electricity: She gaped at me wide-eyed for a moment and then immediately fell to her knees.

"Forgive me, Your Excellency!" she cried through the blood link without moving her lips while pressing her head to the floor. "Forgive me! I meant no harm. This man poses a great danger. I can sense that his spirit is foul!"

"Silence! You can explain later! Help me lift him," I snapped at the woman just as the combat healer stormed into the dining room.

"What happened? Who's ill?" Spotting Krysin turning blue, the healer quickly moved his hands over the man's body, conducting a rapid diagnosis.

"We were having dinner. A bottle of aged wine was served. We each barely took a sip before Arkady Ivanovich collapsed and started gasping for air!" I summed up the situation briefly.

The healer continued moving his hands over Krysin until the man finally drew a faint, raspy breath. His face gradually returned to its normal shade, and within minutes, the baron was able to sit up on his own.

"This was an attempt on his life!" was the first thing out of Orlov's secretary mouth once he recovered. "I won't leave it at this!" he hissed. "I'll run everyone here through the mentalists until I find the perfidious creature responsible for this!"

His eyes had filled with rage and his purple face flushed with red patches of fury. He scanned the room, searching for the culpable party. Luckily, I'd already dismissed the maidservant mentally. Her guilty demeanor would have only provoked the baron further, and I would have had no choice but to step in for one of my own.

"There! He's the one!" Krysin jabbed a finger in my direction. "He didn't drink the wine! I remember clearly! It's him! He's trying to take possession of his cousin's land and he saw this opportunity to remove an obstacle!"

Oh, Krysin's paranoia was blooming gloriously. I'd have to check if the Vinogradovs had any claims to this territory. And yet, even if there were, what did Krysin have to do with it?

"Calm down, Arkady Ivanovich," the healer said politely, sipping the wine straight from the bottle.

The look in Krysin's eyes was priceless. He was, at minimum, calculating whether he'd be declared an accessory in the healer's murder or, at maximum, thinking where to bury the healer and me along with him.

I was curious to hear the healer's verdict. I had my suspicions about Krysin being allergic to some component in the wine, though it clearly wasn't the grapes. Otherwise, the baron would have discovered it in his youth, when all nobles begin indulging heavily in drink and debauchery.

"It was nothing more than an ordinary allergy."

"Inconceivable!" Krysin barked, disoriented. "I've been drinking wine since I was a wee lad and never experienced any side effects."

"That's precisely it — you've been drinking wines aged in contemporary casks of English oak. But seventy years ago, the Vinogradov princes could afford to age certain exclusive vintages in French Limousin oak casks. The quality and taste of this wine is quite different. It was that very type of wine you tasted tonight."

The healer took a deep whiff from the bottle's neck and shut his eyes in bliss.

To be honest, I was intrigued by the healer's depth of knowledge. Apparently, I wasn't the only one with some experience around here.

"And where did you learn about Limousin oak and all the rest?" Krysin eyed the healer suspiciously, practically scooting his chair away.

"My father visited the Vinogradov ancestral

lands down south near Adler when he was young," the healer shrugged, "and he still reminisces about it."

I made a mental note to take a trip south in the future. Who knows? Maybe there were hundreds of illegitimate Vinogradov offspring residing down there.

Krysin meanwhile straightened his jacket, seemingly getting a hold of his temper.

"Gentlemen, forgive me for the lapse in composure." He inclined his head slightly. "Gavrila Petrovich, thank you for your prompt call for assistance, and you, dear healer, for your efforts to revive me."

The healer and I accepted his gratitude and made our exit. But not before I tried that exotic wine myself. The taste was exquisite, so I shamelessly snagged the opened bottle from the table. The baron wasn't likely to need it, and I could savor the heritage of my ancestors.

Peace, however, was out of the question. No sooner had I returned to my quarters and settled in by the fireplace than the wooden wall panel quietly swung open, and in came the same elderly maidservant who'd attended us at dinner.

To avoid eavesdroppers, we communicated strictly through the blood link.

"Welcome back, Your Excellency! We're so pleased to see you again!"

"Thank you..." I hesitated, searching my memory for her name until it surfaced, "Elena. What was that performance at dinner?" I regarded her sternly, sipping the wine slowly. "Grandfather would have ripped your head off for such theatrics!"

"You're right about that, Your Excellency! He'd have ripped it right off!" Elena smiled dreamily. "But we didn't even expect you to still be alive. When we returned in the morning per Agatha Petrovna's final orders half the estate had been leveled and strangers were roaming around claiming to be from the Ministry of Defense. We cleaned up as best we could and waited for you. Even a death mage was here, sniffing around, trying to revive the killers, but no luck!" Elena held up her empty palm before her delighted face. "There was no cleaning up after Agatha Petrovna had done with them."

"And the ones in the swamp?" I asked about my own kills. "Did they find them?"

"They did, of course," Elena confessed. "That damned death mage even got one of them talking! But they didn't learn anything useful."

"Then I don't understand what happened at dinner." I fixed her with a strict gaze. The maid even blushed slightly with shame.

"Forgive me, your honor. Krysin's got a blackened soul. I couldn't help it." She shrugged. "Oh, he's rebuilding the house and not overstepping much, but he's always looking around, sniffing for something... I couldn't hold back. I knew about his allergy all along, and I didn't mind using the wine to let things take their natural course. That bottle was supposed to be for your birthday. Your mother, Maria Vasilyevna, brought it specifically for her wedding."

I looked more closely at the bottle. Nothing special on the outside, just wine. But I mentally thanked Mikhail's mother for the gift.

"Elena, I suggest you avoid Krysin for a while. Better yet, leave the estate entirely," I mused aloud, refilling my glass. "If he does call in a mentalist, even the blood link may not help much."

Elena bowed her head in agreement.

"Forgive us, Your Excellency, for not recognizing you, and for acting on our own initiative. We couldn't sit idly by as those vultures circled around us," she apologized on behalf of all the bloodbound servants. "You don't resemble yourself, not with that ring, the earring... These are all Vinogradov regalia, not ours. But when we heard your call, we faltered for a moment. The late baron and your father could not have summoned us like that! Aedes himself favors you now; we must make an offering to him."

"That's right," I responded immediately to her suggestion. "Offerings and rituals should be conducted as a matter of course. Aedes draws strength from them and that can only benefit us."

"Shall we hold the ritual tonight?" Elena looked at me hopefully. "We've already prepared suitable sacrifices."

Sacrifices? I was caught off guard — did people in this enlightened world still practice ritual offerings?

"Oh, we don't slaughter sheep, of course, but

a voluntary sacrifice can boost my powers nicely," Aedes' voice replied to my question. "Like you drinking blood when you're weak. I can do the same."

"All right, I'll try to come out tonight," I promised Elena sincerely. "Let's just hope I'm not the main sacrifice."

The maidservant withdrew with a silent chuckle.

* * *

At midnight, I was already following Elena through secret, winding passages. The bloodbound maidservant led me beyond the estate to the heart of the marsh, near the spot where Mikhail and I had dispatched the trio of assassins.

I sensed the presence of about fifteen people gathered in the marsh. Ten were bound by vows of loyalty to our family; the remaining five were not.

"Elena, how does a sacrificial ritual like this usually unfold?" I asked her through the blood link.

"It varies, Your Excellence! Your grandfather fed a few murderers to the mosquitoes in exchange for supporting their families. And your own father... well," she hesitated, choosing her words, "he used to take maidenheads at this spot."

"With consent, I hope?"

"Only with consent; otherwise, it doesn't work. He was handsome, your father — girls queued up for their turn," she chuckled. "Plus, it was a righteous thing, and their parents got dowry money afterward."

I weighed both options in my mind, willing to try either, but thought it best to check with Aedes first.

"Which of these is more beneficial and empowering for you?"

"The first option provided more mana, the second a good boost, but more in terms of faith than blood. Both effects were short-lived."

Hmm... what about setting up a mana pool? It seemed like a good idea, though I'd have to see what resources were available.

We stepped out into a circular clearing lit dimly by soft torches along its edges. The blood-bound servants sat apart, quietly exchanging gossip, while the remaining five guests looked rather colorful. Two girls, around eighteen, dressed in loose white sundresses, clustered together at one end of the clearing. Nearby was a bed of evergreen boughs covered with furs. They fidgeted, adjusting each other's clothes and hair. Not far from them, three men of various ages sat on the ground, dressed in rags. Two were eerily similar, like distant relatives, and the third was a mere youth. With their hands tied behind their backs, they chattered and even placed bets on who would die first.

"What are they here for?" I asked Elena, examining the strangely cheerful prisoners.

"Those two are murderers and that one's a thief."

"Has their guilt been established?" Justice often bends to the size of one's purse. In simple terms, those who pay up often end up innocent beyond a shadow of doubt.

"Yes, they confessed, and the mentalists confirmed their veracity."

"And what was the reason?" My question seemed to stump her, so without waiting for a reply, I approached the condemned. At the sight of me, they stood and even bowed. Their cheer faded away as I addressed them: "Good evening."

Their replies were disjointed.

"I have one question for each of you. Your honesty will mean everything."

The men nodded in silence, awaiting my question.

I started with the thief. The young man, younger even than Mikhail, held my gaze steadily.

"Did you kill or steal out of need or pleasure? I'm asking for your true motive. I'm not here to judge the details."

"Need, Your Excellency. My mother is sick and my seven siblings and I all tend to her. I tried to steal an herbal remedy that was supposed to help her."

Once he'd finished, I nicked his shoulder with my trusty dirk and tasted the budding drops of his blood. He wasn't lying. I even caught a glimpse of memories — his mother, his siblings, the trial. He had no regrets, only hoping he'd die before his mother did, so he could leave her his sacrifice money for treatment.

Then it was the murderers' turn. The older one

spoke first.

"It wasn't need or pleasure. It was vengeance," he muttered darkly, avoiding further explanation.

"Details," I insisted, sensing something was off.

"A merchant's son defiled my sister," the younger man growled through gritted teeth. "She lost her mind from grief; we barely saved her from taking her own life. As for justice... the rapist paid his way out and then began harassing her. My father and I couldn't bear it."

I understood, except for one detail: what they needed the money for. I asked, and the father answered again.

"We hoped to pay a mentalist enough to make her forget, then move away. Start afresh."

I checked their words again and found them utterly honest. The "murderers" were telling the truth.

So much for guilt and confessions. Why hadn't the mentalists verified the girl's condition after the assault? Why had her assailant not been held accountable?

Elena shifted from one foot to the other beside me, clearly wanting to speak, but I raised a hand to silence her.

"If these girls are here to trade their honor because they've got a sick or dying relative, I'd be a worthless head of this family if I allowed them to do so," I said, shaking my head and already realizing that there would be no sacrifices tonight. Whatever expectations Aedes had, I couldn't kill people for choices that might be wrong when it came to the law, yet were absolutely logical when it came to my own conscience.

"The girls came willingly," Elena whispered. "They were hoping for dowry money."

Good, then. A dowry they would have.

So, I'd been looking for a release, and here were two willing volunteers. A blond, curvy girl with a high, full chest, and a redhead, small, slender, like a reed in the sun. Both watched me with curiosity and without a trace of fear. Village girls were no timid creatures; they knew exactly what they'd signed up for. I wasn't about to disappoint them, or myself.

"Retreat into the shadows," I ordered through the blood link. "No need to embarrass the girls further."

The bloodbound obediently withdrew into the darkness, taking the volunteer sacrifices with them.

I let my own blood and drew a small ritual circle around the makeshift bed. This time, the purpose was to collect every bit of mana we would unleash, like through a lens.

The girls watched me work with interest, as quiet as mice so as not to disrupt me. After about ten minutes, I finished making my preparations. All the sounds around us became muted and a faint shimmer along the circle's border shielded us from view. Time to begin.

"Just don't let the mosquitoes bite my bare backside," I thought, amused, at the idea of Aedes watching over us.

"Your nerve — that's your blessing. No peeking, no eavesdropping, just a bite on your backside out of spite," Aedes chuckled before adding, "I don't know exactly what you're doing next, but consider protecting the land. Too many outsiders here. It shouldn't be this way."

I silently agreed; I'd thought so myself. I couldn't be everywhere at once, but I could leave something here behind me to protect my territory.

Aedes disappeared, displaying rare tact for a god, while the girls, noticing the misty veil, grew bolder.

What can I say? An eighteen-year-old body with three centuries of experience is better than the reverse. The girls parted with their innocence tastefully and with enthusiasm. It pleased me that while I attended to one, the other didn't stand idly by but joined the play. I'd always known redheads to have fiery temperaments. I can't say how much of the power went to Aedes, but in the process, they praised him, not me. Sometimes, you put in the effort, and all the glory goes to the boss.

An hour later, we left the natural bed of pine needles entirely satisfied with one another. The veil had lifted, and Elena moved to lead the girls away, but I stopped her.

Summoning everyone to gather around me, I proceeded to the next stage of our ritual.

We started by administering oaths of loyalty to the girls and the "sacrifices." When all the usual vows of "doing no harm," "serving until death," and "upholding the family honor" were spoken, I finally had the faithful to launch another, more complicated ritual.

All sixteen people in the clearing were necessary. I drew a large ritual circle with spokes for each person and charged each spoke's point with the fresh blood of my bloodbound servants. The wheel's spokes intersected at the place where part of the mana had already gathered like a lens. The moment I closed the blood circle, the mana completed the loop and surged into me like a torrent.

I was sorely tempted to keep it all for myself — as it could even suffice to break the seal on the rune binding my hand. But I didn't. My god was unfed, my lands unguarded. This was no time for selfishness.

Forcing my will, I directed the blood and mana to the lens, and when both circles united into one construct, a red beam shot up to the sky. I controlled the flow, channeling it in portions, crystallizing a foundation for a future mana pool and a ward for our ancestral lands.

Drop by drop, a thin spire grew from our blood. When it reached about a meter in height, it stopped. My people were exhausted but they held firm. I exhorted them to hold out a bit longer, not to give up. And they did. Blood trickled and filled the pool with mana. I didn't notice who began to pray to Aedes first, but soon everyone was chanting in unison.

I think I even sensed the satisfied rumble of our patron at the edge of my mind.

Time to conclude. The family ring grew warm, demanding to be included. I sent a thin stream of mana into it, and my perception shifted. I was lifted high above, seeing my lands from the sky, with a faint shimmer at their borders. Inside the veil, foreign presences pulsated like sparks. The land seemed to whisper:

"The interlopers don't belong here! Drive them out! Banish them from this land!"

With nearly all my strength gone, I managed to weave a scattering of minor curses into the veil. I thought I felt a slight satisfaction from the land itself, something like "better than nothing, but we'd prefer more."

"There will be more," I promised, "once I'm restored. There will be. I promise."

The spokes faded one by one and my bloodbound slumped to the ground. A red spire stood in the center of the clearing. Once, I could have conjured it from my own blood, but here I'd had to substitute it with my bloodbound' stamina. I'd drained at least half a liter from each, perhaps more. But it was worth it.

Now, all prayers and invocations of Aedes would no longer disperse, losing their potency. Part of the mana went to the god, while part settled in the mana pool, feeding the ward over my ancestral lands, weak still, but as they say — great things come from small beginnings.

Through the blood link, I ordered Arseny to transfer the promised sums to the five new followers of Aedes, who were now my bloodbound servants.

Arseny confirmed the names of the recipients, then briefly acknowledged the task was done. The men looked at me with adoration when they realized the execution was not only canceled but they'd receive the promised amounts. I offered to relocate the family of the violated girl to the village of Little Quagmire, and they agreed gladly. It might be remote, but it's safe, and they wouldn't be bothered there. I promised to pay for the mentalist to treat the girl as well.

Fatigue weighed on me, but I remained calm on the inside. I felt that everything was as it should be. But that feeling didn't last long.

"Baron, we need you at the school," Spider's voice crackled urgently through the blood link. He sounded angry but was trying hard to keep control. "We've been contacted by the assassins who tried to kill us."

Chapter 13

Marcus was angry and frightened. Of his former squad mates, barely more than half were still alive. Hiding hadn't helped; one by one they'd been found and picked off. Nor was there any safety in numbers — an entire squad of five fire mages had been wiped out all at once. Faced with such a deadly onslaught, the plan Marcus now formulated seemed borderline suicidal and yet the only viable option.

With the last favors he still had in the Ministry of Defense, Marcus learned the location of the Mosquitoes' base. That was where his team was now headed, in scattered groups and on their own.

Karelia greeted them with its harsh landscape. Passing again past the site of the massacre felt wrong, but there was no other way. Marcus hoped the Mosquitoes would see their surrender as a gesture of goodwill. He didn't have much information to offer them, but he had some. The assassins were on their way to surrender themselves.

From what Marcus had gleaned, the Mosquitoes had at least some sense of honor — which was more than he could say for the mysterious death mage hunting them.

Honor. Where was their own honor when they had agreed to ambush and murder their victims? And they had prepared for the work so coldly, so professionally, like it was an ordinary military operation with objectives and operational parameters. And now, the tables turned, and a hunt after them, they were hoping to find mercy by running to the very people whose comrades they'd slaughtered.

They passed through Lakhdenpokhya in silence. Everyone understood perfectly well where they were going and why.

They didn't know the exact location of the base, so when an armored vehicle blocked their path — eerily similar to the one they'd recently encased in stone — a sense of unease settled over them. It felt like an encounter with the dead.

Marcus gathered his thoughts and stepped out of the car. Unarmed, hands raised, he announced loudly, "We have information about the murder of your comrades. We're willing to trade it for protection."

The reply chilled him to the bone: "Things must be really bad for you to come and surrender yourselves this way..."

He had no rebuttal to this, so Marcus said the

only thing he could: "I beg mercy for the women."

The deafening silence lasted several minutes.

"Step out one at a time. Hands held out and visible!"

They lined up, willingly extending their hands for the magic-suppressor cuffs. The bracelets snapped into place, severing the mercenaries from what little powers they still had at their disposal.

Some of their spells had already stopped working as they had approached the Mosquitoes' base, something they'd whispered about in the car. Even weak hereditary magic had been stripped from them.

None of them had ever heard of artifacts with such a capability. One thing was magical suppressor cuffs — another was cutting off a combat unit from its hereditary powers as soon as it entered a specific territory.

The further they went, the more Marcus regretted taking on this cursed job. There was a good chance the Mosquitoes didn't give a damn about the information he had. And then what could he offer in return? Marcus had no idea.

The Mosquitoes loaded them into a covered military truck, leaving one person to drive the visitors' car.

"There were more of you during the attack. Why are there only ten of you here?" The cold voice had an edge to it. They still hadn't seen the faces of the people they were surrendering to. The Mosquitoes wore protective uniforms without insignia and masks over their faces, leaving no indications about their identities. Their reliance on magic had played a cruel trick on them here.

"Three others are making their way on their own — a wind mage, a water mage, and a life mage. The rest are dead."

The stranger scrutinized the prisoners' faces, lingering on the squat, stocky earth mage who had once identified the Mosquitoes' insignia.

"You'll spend the night in solitary. We'll talk tomorrow."

* * *

Judging by my chaotic movements, our family totem could've been a flea instead of a mosquito.

It would have been too suspicious of me to leave immediately after receiving Spider's message. So, I spent the rest of the night in the guest quarters, finishing my mother's wine and experimenting with the roses I was cultivating for the florist competition. Sometime before dawn, Krysin's spies came to check on me, only to find an exhausted young man engrossed in his experiments without rest.

I went down to breakfast looking haggard. A sleepless night and my blood loss had taken their toll, but they'd also provided a perfect alibi to feed to Krysin.

"Gavrila Petrovich, you don't look well this morning," remarked the baron politely, sipping his fragrant coffee. "Couldn't sleep?"

"You are quite perceptive, Arkady Ivanovich. I couldn't resist — I started experimenting with the buds I collected," I confessed with feigned guilt. "You see, I don't have much hereditary power, but I've got plenty of ambition. Hence my exhaustion, both literal and figurative."

Krysin nodded understandingly and seemed to lose all interest in me. Not ten minutes later, the healer from the day before stormed into the dining hall.

"Arkady Ivanovich, you need to rein in your people!" His voice dripped with indignation. "It's unbearable — one incident after another! One worker nearly got a nail through his skull, another fell into a cesspit, and yet another, a carpenter, fell off the hayloft ass-backward onto a bull's horn. And that's all just in the last hour!"

When he mentioned the hayloft, Krysin and I barely managed to stifle our laughter, picturing the scene.

I understood the magnitude of troubles the intruders were about to experience. The baron, however, still had to learn what the inevitability of existence meant. Ever since we'd invoked the protective spell, anyone worshiping foreign gods was just a hair's breadth from having a terrible mishap.

Of course, this could only be avoided by worshiping Aedes. That way, the mana pool would be replenished and minor curses would bypass those who suddenly found their faith.

It was a simple and effective system. Our patron god was appeased and his faithful remained unharmed. That said, I had instructed my blood-bound not to mention the solution for a few days.

Doing so would only strengthen gratitude and Aedes would gain more faith.

Krysin promised to talk to his people, while I, after breakfast, invited the baron to the florist competition in Saint Petersburg, where I planned to present my new rose variety.

After he politely refused citing his busy schedule, I excused myself. Just as I was leaving the dining hall, I heard a muffled curse.

It seemed the baron's cup of freshly brewed coffee had just shattered in his hands.

"This is only the beginning, Baron…" I chuckled to myself. "Only the beginning."

* * *

Portal scrolls are truly a brilliant invention, even if some legs of the journey still have to be made by conventional means. I traveled via Saint Petersburg, where I had to endure a siege from Teimei. Tilda stayed out of sight, seemingly unwilling to revisit our interrupted discussion about the past.

Teimei, on the other hand, with her characteristic persistence and recklessness, began pestering me to let her go home.

The conversation quickly escalated into an ugly row, where one side was inherently guilty of everything, and the other was a blameless victim. The girl ranted, raged, and threatened until I laid the issue bare:

"Are you certain your family won't shell out for something deadlier? We barely managed to treat that junk together, and I'm still not fully recovered. The containment rune continues to drain my strength, and just because you've crawled out of your inner sanctuary doesn't mean you're cured. All it'll take is one dose of that junk and everything will collapse like a house of cards!"

"You're underestimating me! You've locked me in this mansion and forbidden me from appearing in public! I'm suffocating! I need mana! I need to go home!" Teimei wailed, tears streaming down her cheeks, playing the role of the wounded victim. Someone, it seemed, had completely lost touch with reality.

"My dear, you're not my bride, sister or lover. Honestly, I couldn't care less how you choose to meet your end. But until you've repaid your blood debt, you'd better keep your mouth shut." I stared coldly at the overindulged aristocrat who thought she could boss me around on a whim.

It seemed the Kitsune heiress finally realized she'd gone too far. Her tears dried up instantly, and her cheeks flushed. With a look of meek submission, she seemed on the verge of hanging on my every word. The transformation was too sudden, though, and my own blood within her betrayed her true intentions to me completely.

"I've got enough problems without dealing with your theatrical tantrums. I've already given you a generous deal: your life in exchange for help within your field. Don't like it? I can send you back where I found you — in the same condition."

Hearing this, Teimei wisely fell silent, bowed

ceremonially, and backed out of the office. Barely two minutes later, Tilda contacted me.

"What did you say to the girl? She's pacing the room, thinking so hard I can hear her brain creaking."

I swore colorfully, mentally sending all the women who tried to control me to the shabbier parts of the nether plane. Tilda snorted at my indignation.

"Got it. I'll keep an eye on her so she doesn't cause trouble."

"Thanks, Tilda! You're the best!" I said gratefully. "When I get back, I'll bring you a gift!"

"I know your gifts — baubles or potions or cheap knicknacks," my friend grumbled. "Surprise me for once in two hundred years!"

"You'll get a surprise! Promise!"

*　*　*

I think I may have overpraised portal scrolls earlier. I was just one more jump away from the Mosquito school when something went terribly wrong. I only realized this already in free fall, moments before plunging into ice cold water. My clothes soaked instantly, dragging me into the murk.

Not a chance. I didn't burn at the stake in another plane just to drown in this one!

Kicking my arms and legs, I worked my way to the surface. Fortunately, the setting sun's crimson light pointed me in the right direction.

Sputtering and coughing, I looked around me.

The scenery was stunning: I was surrounded by the sheer, white, marble walls of a flooded quarry, with emerald-green pine trees peeking over the rocky rim overhead… and there I was, bobbing like a buoy in the middle of the still, placid water. A beautiful place — odd there weren't any tourists around.

I picked the bank that seemed easiest to climb up and swam toward it. Physical activity seemed to help me think. I'd have to figure out the quarry's name and bring Tilda here. She'd appreciate it, since she loved nature. And this place was beautiful, romantic and secluded enough for her to swim in her true form if she wanted.

With those thoughts in mind, I crawled up onto the shore, only to discover that my remaining portal scrolls were soaked and utterly and irreparably ruined. So much for magical scrolls which were supposedly protected against everything.

Whoever made these deserves to have their hands ripped off and shoved up where the sun don't shine! These things cost a fortune! Not only did they drop me in the middle of nowhere — admittedly a beautiful middle of nowhere, but still nowhere — and now I had to find my way out on my own.

I contacted Spider through the blood link to let him know I'd be delayed.

"Need help?" asked the chief of my bloodbound, alarmed.

"Only if you know every flooded marble quarry within a hundred kilometers of Saint Petersburg."

"Why? Just use another scroll," Spider replied, puzzled.

"Here I am, soaked to the bone, drying my clothes in the setting sun, and I thought, why not take a little vacation?" I joked with a laugh. "I've no working scrolls left. The whole batch is ruined. At least they didn't disintegrate me into dust during the transfer. And it was only a quick swim."

Spider cursed vividly.

"Mikhail Yuryevich, maybe you should contact Aedes?" my bloodbound suggested hopefully.

"Relax," I said, laughing as I tried to calm him down. "You're the one who trained us for endurance marches, and I've still got my stamina. I'll find my way out. As soon as I find someone alive, I'll figure it out. Just make sure our unlucky would-be assassins don't kill themselves while I'm gone."

"They'll be in solitary the entire time. It'll do them good," Spider grumbled. "They tried to kill us, and here you are fretting about them."

"I'm protecting our sources of information," I said, sharing my thoughts on the deserters. "You should consider them as potential recruits. If they came to us, it means the ground is burning under their feet. They were effective enough when they had to kill us, you will admit. All of them are former military, judging by their training, while our own guardsmen has one foot in their graves. We're short on people. Ten in Hmarevo, and another twenty at the school. I don't have time to train new ones. We'll bind these mercenaries with an oath using their guilt as leverage. They'll serve us if they want to live, and they do want to live — otherwise, they wouldn't have come to us."

Spider fell into a stunned silence at my reasoning. He'd probably already envisioned torturing them to death in his head, and now here I was being all practical. For my part, I cut the blood link and turned my attention back to dealing with my current situation.

The sun dipped quickly toward the horizon, lengthening the shadows. The air grew damp as it rose from the water. My clothes had dried a bit and would dry further as I walked, especially if I got my blood circulating to warm up.

Oh, Aedes, it's good to have a patron like you. Not only can I summon every mosquito in the area to scout the forest for signs of life, but the ones busy with reconnaissance won't have the time to bite me.

After spotting the sturdiest-looking ladder I could find, I began climbing out of the quarry. Might as well do it now — there was no point waiting. Oddly enough, I felt calm and even a little amused by the situation. A world filled with magic and advanced technology, yet people still managed to mess things up just the same.

An hour passed, and not one mosquito returned. This began to worry me. What kind of wilderness was this — with not a single person nearby? It made no sense to wander aimlessly without some sense of direction, so I sat on a rocky ledge, gazing at the violet sky. My blood sense spread like a wave through the forest, searching for nearby predators. There were none of significant size, though there were plenty of smaller critters.

I wondered whether if I commanded a few thousand mosquitoes to bring me a squirrel, would they manage it? It might be more practical to simply dominate one and make it come to me, but the idea of a mosquito delivery service was oddly amusing.

My idle thoughts were interrupted as my blood sense encountered four living beings that had suddenly appeared about a kilometer away. Three were unmistakably human, but the fourth...

I quickly ordered the nearest mosquitoes to retrieve a blood sample from the creature and shook myself alert. Constantly checking their movements, I set out first running, then sprinting to intercept the group.

It was a hunt. The hunters were closing in on their quarry, tightening their circle. The closer I got, the more clearly I understood that something about this situation was terribly wrong. I could hear two heartbeats inside the hunted creature. Two!

The hunters were chasing a female, and she was injured. I smelled the blood even from a distance — powerful blood, sentient blood. In my home plane, creatures like this were called ergs — beasts that had evolved to possess self-awareness and human intelligence. My Tilda was an erg, and now, nearby, these hunters here were after another being like her — a creature capable of feeling fear, love, compassion and suffering. And I wasn't fast enough.

I tried to take control of all three hunters but couldn't hold them due to the seal on my hand, which blocked two of my three control contours, leaving me just one to work with. Focusing all my strength, I targeted the hunter closest to the erg, disrupting his aim.

Those bastard inquisitors! When I return — and I *will* return — I'll place seals on you so powerful, my parting curse which popped your blood vessels will seem like a lullaby by comparison!

To distract the other two hunters, I sent every available mosquito after them with orders to attack. But there were too few of the insects in the area. The rest were too far away to make it back in time.

Damn it, history was repeating itself. Once again, I wasn't going to make it in time. The staccato of automatic gunfire shattered the twilight stillness of the forest. I could hear guttural cries in an unfamiliar language — excited, greedy. Animals!

The cry of pain and despair from the female tore at my heart. She wasn't running anymore; she was crawling, desperately trying to save her child.

I leapt onto the first hunter from behind, sinking my teeth into his throat. Hot, adrenaline-laced blood gushed out, invigorating me. I drained the life from him, not defending myself but defending her.

Through his blood, I glimpsed how these hunters had massacred a pride of milk-white wild cats that resembled tigers. They hadn't just killed them — they'd tormented them first. This female was the last survivor, protected and defended by her kin until the end. But the hunters had reached her too.

The limp body collapsed at my feet, the blood restoring my strength just as the mosquitoes arrived. In swarms, they attacked the hunters, drawing their blood.

I managed to kill the second hunter by simply snapping his neck. But then the mother's agonized scream tore through the forest.

The third hunter, paying no attention to anything around him, slashed the injured feline's belly with a knife, trying to pull the cub from her.

A red haze enveloped my vision. I saw everything, understood it even, but I neither wanted to nor could control myself.

I severed his spinal cord with the knife, paralyzing him, then laid him next to the dying mother and began a ritual. The hunter and the prey had now swapped places.

Piece by piece, I dismembered him, extracting every ounce of pain and terror, channeling it into warmth, care, and love. That flood of emotion trickled gently into the dying cub.

I saw the intelligent eyes of the tigress, filled with pleading, and I apologized to her for being too late. I pressed my fingers into the erg's blood, absorbing it and establishing a connection with the dying mother.

"I'm sorry. I can't save you both."

No matter how much I wanted to, ergs weren't humans. Their mana structures were entirely foreign to me — and to anyone, really. Each was unique, following its own path to self-awareness. All I could do was try to save the cub, still closest to its animal form. The tigress seemed to read my thoughts.

"Thank you," came a faint mental whisper. "Look into my eyes."

I shifted my gaze from the cub to the tigress, and it was like I'd been struck by lightning. The emerald depths of her eyes pulled me in, stripping me of my will, dissolving every wall and barrier into dust.

"Don't resist," came the gentle purring. "Accept and share."

I dipped my hands into the hot blood. My mana channels strained and stretched, like steel cables ready to snap. Waves of power, unfamiliar gifts, and unimaginable energy surged through me, passing through my heart — the core of my magic — and into the cub. Maternal love, mingling with my emotions of care, protection, and tenderness, wove a fragile web of attachment. I watched the process unfold, utterly unable to control it.

The alien force reshaped my body with careful precision, drawing resources from the tigress's blood to offset the immense cost.

Her body grew translucent, then faded into mist, leaving behind a snow-white cub curled up and softly snoring.

"Well, what am I supposed to do with you now, huh?" I wiped my hands as best I could on the damp grass and gently stroked the cub's scruff. It immediately started purring without opening its eyes.

Taking the kitten and tucking it into my coat, I turned to the hunters' bodies. Leaving them here, even in a deserted place, didn't feel right. Sure, the wildlife would eventually devour anything left unattended, but still. I ordered the mosquitoes to drain all the blood from the bodies. It would give the little ones nourishment and leave me with fewer headaches dealing with the remains.

While waiting for my winged minions to finish their feast, I stroked the kitten, making it stretch out and expose its belly for more attention.

Its snow-white fur glistened in the light, shimmering like silver threads, occasionally standing on end and making the kitten look like a fluffy ball. Each strand of fur seemed to crackle faintly with static, tickling my palm with every touch.

Such a bold, adorable fluff ball — and not one that would trust just anyone.

For some reason, I thought of the blond-haired Hawthorn. My thoughts drifted to memories of her slender figure and fiery temper. The crackling sensation grew stronger. How was she doing? The little sparks pricked my fingertips like tiny needles. Had she managed to ward off that Bear?

A flash of light burst before my eyes... and I was suddenly underwater again. Only this time, the water enveloping me wasn't that of a quarry pond but falling from an ordinary barracks shower — and standing just a step away, soaking wet and wide-eyed with shock, was a completely naked Svetlana Hawthorn.

Chapter 14

"Poor, lost, little kitten," came an unexpected thought, and I wasn't wrong.

As my initial shock passed, Svetlana transformed from a startled maiden into an enraged fury.

"Shut your eyes!" she hissed, sounding as fierce as a wild tigress, as she tried to cover her breasts with her arms. "If you tell anyone about this, you'll hang half-mast for the rest of your life."

"Where have I heard that before?" I blurted out self-destructively as I shamelessly took in the sight before me. And oh, what a sight it was. Pert, firm breasts with pink nipples, a flat stomach, a toned, perky ass — all glistening under streams of water and soap suds...

Any man would understand me. Not only did I *not* close my eyes, but taking advantage of the fact that her hands were occupied, I pressed her against the wall and kissed her — ravenously, insistently and dominantly. To hell with the consequences! I'd deal with that later!

Hawthorn squirmed but didn't push me away. That was my cue to end my bold move — after all, I wasn't roughing up some servant girl but a noblewoman. Reluctantly, I pulled back.

"My shower is always open to you," I teased, winking at her before stepping out, lest I really lose certain key, masculine ambitions.

I darted out of the showers, making my escape in short dashes. Luckily, there was a small window in the locker room through which I managed to climb outside, avoiding the indignity of parading through the barracks in wet clothes.

"I'll be at the instructors' barracks in five minutes. Have dry clothes ready for me," I sent a message to my bloodbound. The response was stunned silence, followed by a flood of questions:

"How? By what magic? Did the contour fail?"

Ignoring the questions, I added another thought:

"If anyone spots a white, fluffy, blind kitten on the grounds, don't touch it. Call me immediately."

Fifteen minutes later, dressed in clean, dry clothes and sipping herbal tea, I was listening to Spider's report.

"There are fourteen deserters — mages with levels ranging from three to five, though some aren't fully developed. In addition to the elementalists, we've got two unusual ones. A life mage and a nature mage. The first can function as both a healer and a radar, detecting all living beings within a kilometer radius. The second…" Spider nearly smacked his lips with excitement. "We need her as a master of camouflage. She cleaned up the site of the ambush so thoroughly that when our guys went to check it, they couldn't even find the place."

I nodded in agreement, inwardly pleased that Spider was focusing on practical matters. Fourteen people, plus their families — that would be a decent addition for Aedes. Spider's next words interrupted my train of thought.

"But there's a problem."

"What is it?"

"There's a death mage after them."

* * *

Svetlana remained standing under the shower for a long time, trying to regain her composure.

Who? Who in the world could cast portal scrolls right into the women's shower? The answer was obvious: no one. That meant it had to be magic. But hereditary magic wasn't supposed to work here. Personal magic, then? But who'd ever heard of teleportation magic being personal? The answer to that question was worse than the previous one. If anyone knew about such magic, that person would either be working for the Emperor and the state — or they'd have been dissected in a lab by now.

Svetlana imagined being forced to repeatedly

escort and deliver people and cargo to places she didn't want to go. The constant control, the lack of freedom — it would drive anyone to despair.

She'd fled here for that very reason. Her father's position ensured that Svetlana had never truly belonged to herself. Her life and destiny had always belonged to the whims of the imperial family. So, it made sense that this man would keep his powers secret at all costs.

Who was he again? A Vinogradov, judging by the ring and the bold earring in his ear. Insolent, of course, but with a sense of boundaries. He hadn't overstepped, hadn't forced anything, and had made a quick exit before things got truly indecent.

Svetlana tried to recall what she knew about the Vinogradovs. All she remembered was that about a hundred years ago, they'd been a princely family under the protection of Muscadine, the god of the vine. She couldn't recall any recent events, even though aristocratic gossip was all that Princess Maria ever talked about. Either the Vinogradov family had fallen into obscurity or disgrace, or it had simply remained out of the spotlight for a long time.

But he'd certainly made an appearance in the shower. Svetlana recalled the bold way he'd kissed her, his wink and his escape. She even switched the water over to cold to clear her thoughts. Acting like a child — by the Holy Hawthorn, really! One kiss and a suggestive look, and she was thinking Hawthorn knows what... She resolved to find out everything she could from Princess Maria about the latest news on Aedes and Muscadine. If heirs from two families had suddenly resurfaced, Maria would know. For the first time, Sveta saw the princess's obsession with gossip in a new light. Knowledge was power. Maybe Maria Krechet wasn't as foolish as she seemed, always staying at the center of the Empire's social web.

*　*　*

The solitary cell held a table and two metal chairs. A dim candle barely illuminated the dark room, and the cold was palpable. A red-bearded man in camouflage breathed on his shackled hands, bound by magic-suppressing cuffs.

I'd spent a long and detailed session with the defectors' commander, Marcus, both in conversation and in methods beyond words. To fully test his sincerity, I conducted an interrogation using blood magic. Spider and Beetle tried hard to pretend nothing unusual was happening, but even they couldn't entirely mask their surprise at what I was doing.

What infuriated me the most was how, due to my seal's limitations, I had to devise extra rituals for what should have been straightforward blood techniques. It made me feel like a dilettante — or worse, some kind of deviant.

This interrogation was no different. In the past, I'd have sunk my fangs into him, lulled him into a trance, and wandered through his memories until I found the answers I sought. But now? Nothing of the sort was possible. I couldn't even infuse my blood into him — it might not take.

"Aedes, what if I make him a servant of the family, then kill him later if he proves unreliable?" I asked, voicing the most obvious question about using a blood oath.

"Our followers are scarce as it is and now you want to conduct experiments with the blood-bound?" my patron retorted, clearly irritated. "You're a blood mage, aren't you? Torture's perfectly legal here you know."

I sighed heavily. That idea was a dead end. Still, it had been worth a try. Torture wasn't an option for me — not out of compassion, but because it risked weakening the clan's future defensive capabilities.

I resorted to a process I found deeply unpleasant. For Marcus's body to accept my blood, I had to craft it into a weak approximation of a macro — a substance usually extracted from the essence of slain creatures in the nether plane. Cutting myself had become a bad habit in this world, one I needed to break, but for now, it was my only viable option. After all, I wasn't just skimming through his last half-hour of life; I needed at least a week's worth of his memories.

Marcus eyed the offered macro warily — it was unlike anything he'd seen before in both color and texture. I waited a cautious ten minutes, ensuring the effects would set in, before beginning my questioning.

By then, the power of my blood had infiltrated the deepest corners of Marcus's memory. I saw more than he'd ever willingly share. His lover's death in war, his helplessness, his adoption of a fallen comrade's child, even the sacrifices he'd made to pay for the child's magical training. I saw his attempts to unite his former comrades, his struggles to find his place in civilian life, and the eventual descent into mercenary work.

Marcus wasn't a good man or a bad one. He was a soldier, with decent leadership instincts but little experience in the murky waters of political intrigue. That inexperience had cost half his squad their lives and left Marcus here, sitting before us, trying to save the other half. Had someone else been in our place, his team would already be dead — an eye for an eye. But we were alive and in need of loyal people.

I asked simple questions as I delved through his blood memories: How did they receive the job? Who was the intermediary? When was the payment made? When did the first squad member die? I rephrased questions, searching for leads. The most useful piece of information I uncovered was the name of their contact for the job — a mobster known as Nikolai Vorobey, the boss of Saint Petersburg's Sparrow gang. Beyond that, Marcus knew little; he was merely a hired gun, not the mastermind.

Wrapping up the interrogation, I stared at Marcus thoughtfully, weighing his fate.

My decision hadn't changed. I was pleased

that Spider had taken an interest in the two mage women in their group; the elemental mages, however, raised some qualms. They possessed hereditary spells and powers, which wouldn't function in our lands. Still, that didn't mean they couldn't be retrained, like the noble children we'd recruited.

"Marcus, what do you want from us?" I finally asked, posing the most important question. Feeling my blood within him, I waited for his answer. Would he lie?

"To get another chance and atone for my past actions," the leader of the mercenaries replied, holding my gaze. "To live by the warrior's code."

"Well, that's honest. But you've come to the wrong place," I replied bluntly, cutting through his lofty words. "We're not noble knights without fear or reproach. We stand as a shield between beasts and humanity. We kill and we're killed. But we never strike first. All of us are bound by a blood oath and a vow of secrecy. So, Marcus, you have two options: either you become bloodbound to Baron Komarin, swear the oath of secrecy, and do whatever is required of you, or..." I let the pause hang in the air before continuing: "That death mage will find his work has been done for him."

Marcus flinched but didn't look away. Instead, he seemed to be deep in thought.

"I can't decide for the others. Let each soldier make their own choice."

We arranged just that. All the defectors were gathered in a single cell. They held themselves with dignity, though fear flickered in their eyes.

Scanning each other for injuries, signs of torture or beatings, their attention quickly settled on Marcus. They were concerned for their commander, and that was a good sign. Marcus took the floor:

"It looks like we got involved in a conflict far beyond our understanding. The Mosquitoes are a true special unit, but we'll only learn the nature of their work if we take a blood oath and an oath of secrecy of the highest level. The oath will bind our loyalty to their god until death. We will have to change our patron deities and become servants of the Mosquito clan. There's no other way to leave this place alive."

Marcus earned my respect with his speech. He explained things clearly and emphasized the right points. The fighters remained silent, processing what they'd heard. Only the life mage broke the silence with a comment:

"That's why we came here. I see only one issue. Changing a patron deity can have consequences. No one talks about it openly, but be prepared for debuffs to hereditary spells, curses — possibly severe ones — and other unpleasant surprises, depending on your god's temperament."

It was a valid point, but one I could easily address for my future clan members.

"On this land, all bow to Aedes, be they Baron Komarin or the Emperor himself. Other gods have no power over you here. As far as they're concerned, you've vanished — died," I said, scrutinizing the group before me. "As you've likely noticed, your hereditary powers don't work here, so only personal strength matters. The rest you'll learn after joining our bloodbound."

Whether they believed me or not was their choice, but they didn't have any real alternatives. Five minutes later, I was administering the oath to fourteen individuals. Aedes' followers were growing in number, and I could hear a satisfied grumble in the back of my mind.

By the way, it's curious how I can communicate with Aedes while others lack any connection to their gods. And yet, at the same time, here in this domain, I can't even use the one power Aedes granted me — summoning mosquitoes.

Something to ponder for later. For now, I needed to replicate the mana pool process we'd used in Hmarevo. I selected the deepest basement in the school's fort for the ritual. Luckily, there were bloodbound available for the ceremony, and the congregation in here proved even more grateful than in Hmarevo, so the mana pool would be consistently replenished.

Spider, for his part, had done an excellent job explaining things to the local populace. Baron Komarin and his patron deity were sincerely revered in the village. It wasn't surprising — nothing bolsters faith in a god or lord like sealing a portal through which a massive beast threatened to obliterate the entire village.

This time, creating the mana pool was both easier and harder. No virgins had been brought, but my blood was far more mana-dense. It seemed my connection with the erg hadn't left me unchanged. The new bloodbound didn't betray any feelings about the process. If it had to be done, it had to be done. Especially since only about half a liter of blood was taken from each of them.

Still, I sent everyone to the infirmary to be checked and treated if necessary. We finished everything just before dawn. As I was leaving the infirmary, I unexpectedly ran into an alarmed-looking Hawthorn.

*　*　*

Svetlana couldn't sleep. She tossed and turned for two hours before giving up and deciding to take a walk outside the barracks. A vague sense of unease gnawed at her. Her father had mentioned something similar once.

The least favorite hour of every healer is between four and five in the morning, which is when the most patients die. It's inexplicable, but true. During this hour, healers feel as though death is making its rounds, collecting its due. No matter how hard they fight, people pass away.

Now, Sveta felt death stalking nearby. She checked on the cadets carefully, but they were all sleeping the sound sleep of the exhausted. Slipping quietly out of the barracks, she wandered beneath the sprawling branches of the pines. The fresh, clean air made her shiver in the predawn chill. Tilting her head back and closing her eyes, she inhaled the scent of pine. It calmed her, as if promising that everything would be okay.

Amid the creaking trees, a faint, weak mewling reached her ears.

Opening her eyes, Sveta couldn't believe what she saw. A snow-white kitten hung suspended from a branch just above her head, mewling softly with its eyes tightly shut. A quick diagnostic spell made her gasp. The kitten was emaciated to the brink of death. Its life force flickered faintly. Conjuring a sphere of healing mana, Sveta tried to infuse the kitten with vitality, replenishing its reserves, but nothing worked. The mana passed right through without taking hold. That couldn't be possible!

Scanning its body for injuries revealed nothing.

"What's wrong with you, little one?" she murmured, cradling the nearly weightless kitten in her arms, desperate to help. She tried every regeneration technique she knew, but nothing worked.

Clutching the kitten tightly, Sveta sprinted toward the healers' building, hoping someone there might save it. At the entrance, she ran into Vinogradov. He stepped aside to let her pass but then abruptly blocked the doorway.

"What happened? You look like you've seen a ghost!"

"Move! I don't have time for this!" Sveta snapped, struggling against his strong arms while holding the kitten, which seemed even lighter now. "This is a matter of life and death!"

"Stop!" Vinogradov barked, his tone brooking no argument. Sveta froze involuntarily.

"Show me," he ordered.

Reluctantly, torn between urgency and frustration, she pulled the kitten from her cloak. Its fur had dulled, turning almost ashen gray.

"Son of a — !" Vinogradov cursed, grabbing her by the arm and dragging her into the nearest room, which turned out to be a dressing room. "Put it on the table."

Vinogradov shrugged off his instructor's dark jacket, leaving only a black short-sleeved shirt, and gestured for her to lay the kitten down.

Sveta placed the tiny creature on the table, but it didn't even stir.

"Come on, you're a healer! One of the best! Do something!" The young man stared helplessly at the gray, furry bundle growing smaller before his eyes.

"I can't! I've tried everything!" Svetlana snapped, running another diagnostic. "My magic just passes through it without taking hold!"

Vinogradov hesitated for only a fraction of a second before grabbing a scalpel from the surgical kit.

"Do you want it to survive?" he asked her, and Svetlana's eyes widened in horror, unsure why he needed the scalpel, but she nodded anyway. "Then swear a blood oath that you won't speak of what you're about to see."

Hesitantly, Svetlana repeated the strange oath Vinogradov recited, word for word. When she said the final "I swear," he slashed his palm. Blood bloomed from the cut like a crimson flower, its "petals" forming fine veins that twisted and intertwined, creating something resembling a macro.

A macro formed from his own blood. Svetlana couldn't believe what she was seeing. Macros were only ever extracted from creatures of the nether plane. They were effectively concentrated energy cores. But how? Why? Who... *What* was he?

Questions crowded her mind, but Vinogradov worked quickly, carefully forming a red pebble-sized macro and placing it in the kitten's mouth. He gently stroked its throat, encouraging it to swallow. The kitten complied.

Moments later, its fur turned from ashen gray to a soft peach tone, then deepened to a shade reminiscent of garnet. Another moment passed, and its eyes fluttered open. The kitten purred softly and climbed into Vinogradov's arms.

The young man, however, looked far from well. His face was pale, his lips blue, yet he cradled the kitten tenderly, whispering something inaudible.

Svetlana quickly scanned Vinogradov, determined to heal him if she couldn't help the kitten. She was a healer, after all. But as soon as the scan results appeared, she froze in stunned disbelief.

In this completely unfamiliar man, she recognized her own handiwork. His fully restored mana channels bore her distinct signature. His guise might have been fake, but the family crest on his ring couldn't be.

"By the Holy Hawthorn," she thought, "what on earth are you?!"

Chapter 15

I FELT AWFUL. Two days without rest, two mana pools formed and two macros conjured from my own blood. I was running a mad race, and on top of it all, the erg cub had nearly died.

When Hawthorn had shown me the kitten, practically melting away before my eyes, I'd hoped she could help. She was a healer, after all. But my hopes turned out to be futile. I had no choice but to share my own blood, which still held traces of its mother's energy, with the cub.

The kitten had taken the sustenance, opened its eyes, and completed the final bond with me. Now I could sense its insatiable curiosity mixed with concern for me.

"Don't worry, I'm fine," I assured the kitten in a murmur, stroking its head. "I'll get some sleep and it'll pass."

The kitten licked my hand with its raspy little

tongue.

"Are you a boy or a girl?" I teased. The kitten tilted its head, spun in a circle chasing its tail, and then looked up at me with a charming expression.

"Memeow is still meow-small!" The kitten puffed up its fur, resembling a fuzzy ball. "Memeow knows how-meow to hide!" Sparks danced across the kittens coat again.

"Listen, Memeow," I said, stopping the kitten before it could vanish again, "don't disappear like that without warning. I worry about you, and it drains a lot of mana from you when you do that."

We conversed mentally as I slid down to sit on the couch. Hawthorn was staring at me wide-eyed, as though she'd just witnessed a monster from the nether plane. Maybe that's what she decided I was after everything she'd seen. Thankfully, there was the oath to keep her from talking.

"This didn't happen," I warned sternly, meeting her gaze, and she nodded numbly.

"If you help me now, I'll be truly grateful," I added.

Another nod, this time more deliberate.

Her magic flowed into me again. The mana sphere she conjured this time was much smaller, fitting neatly into her palms, but it was enough to clear my head and restore some strength.

"Thank you," I said sincerely. "Now, go back to the barracks. Reveille is soon."

For all her defiance, Hawthorn obediently headed for the door. She paused at the threshold, gave me a crooked smile, and said, "My name is

Svetlana. And you owe me for two healing sessions now."

Svetlana left and I remained with the kitten, who purred softly in my lap.

"Nice Svet-lau-na," it murmured, "kind and br-r-rave."

"I know, kitten," I replied. "Oaths are oaths, but I'll need to keep a close watch on her now. Family secrets have to be kept in the family."

*   *   *

I returned to Saint Petersburg by midday, having indulged in a good nap before my departure. Before I left, Spider handed me an unassuming amulet with three small oak pendants strung on a chain.

I was about to pocket it when Spider stopped me.

"Put it on. It's a ward against the death mages. Each pendant can absorb three spells or physical touches. We dug them up from our old stocks today and we're issuing them to everyone in case of an attack."

"I didn't know there was protection against death mages," I said, inspecting the simple amulet. "I thought only life mages could counter them."

I couldn't even imagine what a fight between life and death mages would look like. Life mages were far more common, while death mages were true anomalies. I'd read in *The Social Bulletin* that for the first time in a hundred years, a powerful death mage had emerged in the southern lands of the Empire.

It made me wonder how much someone had paid to hire such a rarity to eliminate the assassins who'd failed to kill me.

The price must have been astronomical, considering Marcus had mentioned that the contract alone was worth nearly half a million.

This was a high-stakes play then. On one side, someone with immense financial and administrative resources. On the other, my three hundred years of experience and my grandfather's uncanny foresight.

Baron Komarin might be dead, but he could still send greetings from the afterlife to keep his killers on their toes. And that was precisely what I intended to do.

*   *   *

Arkady Ivanovich was furious. An endless string of mishaps had forced all the construction work to a standstill. And yet, however much he wanted to, there was no way to accuse anyone of sabotage or malice. The mishaps were so bizarre and absurd that no one could have possibly engineered them. A full-fledged field hospital was already operating in Hmarevo, with a constant stream of minor injuries coming in. Nothing serious, but the sheer volume...

Even the border guards — the so-called "Eagles" — seemed to suffer less, perhaps because they patrolled the boundaries of the Komarin lands and had begun invoking Aedes' name regularly.

That worked for them — they were untethered by family ties or totems. But Krysin's own people weren't so fortunate. On these cursed lands, their connection to their patron deity, the Rat, was completely severed. Attempts to pray or call upon him only seemed to increase the rate of accidents.

By the third day, Krysin was ready to blame anyone, even Vinogradov, for his misfortunes. But the Eagles reported that Vinogradov himself had suffered an accident — his horse twisted its leg as he left the estate, forcing him to travel on foot to a nearby village before continuing on to the railway station.

For the first time, Arkady Ivanovich began to think he might have been wrong to suspect the man. Coincidences might not be coincidences, but for some reason, Vinogradov inspired more sympathy than suspicion in him.

Deprived of hereditary power, the man still worked tirelessly for his family's sake, much as Arkady Ivanovich had in his younger days. Men like that were often undervalued in the clan system, which prioritized personal power in the empire.

Still, Krysin was more preoccupied with his own problems than by the affairs of some aristocrat. By evening on the third day, a curse specialist from the Ministry of Defense had arrived in Hmarevo.

The young specialist, fresh out of the academy, was highly promising and eager to fulfill personal requests from the leadership.

The former student practically buried his nose in the ground, searching for the root cause of the accidents. And that wasn't a metaphor — he literally dug through the earth, uncovering even traces of a poorly cast curse left by Krysin's own nephew. Something Arkady Ivanovich had certainly not expected.

By lunchtime the next day, the bleary-eyed young man, with dark circles under his eyes, came to present his findings.

The specialist downed three cups of coffee as Krysin waited, unhurried. His sources had reported that the young man had worked diligently, so Krysin was willing to overlook the simple human weakness of needing caffeine.

Finally, Arkady Ivanovich heard the specialist's findings. They were anything but reassuring.

"Your Lordship, what we're observing here is, I dare say, unique," the young man began, laying out a topographical map with the Komarin lands outlined. "There is clearly an magical anomaly on this land. More importantly, it is of divine origin. Over the past day, I've conducted experiments and measured mana fluctuations for unaligned individuals versus ones with a patron deity. The results are staggering."

The specialist gestured nervously, adjusting his round glasses.

"The local patron deity is actively expelling anyone who does not revere it. Or rather, it is making it abundantly clear that such individuals are unwelcome here."

"Listen, my dear boy," Krysin interrupted, barely concealing his irritation. "I already know that much! Tell me something that justifies the cost of your services."

"Very well," the specialist replied, his tone tightening. "In the past two weeks, three sacrificial rituals have been performed here, triggering a chain reaction. Essentially, the lands of this family are now in the initial stages of conservation. If a legitimate blood heir does not appear within six months, the local patron deity will escalate its actions. Most likely, it will begin outright killing those it deems undesirable."

"But... that's tantamount to a declaration of war between families!" Krysin's left eye twitched uncontrollably at the news. "Other clans didn't face this kind of trouble when annexing foreign lands."

"Who is the patron deity of these lands?"

"What does it matter who it is?" Krysin snapped.

"It matters greatly," the curse specialist retorted. "Taking land from a plant or minor animal deity is one thing. You might see dying trees, an influx of rodents, or an overabundance of frogs. But if someone tries to claim land belonging to a predator deity, their totemic creatures could orchestrate a bloody campaign against the invaders. Especially if the deity perceives the claims as unjust."

Krysin fell into a deep, brooding silence. For ten years, he had systematically besieged and strangled a seemingly insignificant family, finally achieving his goal. And now he was being told that their patron deity might retaliate with vengeance?

Why should anyone care about these gods? They didn't interfere in human affairs. Where had this god been when the family was being wiped out? And more importantly, what was he supposed to do now? Where could he find a blood relative of the Komarin family to use as a puppet?

A surprised exclamation interrupted Krysin's troubling thoughts, irritating him further. The curse specialist was calmly sipping another cup of coffee while reading a slightly outdated newspaper.

"You're still here?" Krysin barked. "This meeting is over!"

The former student carefully set down his cup and folded the newspaper, leaving one section visible. He seemed calmer, even sterner.

"I think I know which family we're dealing with," he said, setting the paper on the table. "Good luck waging war against the Mosquito god!"

With a sly grin, he gathered his materials and left, leaving Krysin to stare at the paper. On the front page of *The Imperial Gazette* was a public notice offering a reward for any information about Baron Mikhail Yuryevich Komarin.

"What in the name of the Rat is going on here?" Krysin growled.

As if in response to his invocation of his patron, his stomach churned violently, forcing him to leave the dining hall in haste.

* * *

I returned home without incident. A shower and a hearty lunch did wonders for my mood. The number of bloodbound was growing, the two mana pools were working perfectly, and even Memeow had found her spot — on the pillow next to mine. The little cat followed me everywhere with an air of importance. When she had time to tear through the mansion like a hurricane, I couldn't say, but the next time she appeared, her face was smeared with blood. Alarmed, I called out to her.

"What happened? Are you hurt?"

"Memeow feels good! Imewo had yummy-meow!" She licked her lips with a dazed expression.

"Tilda, could you come to my study, please?" I called out to my friend. "I have... uh..." I hesitated, unsure of how to describe Memeow. She wasn't a pet, nor a beast, nor a guest. She was... "...a child here with me."

Through the blood link, I could sense Tilda's stunned silence. For her to be at a loss for words? Impossible. Moments later, she burst into the study, and I found myself momentarily paralyzed, oblivious to all other stimuli. The reason? Her outfit — or rather, her lack thereof. No, not quite. She was wearing something. A dress, if you could call it that. Layers of semi-transparent fabrics in varying shades, embroidery and chains in the most unexpected places. It was similar to what women of the dune tribes wore in our world, where the belief was that the more powerful the warrior, the more revealing her attire.

I nearly drooled, while the stir her appearance caused in my trousers is best left unmentioned.

"You look stunning! Simply exquisite!" I exclaimed with genuine admiration, watching as Tilda twirled, relishing the effect she'd achieved. "At the flower exposition, every man's eyes will be on you, not the flowers!"

"What flower exposition?" she snapped, latching onto the new piece of information. "Although, hang on, what about the child you mentioned?"

I called Memeow, who shuffled out from under the curtain, her face now sticky with raspberry juice.

A kaleidoscope of emotions swirled across Tilda's face: delight, caution, amazement, and finally, the realization of how much trouble lay ahead. She crouched cautiously near the little cat, letting her sniff her hand. Memeow's eyes widened into round saucers. Within seconds, she was nestled in Tilda's arms, purring contentedly.

"I don't know anyone else who draws ergs to them like you do," Tilda said as she sank into the chair across from my desk, stroking the kitten absently. "Me, then Lana... now Memeow. You understand this doesn't just happen normally, right?"

I nodded, unwilling to delve into the topic, especially after she mentioned Lana.

"I guess I always stick my nose where it doesn't belong, and this is the result."

"You don't get it," Tilda sighed. "Macros, which in this world are harvested from creatures of the nether plane, are underdeveloped, calcified magical cores. Ninety-nine percent of beings remain stuck at that stage of development. Less than one percent push past the barrier and become ergs — sentient, magically gifted creatures. You — " she jabbed her finger at me, " — you treated all of us like equals, like reasoning beings. You talked to us. That gave us the push we needed to evolve, to understand, and to become self-aware. Why do you think, after your death, the creatures of the nether plane, led by ergs, waged war against the Holy Inquisitors who burned you? Because the seals on the nether plane burst upon your death? No! It's because there's something about you that's dear to us. I've spent two hundred years trying to figure out what it is. But ergs... we sense it and come to you across worlds and dimensions. Want me to guess how this little one ended up with you?"

I nodded, mulling over her words.

"A natural rift must have occurred, and this miracle fell almost literally at your feet."

"Not quite, but close enough," I admitted reluctantly. "Let's shelve my uniqueness for now and figure out what to do with her."

"What's there to figure out?" Tilda smiled, gently combing through Memeow's snowy fur. "Feed her regularly, love her, don't hurt her, and play with her so she doesn't cause trouble. By the way, what's her ability?"

"Teleportation, apparently. She transported me the moment I pictured the place I wanted to go."

Tilda whistled with amazement.

"That's no simple shape-shifting. That's..." Her eyes lit up with excitement. "Oh, the possibilities!"

I had to bring her back to reality.

"She's still a cub. She needs to grow first. Otherwise, she might end up somewhere she can't come back from, and I won't be able to find her."

I poured myself a glass of brandy, mulling over how to keep my kitten safe.

"Have you established a bond with her?"

"Yes. I gave her a macro made from my blood, with traces of her mother's energy," I said, shuddering as I recalled the sensation of creating the macro. It had felt like being consumed alive.

"Then she won't leave you unless you drive her away," Tilda shrugged. Her tone, however, carried an unfamiliar weight, as if her usual carefree demeanor had cracked, revealing emotions she rarely showed.

"Tilda," I began, trying to broach our past, but she cut me off with a wave of her hand.

"Let it go. It happened, and it's over. Don't repeat your mistakes — with her." She gave me a crooked smile and turned to leave the study, but I stopped her.

"How about a night out on Friday?" I asked, formally inviting her.

"Dress code?" she asked, pausing at the door but not turning around.

"Exotic is fine, but you and Teimei will need costumes. We'll be attending the International Flower Exposition and Florist Competition, where your humble servant will have the honor of dazzling Their Imperial Highnesses Princess Maria and Prince Andrey," I said with a theatrical bow.

"Oh, if you want exotic, we'll give you exotic!" Tilda laughed, clearly amused, and left the room.

I was alone again, but peace was a luxury I couldn't afford. Activating the blood link, I issued instructions to my loyal butler, Arseny.

"I need a thorough survey of all flooded marble quarries near the city," I said, describing the location Memeow's mother had diverted my portal scroll to. "Within a kilometer radius, there might be the remains of three people there."

"Shall I have the remains destroyed?" Arseny asked matter-of-factly.

"It would be nice, but I think the wildlife has already taken care of it. Oh, and Arseny, I need a meeting with the most cunning and scandalous journalist from *The Imperial Gazette*."

"Perhaps someone from *The Social Bulletin*?" he asked with interest. Honestly, I couldn't think of an area where he didn't have connections.

"No, I need a serious investigator — a bona fide sleuth! Meticulous, well-connected, and uncompromising!" I described the kind of detective I wanted to uncover my enemy's secrets. I had my suspicions, but I needed proof.

"Understood! I'll arrange a meeting for you at the Vidrin estate. You're a welcome guest there now; a personal invitation arrived the day after you left."

"Perfect. A 'chance' meeting is exactly what I need!"

* * *

Vidrin's mansion was unusually quiet and deserted compared to our last visit. I had confirmed my courtesy call in advance, but I couldn't shake the worry that the meeting with the journalist wouldn't happen. In hindsight, I was wrong — but how could I have known?

I was greeted by the count himself. Pyotr Semyonovich looked elegant and, most importantly, sober. He scanned my bespoke suit from the Arachnid atelier, noted the family crest on my ring and the earring in my ear, and nodded as though coming to some internal conclusion.

After exchanging the usual pleasantries about the weather, politics and the gossip of the day, the count finally got to the point.

"During your last visit, Gavrila Petrovich, you demonstrated a rather specific family skill. I'd like to propose a way for you to monetize it."

To say I was stunned would be an understatement. During our last visit, it was Teimei who had shown off her abilities. I had nothing to do with it. Just to be safe, I decided to inquire what exactly he was talking about.

"No need to be modest; I've peeked into the archives. Your distant ancestor had a similar skill and learned to use it very effectively. I'm offering you a share in an established winery and am even willing to buy you land with a mansion for your own use," Vidrin said, growing more excited as he laid out his proposals, clearly trying to get them all out before I interrupted with the usual line about family secrets.

The thing was, I had no idea what skill he was referring to. Listening to Vidrin wax lyrical about the prospects of a joint business venture, I reached out internally to my adopted Wine God.

"Muscadine, do you know what he's talking about?"

The response came quickly: a chuckle followed by contented sniffling.

"Oh, I know! You started handling family affairs, so I gave you a little perk," Muscadine said smugly. "You're not the only one who enjoys a good joke."

"And what exactly is this little perk?" I asked cautiously, wary of his sense of humor.

"At Vidrin's party, all wine-based alcoholic drinks suddenly skyrocketed in potency. Congratulations, you're now a walking distillery! Enjoy!" Muscadine quipped before vanishing.

Well, I was in trouble now. How was I supposed to explain this to Aedes?

"What's this all about then?" my patron deity's voice chimed in as if on cue.

Chapter 16

In the end, I told the count I'd consider his proposal later, as family matters took precedence for now. A little extra income never hurt, but if Muscadine's "perk" truly worked, I could revive my own winemaking operation. We'd buy land, restore the vineyards — it wouldn't happen overnight, but if the Muscadine family was to rise again, we could even merge into a larger clan.

For now, though, I had no time to delve into this new skill or the intricacies of the proposal. Vidrin took my response in stride, pleased that I hadn't outright declined, and our personal acquaintance got off to a good start.

I spent the evening in male company. Vidrin was hosting a meeting of his gentlemen's business club, most of whom had prominently featured — bare bottoms and all — at the previous orgy. I had collected blood samples from them then; tonight, I reacquainted myself with Vidrin's inner circle.

It was quite the gathering: bankers, industrialists, shipowners, builders — the list went on. Men aged twenty-five to forty. By the standards of high society, they were mere youngsters, still learning the ropes of managing their family affairs.

"So, Gavrila Petrovich, what is it you do?" one aristocrat, seemingly connected to river shipping, asked me.

This was the question I had been expecting. Staying silent wasn't an option, and citing my youth would be tantamount to admitting weakness, costing me any authority in the future. Fortunately, I had prepared my answer in advance.

"Gentlemen, I am currently fulfilling the will of the late Count Vinogradov. We have recently discovered previously unknown annexes to his last will and testament, in pursuance to which I have the honor of addressing certain family matters," I said, sticking to the cover story I'd fed to Zubrov. What I didn't anticipate was how quickly the conversation would pick up.

"That was clever of you, involving the Heraldic Service," said a stocky man with deep-set eyes and rough features — Kabanov, the Boar, if I wasn't mistaken. He raised his snifter of brandy in a toast. "I can only imagine how all the bloodline heirs must be scrambling now. The count's estate was estimated at several hundred million gold rubles a century ago, including antique and art collections. With compound interest and Imperial family guarantees, the accumulated wealth must be astronomical. Anyone in the know would be envious."

I smiled modestly, though inwardly I whistled at the sheer scale of the fortune. Surely, it wouldn't hurt to work for two gods at once?

Muscadine's smug voice chimed in: "Told you so!"

Aedes, clearly irked, retorted, "What is this nonsense?! Everything was fine! Besides, we're not exactly starving here!"

I responded to Kabanov in his own manner.

"Yes, the prince's wealth isn't exactly a secret, but the terms of inheritance…"

I trailed off modestly, taking a sip from my snifter and allowing the light to catch the adamantine family ring on my finger.

Much later, when the noble gathering had splintered into smaller groups, Kabanov found me again by the fireplace.

"You're remarkably modest for someone of your current status, Gavrila Petrovich," he remarked. His gaze flicked from the fire to the brandy swirling in his snifter. "Your earring, paired with that ring… let's just say, I know enough to recognize what that means. A tiny drop of Muscadine blood flows through my veins — a grape from the same vine. Even so, I know that only someone capable of communicating with the patron deity wears that combination."

He leaned in slightly, lowering his voice.

"And as for that little party at Vidrin's… I let him know the reason it was so spectacular only after he tried to cure his hangover with a random glass of wine. You may not believe me, but I'll be truly delighted if the Vinogradov family establishes a new vineyard. The Kabanovs will always welcome you in our home."

As we parted ways, I handed him my calling card to solidify the new connection. Vidrin and Kabanov escorted me to the carriage, both looking slightly awed by the princely crest emblazoned on its side.

"My grandfather was a staunch traditionalist," I said with a shrug, then added with a mischievous wink: "and it doesn't hurt that the ladies find it romantic."

Vidrin nodded in understanding.

Before opening the carriage door, the coachman spoke to me through the blood link.

"Master, Arseny has scheduled a meeting for you tonight. Your guest is waiting inside."

"Thank you for letting me know," I replied, then bid farewell to Vidrin and Kabanov before moving on to my next negotiation.

* * *

Anonymity was essential for both parties, so my meeting with the reporter was brief and to the point. The dim light of the carriage lent the atmosphere a certain criminal undertone.

"I was promised the story of the decade. That's why I'm here," the visitor said in a gravelly, smoky baritone, skipping any pretense of polite introductions. "This isn't about another salacious affair, is it?"

"Do you have sources inside the Ministry of Defense?" I cut straight to the chase. "If not, there's no point in continuing."

A long silence followed, broken only by a sharp, scrutinizing look and an eventual, cautious nod.

"In that case I want you to investigate the destruction of the Komarin family. Officially, it's been ten years of tragic accidents. But I have reason to believe otherwise."

"What does the Ministry have to do with this?" the reporter asked warily.

I reached into my jacket and pulled out a few pages of my grandfather's notes, edited and supplemented by me. Certain sensitive information had been omitted, but the names of five individuals — those with the power, money, and influence to destroy our family — remained.

The reporter moved to pocket the notes, but I stopped him.

"Read them here and burn them when you're done."

With a shrug, he pulled out a small pocket lantern and began reading. As his eyes scanned the pages, his eyebrows rose higher and higher.

"How confidential is this information?" he finally asked, lighting the document with the lantern and waiting until the pages burned to ash.

"Top secret," I replied bluntly. "This investigation could very well be a one-way ticket to the nether plane. But if you find any proof — any at all — the reward will set your grandchildren up for life."

"You underestimate my grandchildren's appetites," he said with a crooked smile.

"And you underestimate my wealth," I shot back with an equally wolfish grin.

The reporter thought for a moment before knocking on the roof of the carriage, signaling the coachman to stop. As the carriage came to a halt, he said, "It's dangerous. But interesting. I'll take it. I'll relay my findings through your man."

With that, he leapt from the carriage and vanished into the night.

I liked the guy. He was no simpleton. I couldn't identify his patron deity or magic, but he was undeniably powerful. His blood carried a rich mana signature and I kept a sample of it for my library.

The "library" was still a makeshift collection in the mansion's basement. But at this rate, I'd soon need to dedicate an entire underground bunker to it — preferably in a remote location where no one would think to look.

* * *

Saint Petersburg was proud to host the International Flower Expo and Florist Competition that year. Massive iron and glass conservatories had been built just outside the city for the event. The imperial interior and landscape designers had truly outdone themselves.

There was more to see than just flowers. Foreign and domestic companies showcased new carraiges, reasoning that while the ladies admired the blooms, their consorts should have the chance to relax and spend some money.

That evening, the Imperial Opera and Ballet Theater was staging a premiere performance in honor of the occasion.

One pavilion was dedicated to cosmetics derived from plants of the nether plane. The number of exhibitors in this category was staggering. At the last minute, even the Japanese Empire had joined, presenting an exclusive elixir made from their nether plane's counterpart of the sakura.

Of course, Russia had its own treasures to boast about. From Krasnodar came a youth-restoring potion that was so potent that it had even been banned from export.

The "Nipponites," as Her Imperial Highness Princess Maria liked to call Russia's perpetual adversaries in the East, rarely appeared in foreign lands except for private visits. But this time, they were here quite officially and publicly — led by none other than Akira, a scion of the Inari family.

As the official hostesses, Her Imperial Highness Princess Maria was now on her way to the special pavilion to greet the distinguished guest. She was accompanied by the daughter of the imperial physician — young Svetlana Hawthorn.

Svetlana gazed at the chaos around her with quiet disdain. The tightly laced dress with a corset running the length of her back, the heels, gloves, parasol, and hat — all of it grated on her nerves. The field uniform of the Mosquito unit seemed heavenly by comparison. She was ready to march ten miles that very instant if it meant marching away from this place. Bodyguards flitted about them, never in sight. Noise, chatter, frivolous social gossip — it was enough to make her scream at the thought of trailing behind Princess Maria all day like a lapdog.

"Svetlana, if you keep up that sour face, all the flowers at the exhibition will wilt and wither," purred Her Imperial Highness, the Crown Princess of the Russian Empire, ignoring yet another flattery from a nearby aristocrat. "At least pretend to be interested!"

"Yes, Your Highness!" Svetlana replied with a saccharine smile and turned to admire yet another wisteria, then an eye-searingly bright gerbera, and then some maniacally grinning Venus flytraps.

"Just hang on a while longer," Maria teased her, leaning closer. "We'll perform our mandatory waltz with Akira, and then we can go see your special 'someone!'"

"He's not mine," Svetlana muttered irritably, her tone dripping with denial.

She already regretted a hundred times over having mentioned the heirs of the Komarin and Muscadine families to Maria. The princess was now determined to meet the young men who had piqued the interest of the "Icy Maiden" at her side.

That nickname had stuck to Svetlana since childhood, thanks to her blond braid and icy blue eyes, which were the color of Lake Baikal's frigid waters. No doubt it was born of her unshakable stoicism in the face of the imperial family's frequent meltdowns.

Next to the statuesque, green-eyed Maria, whose every movement exuded grace and understated sensuality, Svetlana often seemed like a pale moth. Her role was simple: to highlight the princess's fiery presence with her icy demeanor and provide medical aid if necessary.

It was precisely this contrast that made Svetlana grit her teeth at the idea of appearing before Vinogradov-Komarin alongside Maria. Outwardly, he would look far more harmonious with the princess than with her. Yet envy was not an emotion Svetlana could afford at her station, so instead, she roiled inside like a boiling kettle, anticipating an inevitable disaster.

If Vinogradov, who had entered the exhibition as a contestant, really drew Maria's interest, the princess would waste no time playing with her new toy.

"Oh Holy Hawthorn, why is this taking so long?" Svetlana thought as they finally approached a pavilion that looked entirely out of place — a miniature palace of the Japanese Emperor, surrounded by blooming sakuras.

The crowd of onlookers here was overwhelming. Unlike the sterile beauty of the glass and iron greenhouses erected by the imperial architects, this place felt alive, radiating a tranquil energy that drew and held the eye, like an earthly paradise.

"It is beautiful indeed," Maria admitted reluctantly, stepping gracefully through a cascade of falling petals. She smiled warmly at her subjects and the guests, performing her duties on behalf of herself and her brother, but Svetlana could see the irritation smoldering beneath her mask of composure. Princess Maria was not pleased to see Akira Inari excelling in anything.

Lord Akira waited at the entrance to greet his esteemed guests. Tall, dark-haired and clean-shaven, with a long braid and a piercing crimson gaze, he offered a deep ceremonial bow, acknowledging his lower status.

Maria said nothing at first, her sharp gaze taking in every detail of their host. His attire defied the formal dress code for the exhibition and the protocol for interacting with the Russian royal family. The white mourning kimono, paired with wide trousers, was one thing, but the pair of samurai swords, a daishō, hanging at his waist, was a blatant insult to security and the traditions of the host nation.

Carrying weapons in the presence of royal family members was strictly forbidden.

Though often perceived as impulsive and capricious, the princess was the picture of composure now, extending the diplomatic silence. Only a slight furrow in her brow hinted at the storm brewing within.

But Akira was no novice. He knew the rules well. Bowing once more, he addressed the princess:

"Evening bindweed has ensnared me... I stand transfixed in forgetfulness," he said, his voice smooth. With a wave of his hand, the swords vanished from his waist. "Forgive me, Your Imperial Highness. Captivated by your beauty and still mourning the untimely loss of my sister, whom you so remind me of, I forgot all laws and customs, neglecting to disperse the illusions I carry as a son of the Goddess Inari. Rest assured, no thought, word or deed of mine was intended to trouble you. What you see is but a modest gift of my goddess."

Maria smiled charmingly, batting her lashes at the pavilion's host.

"We are delighted to welcome Akira-sama of the Inari house to our lands. Your wisdom is rivaled only by the beauty of your art. Truly, your creation is the crown jewel of this exhibition!"

As Maria Krechet exchanged pleasantries with the Japanese prince, Svetlana found herself bored to tears. She distracted herself by examining the crowd of elaborately dressed courtiers and exhibition guests and didn't notice until too late that Maria had stepped aside to introduce her to Akira Inari.

What she couldn't miss, however, was the fanatical gleam that lit up in his eyes when he saw her.

"Oh no, I can find no ready comparisons for you, third-day moon!" The words flowed from the prince's lips as he handed Svetlana a sakura branch that was abloom despite it being September.

"Thank you, Akira-sama. I am flattered that your lips echo the words of the great Bashō," Svetlana replied, recognizing the haiku of the famed Japanese poet.

"As autumn deepens, a butterfly sips chrysanthemum dew," Akira continued, showering Svetlana with poetic compliments foreign to her ears.

The healer began to feel distinctly uncomfortable under his concentrated gazed. She remembered her father once telling her about his studies in the Land of the Rising Sun. The Japanese court was fascinated with blond, blue-eyed women, who were highly prized in their imperial harems.

Svetlana wasn't born yesterday, and with her healer's gift, she could sense the faint excitement beneath Akira Inari's poetic flattery and outward admiration. She forced herself to think quickly, searching her memory for an appropriate response — something neutral but polite, to deflect his attention. Another verse from Bashō came to mind:

"In a field of grass, each flower a victory. This is the flower's greatest triumph!"

Akira bowed, acknowledging Svetlana's graceful reply, and shifted his attention back to the princess.

"Your Imperial Highness, may I become the happiest of mortals by daring to offer you my company as you make your way through the exhibition?"

Maria might have refused, but the intricacies of lineage in the Japanese Empire complicated matters. Akira, a member of the Inari clan, descended from an emperor's son and was effectively on par with a Serene Prince or a distant member of the imperial family. Refusing such a minor request could be interpreted as an insult to the monarchy of a neighboring empire. So, with regal poise, Maria accepted his proposal and proceeded alongside the Japanese heir.

The sight of their procession was undeniably striking. A path of sakura petals unfurled before the pair of imperial blood, bordered by ponds of lotus flowers and bamboo groves. All eyes were drawn to this unusual couple. Svetlana followed demurely behind, noticing that Akira's illusion extended to include her — ensuring she walked through the same enchanted scenery. But the magic dissolved into mist the moment she crossed its boundaries, leaving her in the mundane reality of the exhibition.

It was a dangerous game Akira was playing, equating the healer's daughter with figures of imperial blood so openly.

In one of the final pavilions, however, the entire procession halted, stunned by the spectacle before them.

The Japanese illusion paled in comparison to the work of this mysterious florist.

In the center of a cavern glittering with clusters of gemstones, a waterfall tumbled from above, filled with iridescent fish. The interplay of water and light transformed the grotto into a kaleidoscope of pearls and diamond-like droplets. The only sound in the awestruck silence was the splash of water, as two half-naked mermaids frolicked in the pool at the waterfall's base.

Gasps of wonder were quickly followed by the audible grinding of Akira's molars.

The mermaids dove beneath the surface, only to reappear moments later with a dark-haired, half-clad Triton — the undersea king. Svetlana was astonished to recognize Vinogradov-Komarin in the role of Triton. He held a casket shrouded in a magical dome, within which a rose shimmered in every color of the rainbow. Its beauty was mesmerizing, drawing all the audience's eyes to it.

The trio of mythical beings advanced toward Princess Maria and Lord Akira. The princess, however, would never have earned her reputation as an impulsive maverick without her true nature coming into play. Leaving Akira behind, she stepped to the edge of the lake, watching in fascination as the hem of her dress grew wet. The illusion was tangible!

What happened next was a blur that Svetlana could never fully piece together.

Maria, disregarding all decorum, pushed off the shore and dove into the enchanted lake. As she did so, silver needles shot from all directions toward one of the mermaids, threatening to turn her into a pincushion.

The princess surfaced before the mermaid, laughing as she shielded her with her body. At the same instant, crimson tendrils erupted from Triton, spreading outward. Some coiled protectively around the princess and the mermaids, forming a cocoon, while others lashed out into the crowd, reaping a bloody harvest. Chaos erupted as people screamed and scattered in all directions.

The only ones left standing were Triton, several would-be assassins impaled on his blood-red vines, and Akira. The Japanese prince was shielded by a transparent barrier, but it was already thinning under the relentless assault of the predatory tendrils. Sweat dripped from Akira's face, blood trickled from his nose, as the blood vines continued to lash his protective barrier.

Svetlana watched in horror, realizing that the technique she was witnessing had combined the power of two divine totems. Then a voice rang out behind her:

"In the name of the Emperor, I command you to stop!"

Chapter 17

Count Orlov twirled a fountain pen thoughtfully in his fingers. The curse specialist whom Krysin had summoned to Hmarevo had just left his office.

The young man had delivered intriguing results. Three sacrificial rituals had occurred within a ten-day span on the Komarin lands. The first two coincided with Komarin's coming-of-age ceremony, though there were no traces of the victims or rituals due to an explosion which had wiped out all evidence of the ceremony. The third and most recent ritual had been performed by a powerful mage. Attempts to reach the epicenter had been blocked by Komarin's retainers, indirectly confirming that the young man was not only alive but actively overseeing his family's affairs.

This theory was further supported by two checks that had been verified by the mentalists. One check had gone to a Sparrow gang coachman who had transported a young nobleman from a brothel, a girl slung over his shoulder. The trail had gone cold in the city. The other check was for another coachman who had taken the man from the train station to the Sparrow gang's territory. Both drivers had noted the family ring adorned with a mosquito.

Returning to the curse specialist's findings, Count Orlov was particularly intrigued by the predicted chain of events triggered by the sacrificial rituals. The conservation and expulsion of invaders through divine intervention were no trivial matters.

As the patriarch of his own family, Count Orlov rarely communicated with his patron deity, who preferred to stay in the shadows, believing his past deeds spoke for themselves. Achieving such a level of interaction, where a god actively intervened in human affairs, was no small feat.

Earlier, Orlov had received a report from one of the Eagle commanders about the situation in the Komarin domain. Strangely, the Eagles seemed unaffected by the curse, while Krysin's people suffered significantly.

This led to certain natural conclusions about Krysin, yet the chronology didn't add up. Arkady Ivanovich had served as Orlov's personal secretary for over twenty-five years, while the attacks had begun ten years ago. Orlov was reluctant to suspect his subordinate, but Komarin's words about betrayal against the crown and the Emperor lingered in his mind. For personal gain, one might betray not only a provincial family but even the homeland itself.

Count Orlov dialed a short number on his commulet, summoning one of the Empire's most elusive but indispensable individuals. Within half a minute, there was a knock at his office door.

"You called, Daniel Andreyevich?" asked the Empire's chief "shadow."

"I did," the Minister of Defense replied, gesturing to the chair by his desk. "I have a request for you... strictly internal. I don't want counterintelligence involved."

"I'm listening. But you know my methods..." the shadow disclaimed, distancing himself from any potential fallout.

"I know. There's no official evidence," Orlov admitted, gripping his fountain pen so tightly it shattered into pieces. "But I need to be sure."

*　　*　　*

The exhibition had been a resounding success. The Imperial Security Service, however, had arrived at the worst possible moment. A little longer, and there would have been nothing for them to do. The throne would've had a would-be assassin targeting the princess to negotiate political advantages with the Asians. Teimei would owe me her life and her position. But as the saying goes, "Tuck in your trunk, old boy; take what you've got." The fun was just beginning.

I had been comfortably accommodated in one

of the private rooms at the imperial residence in Saint Petersburg. No windows, unfortunately, but they did provide me with some form of clothing. It was one thing to strut around like a sea king in the middle of an illusion, quite another to do so at court. As my grandfather would've said: "Why, it's unseemly!"

"Be grateful it's not a prisoner's uniform," came an unwelcome thought. "They could've provided it free of charge."

In addition to clothing, the Imperial Security Service had generously supplied me with handcuffs that were supposed to suppress any magical abilities.

Magical suppressors in this plane, I must say, are subpar. I couldn't sense Misha's hereditary powers, but my blood magic was still available to me and I could sense Muscadine's artifact as well. In theory, I could replicate the spell I'd instinctively conjured at the exhibition, but the thought of ending up a convict in the nether plane was unappealing.

Meanwhile, in some divine realm overhead, a heated debate raged about my recent exploit.

"It shouldn't have worked at all," Aedes fumed. "It's taboo! Two patron deities — the height of taboo! Mixing their powers — taboo! He's disrupting the balance between the higher and nether planes!"

"Oh, come off it," Muscadine replied nonchalantly. "He acted reflexively in a critical situation to save an imperial heiress. And frankly, I'm starting to think this whole separation of divinities business is absurd. Look, the boy combined two abilities into one technique, and the world didn't collapse. If anything, he's a living example of that divine balance everyone likes to go on about."

"Uh, what is this balance between the higher and nether planes we are talking about?" I cautiously interjected.

"Shut up and sit still, you miracle worker!" Aedes barked. "How are you going to explain what you did to the security officers? Any mentat will send you straight to the gallows."

"Not a mentat — a mentalist," Muscadine corrected again, "and they won't find anything. I've already checked, just out of curiosity. His memories? Soul-bound. Misha's bodily memory? That's another story, but the familial secrecy oath covers everything. So don't panic — he won't die prematurely. Besides, Princess Maria will likely pull some strings for her savior. And if you doubt me on that, I'll be happy to accept your wager."

*   *   *

Svetlana was watching a battle of titans. The head of the Imperial Security Service, known for bending the strongest mages to his will and standing toe-to-toe with the shadowy rulers of Siberia, the Tiger Lords, was now slowly but surely losing ground to the wily, snake-like Maria Krechet.

"I repeat, Dmitry Fyodorovich: This young man is neither the plotter nor an accomplice in the assassination attempt against me," Maria Petrovna explained, smiling sweetly at her father's subordinate. The smile sent a chill down Duke Medvedev's spine. "Risking his own life, he used a unique spell — a classified family secret — to save me! His actions were timely, albeit extreme. And where, pray tell, were your men during all this?"

Svetlana shivered at the barely concealed menace in the princess's tone. To be fair, Maria had every right to be furious. Not only had technomagical weapons been smuggled into the exhibition, but they had also been used in an attempted assassination. Even if Maria hadn't been the intended target, the mere attempt was a slap in the face to Medvedev's security service.

The needles had contained a rare magic-narcotic substance that clouded the mind, overrode free will, and caused instant addiction. Judging by the quantity of needles and the amount of the substance, Maria had no chance of surviving.

Akira Inari was currently in a magical coma and unable to answer questions. Given his foreign nationality and imperial lineage, the security officers had decided to sink their claws into the princess's defender instead. But they hadn't accounted for Maria Krechet, who had meticulously cultivated her reputation as a frivolous, air-headed young woman — whereas the truth was that she was anything but.

"Your Imperial Highness, I understand your confusion and your feeling of gratitude. However..." Medvedev began tentatively.

"No, Duke! You have no idea the extent of my anger," Princess Maria hissed, her gaze fixed on the military officer. "I will not allow you to shirk your responsibility by scapegoating an aristocrat from an extinct noble family! It was *me* they nearly killed! And if you lack the spine to act, I'll speak to Akira Inari myself — and I assure you, my methods of conversation will be far from pleasant! An eye for an eye, a tooth for a tooth! And I'll personally prepare the recording of the assassination attempt for the Nipponites. Then we'll see how many islands in the East China Sea they'll concede in exchange for this... illusionist!"

"Your Imperial Highness, there's no need for that," Medvedev, the head of security, finally relented. "We'll handle it ourselves."

"Well you're doing a poor job of it so far, Dmitry Fyodorovich!" Maria jabbed, her tone sharp. "Today, the Empire nearly lost its heir, and it wasn't you who salvaged the situation!"

"May we at least interrogate the young man?" Medvedev ventured cautiously.

"Why stop there? Shall we march him straight to my father for a session of his vaunted 'righteous wrath'?" Maria smiled sweetly, her words laced with venom. "No, I'll join you for the conversation. I'm curious myself how he managed to react so quickly!"

Svetlana groaned inwardly and mentally clutched her head. Considering the tangled mess of this young man's biography, any interrogation could unearth so many inconvenient truths that he might regret saving the princess in the first place. Hardly believing her own audacity, she decided to speak up:

"I am willing to conduct an examination of the young man to detect any falsehoods."

Medvedev raised an eyebrow, surprised to hear the typically reserved daughter of the imperial healer step forward this way. The girl was highly promising, both in terms of her gift's strength and her close ties to the imperial family. Dmitry Fyodorovich had even suggested his second son as a potential match for Hawthorn, though he had yet to receive a reply.

"An examination?" he repeated, his tone skeptical.

"Yes, an examination," Svetlana said, her voice steady despite the nervous flutter in her chest. "Using my gift, I can detect deception in his responses. It would be more precise and less intrusive than any mentalist's probing."

Maria's lips curved in a faint smile, her eyes glinting with approval. "A splendid idea, Svetlana. I knew you wouldn't let me down."

Medvedev exhaled slowly, glancing between the princess and the young healer. "Very well. We'll proceed as you suggested, Your Imperial Highness. Lady Svetlana, you'll conduct the evaluation under my supervision."

Maria inclined her head regally, signaling her assent.

Svetlana, meanwhile, felt her stomach twist into a knot. She hadn't the faintest idea how this examination would go — or what secrets it might reveal.

At that moment, Medvedev realized he had another witness on his hands — the ever-invisible shadow of the princess. And this girl was not only ready to cooperate but was also offering her assistance. This didn't preclude the use of a truth artifact, but the fact remained: the girl had grown up, and now she had found her voice.

"Svetlana, your help would be greatly appreciated."

*   *   *

A whole procession entered my room: Her Imperial Highness Princess Maria, Svetlana Hawthorn and a large, predatory-looking man with a bushy ginger beard and amber eyes, who carried himself like a bear trapped in a cage.

Oh, he bore a striking resemblance to the Medvedev kid — Bear — from the Mosquito school. Could this be his father? Judging by the fact that I was still in the Winter Palace and not locked in the dungeons of the Peter and Paul Fortress, I knew that I wasn't under suspicion — yet.

My girls, meanwhile, had been questioned amid the chaos and sent home. Tilda had already reported back via the blood link. They had claimed to be hired illusionists tasked with presenting the rose at the exhibition. The mentalists had even confirmed their honesty. Of course they had: Tilda and Teimei's last two days of memories were filled with preparations for the exhibition, rehearsals, and fine-tuning the details of the performance.

When they had first approached me with their idea to create an undersea tableau, I had been ecstatic. And I'm sure the imperial mentalists who reviewed their memories thoroughly enjoyed witnessing our creative process.

Now, however, I had to answer for my actions and motivations alone. Well, balancing on the edge of utter destruction had become a personal hobby of mine lately.

Svetlana approached me without raising her head. Standing before me, she blocked my face from view and placed her trembling hands on my temples. Her lips barely moved as she whispered:

"There's a truth-detecting artifact here. I'm here to help."

"Thank you," I whispered back, winking. "Don't worry. We've got this."

As I looked at Svetlana, I couldn't help but think she was just as alluring in her gown as she had been in the Komarin uniform. I wondered how she'd look in the desert raiders' attire — layers of fabric forming a translucent silhouette, no corsets, semi-concealed nudity... I had to force the distracting image out of my mind through sheer willpower.

Healing magic began to flow from Svetlana's hands. She checked my condition and seemed surprised to find I was unharmed. Small wonder — when the needles had struck my vines, I had expected to drop dead on the spot. But the vines had absorbed enough blood from the assassins to block the needles' poison and keep it from entering my body. I'd even siphoned off some energy from the Japanese prince's shield, boosting myself in the process. Honestly, I rather liked this energy-vampirism effect. I might need to develop something similar, but without relying on the powers Muscadine had loaned me.

Or perhaps... If I had managed to merge a spell I'd only seen once before with my own magic, maybe I could create something else at the intersection of these different magics.

"Gavrila Petrovich, first and foremost, I'd like to personally thank you for saving me!" Maria Krechet broke the prolonged silence. In the calm setting, I noted just how striking she was. A brunette with a cascade of curls, emerald-green eyes with a witchy glint, full lips and a sultry gaze. Wars had been fought and empires toppled over women like her, and Maria knew it. Utterly shameless, she wielded her beauty like a weapon.

"The extent of our gratitude will be discussed later, but for now, the Imperial Security Service, represented by its head, Duke Dmitry Fyodorovich Medvedev, has a few questions for you as a *witness*," she emphasized the word pointedly.

"I told you!" In my head, Muscadine chuckled from somewhere in the divine plane. "You owe me — you know what."

Oh, I'd have to remember that the gods here are fond of gambling.

Meanwhile, Medvedev, who indeed seemed to be the father of my Bear acquaintance from the school, took the floor:

"Gavrila Petrovich, you must understand that we're simply doing our duty. Protecting the Imperial Family is our paramount duty. And I must inform you that this conversation is being conducted with the use of a truth-detection artifact." He gestured to a ring on his finger, identical to the one I'd seen on Count Orlov. "Additionally, your condition will be monitored by a healer — Svetlana Hawthorn."

I nodded, indicating my formal consent to the stated measures. Thus began my "soft" interrogation.

"Gavrila Petrovich, what were you doing at the flower exhibition?"

"I was presenting a new variety of rose called 'A Surprise for the Princess,'" I replied. This line of questioning did not seem particularly intimidating.

"And what was the surprise supposed to be?"

"The rose produces tears if someone pricks themselves on its thorns," I explained my failed surprise.

"Excuse me," the princess interrupted the duke. "Have a sample brought here. I want to see such a wonder for myself."

The duke nodded and left the room briefly. Maria Krechet's façade of grace evaporated the instant he stepped out the door.

"All right, Gavrila Petrovich," she said sharply. "I just saved your ass from the security service — pardon my frankness — but I've got a few questions of my own. Answer quickly and without hesitation. Svetlana, keep watch!"

Svetlana's hands trembled at the command, but she nodded.

"Were the assassins targeting me?"

"No!"

"Who, then?"

"They were after one of my mermaids. She happens to be Akira Inari's sister. Five years ago, the two became embroiled in a struggle for power in their family. Lord Akira got her addicted to drugs, smuggled her out of Japan to a foreign country and left her to die in one of our brothels."

"What a bastard!" Maria hissed with a mixture of admiration and disgust. "So illusions are their family craft, then? And if Akira's sister can create such tangible ones as your display, she must be inherently stronger!" The princess connected the dots. "How did you manage to react so quickly?"

"That's a family secret."

"Don't lie to me, sweetheart," Maria purred even as her eyes drilled into me. "I can tell even without Sveta here that I'm not supposed to know. Yet, don't you forget who I am! Think carefully and answer in a way that keeps me happy and doesn't change my opinion of you."

"Fine then," I said, meeting her gaze and gesturing toward the earring in my ear. "A divine secret."

Maria coughed, momentarily at a loss for words. "Touché! Looks like I won't pry further. One last thing — what are your intentions with my dear

Sveta? Are you just looking for some bit of fun or are you after something more serious?"

Poor Svetlana's hands trembled as if she was having a seizure, but she kept them on my temples, avoiding eye contact with either of us.

"Something more serious! Right now, my status precludes me from offering anything to someone of her station, so I can only admire her from afar," I replied as honestly as possible. To be fair, I'd already been considering pursuing Svetlana more seriously. But given my family situation and other complications, I decided to hold off for now.

Svetlana seemed to relax a little, even casting a curious glance my way. Without thinking too much about it, I turned my head slightly and kissed her wrist. Her face flushed bright red. Who would've thought the fiery healer could be so shy?

"Oh, I see where this is going!" Maria burst out laughing, clearly entertained.

At that point, Duke Medvedev returned to the room, carrying the rose under a protective dome. It shimmered with all the colors of the rainbow, its pearlescent petals glowing softly.

"Here it is, Your Imperial Highness. I retrieved it from the evidence annex," he said, placing the rose on a small table before Maria. She was about to open the dome when I stopped her.

"Wait!" I said abruptly, halting her hand midair. "I sense another spell layered over it — something deadly. Not mine. Summon the mages and have them investigate it!"

Chapter 18

THERE WASN'T TIME TO SUMMON THE MAGES, HOWEVER. I noticed Medvedev's vacant gaze as he reached for the rose's dome, and I had no choice but to shove Svetlana out of harm's way.

I didn't want to die. But if I had to act, so be it. I threw a stiff straight at Medvedev, slamming my fist into his solar plexus and we tumbled to the floor together.

"He's under mind control!" I managed in between grunts, trying to keep the enormous man away from the rose. The women froze like statues, too shocked to intervene. "Sveta! Put him to sleep!" I croaked as Medvedev's hand clenched around my throat.

Snapping out of her state of shock, Svetlana gently touched Medvedev, slumping him into unconsciousness — unfortunately, not before he cracked a couple of my ribs, broke my nose, and nearly twisted my neck off. We were in entirely different weight classes.

Barely managing to sit upright, I spat blood onto the plush oriental rug — not exactly very aristocratic of me — and muttered, "If the first attack was a coincidence, the second was someone seizing an opportunity to blame it all on the Nipponites."

Stunned, Maria stared at Medvedev's unconscious form, me bleeding on the floor, and Svetlana tending to my injuries unbidden. Then the princess unleashed such a colorful tirade of curses, I almost envied her.

She made to storm out of the room, but I hissed, "Stay put! Someone's likely waiting for this place to blow to Kingdom Come, and you're about to walk right into their trap!"

Maria hesitated, looking uncertain.

"Can you get these suppressor cuffs off me?" I asked her bluntly. Time was running out, and I didn't have enough confidence to summon enough mosquitoes to check everyone in the palace — and even less confidence that I could process all the blood samples quickly enough to identify the culprits. Still, I had to try. "The longer you wait, the more likely the assassin will make their getaway."

The princess made up her mind. Placing her hands over the cuffs, she did something I couldn't quite follow. Her hand seemed to lose form, spreading over the metal like ink. Seconds later, I heard the distinct click of the latch releasing and the suppressor cuffs fell to the floor.

Freed, I commanded any mosquitoes in the area to collect blood samples from everyone in the palace.

To my surprise, the search took only fifteen minutes. Though, judging by their expressions, neither Svetlana nor Maria understood what was happening.

I asked them to give me some time and began sifting through the memories of everyone in the palace. I sought any hint related to the rose, Medvedev, a possible explosion, magic, or even emotions like fear and greed. Sorting through hundreds of memories, I finally found what I was looking for.

"There are three people involved in this incident, and five more targeting your younger sister... soon. They're planning something during the theater season at the resort," I said, opening my eyes, momentarily disoriented. My head was swimming from having plunged into so many lives, so many thoughts and emotions. I held onto the threads of what I'd uncovered — descriptions, roles, abilities — but nausea overwhelmed me. Warm hands on my temples eased the throbbing pain before I realized Svetlana was wiping my face with a cloth, dabbing at my blood-streaked tears.

Gratefully, I embraced her as Maria stood frozen, clutching her commulet, too shaken to make a call.

"Here's the deal," I said, going all in. "If I'm right, you swear never to reveal how you got this information. If I'm wrong, you can drag me before your father and he can decide my fate."

Maria nodded, biting her lip. She made a call, her voice barely rising above a whisper as she relayed my findings, emphasizing the suspects I'd identified.

Meanwhile, Svetlana worked to revive Medvedev, undoing the mind control spell. I stood ready, a porcelain vase in hand, prepared to use it as a makeshift weapon should Medvedev regain consciousness violently. Call it cowardly if you like; I call it strategic foresight to keep my ribs intact.

Moments later, a rapid-response team burst into the room. They took Medvedev away, still unconscious. Two mages examined the rose under artifact-enhanced goggles. The palace was finally under control, but something told me this was just the beginning.

"The spell is on the dome," I interjected, attempting to add my two cents. "If possible, save the rose."

"We don't care about the spell," one of the mages replied dismissively. "It's weak. But the plant..." A sly gleam lit up his eyes.

"Yes, I'm also curious about how you create such flowers," came a quiet but commanding voice from the doorway. Standing there was a tall but alarmingly thin young man. His facial features bore a subtle resemblance to the princess, but his gaze was entirely different — steely and unyielding, as though a powerful spirit were confined in his frail body.

"Andrey," Maria exhaled with relief, rushing to embrace her elder brother. "How's Nastya? Did you catch all the suspects?"

"We got them, Masha," the heir replied, gently stroking her curls to calm her. "Mentalists and interrogators are working on them now. So far, your account checks out. But I'd like to have a word with this young man. Privately."

The mages made curt bows and began to leave, carrying the rose almost under their arms, which implied the spell had already been removed. Maria's gaze lingered on the flower, a pout forming on her lips like a spoiled princess denied a toy.

"Leave the rose. It's a gift for the princess," Andrey commanded promptly. Whether out of affection for his sister or personal interest in the flower, the directive was clear. The mages reluctantly placed their prize back on the table and shuffled out.

Svetlana moved to follow them, but Andrey surprised me yet again.

"And where are you off to, oh Queen? You've been involved in this mess from the beginning."

Queen? My eyebrows shot up involuntarily.

Svetlana, noticing my astonishment, blushed adorably. Ye gods, how she blushed! She really was delightful.

Meanwhile, the prince turned the stone on his ring, and a shimmering barrier enveloped the room. Another artifact. These people were draped in them like a vine in grape clusters. Well, they were imperial heirs, after all. Survival in any situation was probably part of their job description. Still, I couldn't understand why Maria hadn't activated something like this during the exhibition.

"No one will overhear us now," Andrey said, gesturing to a chair at the table. "We can speak freely and without formalities. I have many questions, but considering you exposed two assassination attempts against my sisters in one stroke, I'll rein in my curiosity a bit."

I nodded, appreciating his perspective. They could have sent me straight to the gallows after all. Everyone here seemed so kind and trusting — such a stark contrast to where I came from. There, the rules had been simpler: "Better to torture, curse, and torture again than regret missing something later." But since this trust worked to my advantage, I decided to lean into it.

"I swear to answer honestly any questions not related to family secrets or dealings with divine patrons," I said solemnly. As the words left my mouth, a silver vine with crimson grapes coiled around my wrist, signifying the oath's sincerity and divine approval.

"Oh, what an idiot," muttered Aedes.

"No, actually, that's a cleverly vague wording. It allows a lot of flexibility," Muscadine countered approvingly.

I watched the surprised expressions of everyone in the room.

"Well, that's unexpected," Andrey Krechet cleared his throat. "Let's get to the main questions, then. How did you perceive the spell over the flower's lid while wearing magic suppressors? And how did you identify the assassins in the crowd during the attempt? The healers and security confirmed that all the attackers were from the same clan, marked with identical family tattoos."

"Muscadine," I called one of my patrons, "if I say the vines and the rose were semi-sentient, would that violate the oath?"

"Well, if you equate them to a pet... loosely speaking..." Muscadine replied uncertainly. "But we've never tried anything like that."

"And who can prove otherwise?" Aedes chimed in smugly.

"Wait — are you two just keeping tabs on me now?" I pretended to be outraged. Pretended, because in a dangerous situation, having two gods on my side was infinitely better than none. Their advice, even their arguments, had proven useful.

"You're entertaining, at least. Something to pass the time," said one of them. I wasn't sure which, and it didn't matter. I had to explain myself to His Imperial Highness Andrey Petrovich before his patience — and goodwill — evaporated.

"The answers to both questions lie in family abilities. I can't give a detailed explanation, but in broad terms..." I paused, choosing my words carefully. "Do you have pets? A cat, a dog? Or perhaps a magical companion? No? Then imagine the first option — it's closer to the truth." Andrey and Maria exchanged glances and nodded. "It's the same concept here, but instead of an animal, it's a plant. It's not exactly alive or independent, but it can convey vague sensations — danger, unease. You choose whether to listen to it or not. Like how cats, dogs, or even fish sense earthquakes, plants can sense magical disturbances."

I shrugged, unsure how else to clarify.

Andrey seemed intrigued, but Maria frowned, clearly piecing together the events of the exhibition.

"But that doesn't explain how you bypassed the magic suppressors just now," Andrey pressed, more persistent than Medvedev.

"A divine artifact," I said, pointing to the earring in my ear. "I can't elaborate further without risking my life. It would be less painful to end it myself."

Andrey nodded thoughtfully, but Maria straightened, her posture resembling a cobra preparing to strike.

"And how were you able to both kill and protect simultaneously during the exhibition?" she pressed.

Ah, Princess Snake herself... She'd bailed me out in front of the security chief, but now she latched onto me like a leech in her brother's presence.

"That wasn't me — it was the spell. The vines shared the same sensitivity as the rose, but I granted them a bit more autonomy to protect Your Imperial Highness, myself, and my companions," I replied smoothly, twisting my words on sunbaked pavement.

"And how often can you create something like

that?" Maria, as persistent as a tick or a python, refused to let up.

"I can't, Your Imperial Highness. Doing so drained a significant portion of the artifact's charge. Another portion was used today to locate accomplices," I said, shamelessly attributing it all to Muscadine's aid. In my mind, the mantra was clear: "It wasn't me; it was divine magic. Take it up with the god."

Maria and Andrey fell into deep contemplation. My oath had severed the loose ends, so theoretically, this should have been the end of the conversation.

But to my surprise, the Imperial family held notions of honor and nobility that were far from empty words.

"Gavrila Petrovich, I think it's pointless to press you further. You've shared more than you were obligated to under the constraints of your oath," Andrey said, his gaze shifting between the rose and me. "What would you like as a reward for saving my sisters?"

Oh, now this was a different kind of conversation! A pity he lumped both rescues together — I could've bargained for each separately. Still, one shouldn't look a gift horse in the mouth.

"Would it be too much to ask to disappear from your security service's radar?" I quipped, earning a faint smile from the heir.

"That, my sister and I will ensure as a bonus," he replied.

"Then I'd like a favor — something reasonable.

Nothing treasonous, no financial gain, no lobbying for scoundrels or anything of the sort," I shrugged, playing humble. "Life is long, and my family's standing is humble at the moment. A weak lineage invites trouble from every corner. I'd like the option to request protection if needed."

"In other words, wealth, artifacts from the imperial treasury, magical cores or a beneficial marriage..." Maria interjected, casting a sly glance toward Svetlana. "...none of that interests you?"

"Exactly, Your Imperial Highness. None of it. I'll earn all that myself, including the consent of my future wife."

"So be it," Andrey concluded, silencing his sister's retort with a wave of his hand. He removed an unassuming jasper ring from his finger. With a simple twist, the stone detached, revealing a thin needle beneath. "I, Andrey Petrovich Krechet, hereby grant priority consideration of any petition presented by the bearer of this ring, in gratitude for saving members of the imperial bloodline."

The needle pricked his finger, and the jasper turned a deep ocher, glowing faintly.

"Would you allow me to bind the artifact to my blood?" I asked the imperial heir. "I wouldn't want such a generous gift to fall into the wrong hands."

Andrey nodded and handed me the ring. I didn't echo his declaration; I simply pricked my own finger. The stone shifted from ocher to the rich hue of ripe garnet. Sliding the ring onto my finger, I felt a surge of confidence.

While we conducted this ceremony, Maria's

restless nature had led her to tamper with the glass dome encasing the flower. Carefully removing the cover, she gasped as the rose stirred like a living being, its petals unfurling to catch the sunlight and scattering iridescent rays across the room.

"Ah!" Maria yelped, sticking her finger in her mouth.

"Curiosity killed the cat…" Andrey sighed, eyeing his sister. But before he could finish, Maria interrupted, her excitement bubbling over.

"Look!"

Transparent droplets had formed on the rose's petals. They glistened in the sunlight, cascading down and amplifying the flower's fragrance. The rose was crying.

"The rose regrets hurting you and is apologizing by offering a stronger fragrance," I explained. Maria's eyes shimmered with pure, unadulterated delight.

"How exquisite, Gavrila Petrovich! I know it's against the rules, but could you grow such a miracle outside my window?" Maria clutched my hand, her charm on full display. Behind her, Svetlana pressed her lips together and turned away, while Andrey merely shook his head.

"It would be an honor, Your Imperial Highness, but I'll need time to cultivate buds. They're incredibly temperamental — like all true beauties," I said, spreading my hands and winking at the princess, who blushed in response.

"This surprise has been a success in every

sense," Maria declared, stroking the flower's petals. The rose leaned into her touch, its intoxicating aroma filling the room.

* * *

News of the assassination attempt at the flower expo spread like wildfire. An extraordinary issue of *The Imperial Gazette* described the event in vivid detail, glossing over the unfortunate incident involving the Japanese delegation. The Imperial family extended their heartfelt thanks to me for aiding in the resolution of an unexpected situation.

But rumors, unlike the press, which was tightly-watched by the state, couldn't be contained. Witnesses whispered tales of the assassination attempt against the princess and the valiant intervention of a young nobleman. With every retelling, the story grew more fantastical. By evening, I was reportedly wielding my vines against an army of Japanese assailants who had dared attack the jewel of the Empire — Maria Petrovna Krechet.

In taverns, toasts were being made in my honor. Forgotten noble houses suddenly recalled distant connections and the upper echelons clamored for my presence at their soirées. Invitations flooded in, but something else caught my attention. Two days after the incident, the gods paid me another visit. Muscadine radiated strength and vitality, practically glowing with emerald brilliance, whereas Aedes was palpably furious.

"I should thank you!" Muscadine began, his

tone jubilant. "I never imagined I'd receive such a surge of faith from non-believers. Yet here we are! And as a token of my gratitude, I'll not only restore your artifact's charge but also increase its capacity to hold five spells."

I sincerely thanked the god for his help — having a backup plan was always better than relying solely on one's own strength. Yet Aedes' foul mood troubled me. Muscadine vanished, but my patron god remained in brooding silence.

"You're angry," I ventured, trying to draw him out. Honestly, his brooding silence was unsettling. Normally, he'd rant, make snarky comments or laugh — but silence? That was new.

"I am," Aedes admitted without pretense. "I understand the logic of your actions, but I'm still furious that all that renewed faith went to another deity. You're *my* follower — *I* saved you! And yet the all that faith bypassed me entirely!"

I stayed silent, giving him space to vent. His grievances made sense. I'd been working on long-term gains for him, setting up mana pools, inspiring believers. The faith was trickling to him in a steady, albeit thin, stream. But Aedes, like many gods, wanted it all and he wanted it now.

The assassination attempt, however, had precipitated an unforeseen chain of events — one risky move had catapulted me into high society and inadvertently bolstered another god's strength.

"So... is this why having two patron gods is so taboo?" I asked cautiously, hoping to redirect his frustration.

"Nah," Aedes waved off the suggestion. "Before you, I didn't even know it was possible. Pleasing two gods at once? That's a feat! Most people can't even manage one properly, and you're out here like some kind of... Stakhanovite."

"Who?" I asked, unfamiliar with the term. Neither I nor Mikhail held any reference to it in our memories.

"Forget it," Aedes sighed. "In a different world from this one, it was a movement designed to coax coal miners into working harder, smashing ordinary productivity quotas."

"Dwarves?" I asked, incredulous. Sure, the little folk were fanatical about work, but overproducing? Their mountains and mines weren't going anywhere, whereas ale could be guzzled up by a neighbor, and their wives... well, let's not even go there.

"No, humans," Aedes clarified. "Working triple shifts, surpassing their regular quotas three or four times over."

"Slaves?"

"No, free people, who just really loved their homeland."

We fell into a contemplative silence.

"Impressive analogy," I admitted, breaking the silence, "but it doesn't change the fact that feeding Muscadine wasn't part of my plan."

"I know," Aedes conceded, "which is why I can't stay angry for long. Still, it stings. Look at Muscadine, tossing around artifacts like candy.

Even Kitsune does it. And all I can give you is the power to summon mosquitoes!"

It was hard to tell if his frustration stemmed more from envy or his own divine insecurities, but I decided that a god needed encouragement just as much as faith.

"You shared your own blood with me," I pointed out. "Isn't that the most precious gift a god can offer?"

Aedes became pensive. I thought he'd retreated to his divine realm when he suddenly spoke up.

"Oh I keep forgetting to tell you! There's someone else with Komarin blood — I've started sensing them. But I can't establish contact just yet."

Chapter 19

I froze. How was that possible? I was the last of the line — or so I thought. Aedes, evidently aware of my thoughts, offered an explanation.

"I'm just as shocked as you are. Could you have sired a child while romping around the marshlands with the village girls? I'm not picky — an illegitimate heir would do too — but it's still an odd situation."

I was meticulous in such matters. I wasn't a healer, but I knew enough tricks to avoid any... complications. And yet here we were, just a week later.

"Can you pinpoint the area where this blood-line member emerged?" I asked. Surely, gods had resources I didn't.

"That's the thing — I can't. All I sense is a faint thread of blood linking you to someone. But I can't interact with them."

"Wondrous are your ways, oh Aedes!" I muttered, my mind racing. "Alright, I'll investigate. Thanks for the heads-up."

"Don't mention it!" Aedes replied, then added, almost hesitantly, "I mean it — reach out if you need anything. I'll help however I can."

* * *

Svetlana Hawthorn was enduring yet another lecture from her father. A tall, wiry blond man with storm-gray eyes, he still turned heads among women. Though he swapped mistresses frequently, he'd never remarried.

Sometimes Svetlana wished for a stepmother to deflect her father's relentless attention. But most of the time, she was glad to avoid such complications.

Today, as he prepared to send her off to Madam Duplessis' finishing school, he was droning on about the importance of family, proper conduct and the necessity of narrowing down her suitors.

"Papa, I agree," Svetlana interjected, slipping her own words into his monologue.

"You... agree? With what?" The sudden shift in his daughter's behavior caught him off guard. He paused mid-stride in the middle of his greenhouse, which doubled as his study and examination room.

"With everything you said: That as a dutiful daughter, I should start considering potential suitors," she replied sweetly, her sky-blue eyes framed by long lashes batting innocently.

Her father was momentarily speechless. Then, in a flash, he strode over and placed a hand on her forehead.

"No fever... strange. You're not ill..." he muttered, his hand glowing faintly as he used healing magic to scan her. "Hmm, slight hormonal changes... physical fatigue... but nothing serious."

As he continued his examination, he grew increasingly perplexed.

"This doesn't make sense."

"Papa," Svetlana said gently, "I'm simply agreeing with your reasoning. I even wanted to propose my own list of candidates. After all, I'll be the one living with one of them — and bearing your grandchildren."

Her father stared at her in shock, muttering to himself.

"No change in your heart rate... you don't seem to be lying. All right, my daughter, either confess what's going on or I'll start worrying this isn't really you under that guise. For three years, you threw tantrums at the mere mention of marriage, and now you're on board? This doesn't add up."

Svetlana hesitated for only a moment before deciding to tell the truth. She loved her father, and his affection for her was just as genuine.

"Papa, I wouldn't want anyone to use me to get closer to you or the imperial family. That's why I'll choose candidates who are genuinely interested in me as a person. They may not be highly noble or wealthy, but they'll be honest and sincere with me." Svetlana approached her father and hugged him around the waist, just as she did as a child, seeking refuge under his protective wing.

"So, you've already set your sights on someone…" Her father tussled the curls atop her head. "My little bride has grown up. When will you introduce me to him?"

"Don't rush things, Papa. I want it to happen naturally," Svetlana replied, her cheeks turning a deep shade of crimson as she buried her nose in his collarbone.

"As you wish, my daughter. If it's important to you…" He held her tightly, cherishing his most precious treasure. "But Sveta, if he turns out to be a scoundrel, you'll become a young widow. I couldn't care less what others might say. Though…" He paused, a mischievous smile spreading across his face. "If that happens, I'll leave him to you. No sense in gifting an easy death to a scoundrel!"

They both laughed, knowing full well that the humor in his words was only partly a joke. The most skilled and inventive tormentors are healers. Their knowledge of the human body and pain surpasses that of any torturer. Even life and death mages are merciful by comparison. Heaven help anyone who makes a healer their enemy — it's a condition only death can cure.

* * *

When I returned home, I was greeted as if I'd achieved a grand victory. I'd notified Arseny and Tilda via the blood link that I was on my way back, following a tactical victory. Awaiting me was a full feast, beautiful women, and a jubilant Memeow, who immediately leaped onto my shoulder and licked my cheek.

"Memeow was wor-r-r-ried! Memeow missed you so much! Memeow wanted to br-ring you back!" she meowed.

I stroked the little erg and imagined Medvedev's face if I'd teleported directly out of the suppressive field of his magic suppresors. No amount of ancestral oaths would've saved me then.

"Don't worry, little one," I assured her, scratching behind her ear and basking in the warmth of her sincere emotions. The same warmth flowed from Tilda. Only Teimei seemed like a bundle of exposed nerves. She took a hesitant step forward and, bowing her head, spoke:

"Forgive me! I was wrong to want to return home. When I saw Akira, I thought he had come for me... that the Goddess Kitsune had sent him..." Her voice grew softer and more uncertain.

"And it didn't strike you as odd that he was wearing mourning attire?"

"The clan should have been grieving my disappearance."

I didn't point out her naive joy upon reuniting with her cousin or mention how, through his blood, I'd felt his thrill of the hunt, the satisfaction of impending murder — and lust — intertwined.

"Your clan tried to kill you today, but that's not what concerns me," I said, refraining from the classic "I told you so," since she wasn't a child. "What bothers me is who could've been watching you and tipped them off that you not only survived but recovered."

The thought of a spy gnawed at me. The possibilities were limited: Madam Ju-Ju's staff or... nothing else came to mind. My bloodbound couldn't betray us, so that was out of the question. Yet, here, Teimei managed to surprise me.

"No one needs to watch. Every clan has a great tapestry where all family members, even newborns, are marked as branches. The deceased branches darken and gradually fade, moving on to rebirth, while the living ones grow and spread. My branch probably turned green again and my cousin decided to finish what he started."

What an intriguing artifact! I wanted one.

"And how are these made?" I asked. "Are they crafted, or are they divine gifts granted when a clan is founded?"

Teimei froze, stunned by the simplicity of my question.

"I'll ask my goddess," she finally replied after half a minute. "And I must acknowledge a double life debt. The price you named is too low. You may always count on my help, and when I become the head of the Inari clan," she added with a blood-thirsty smile, "you'll have the clan's support as well."

"Agreed," I said, nodding. "But for now, let's celebrate surviving that murderous exhibition! Ladies, you were spectacular!"

The evening was a resounding success. We feasted, drank champagne and laughed a great deal. Only fresh raspberries could coax Memeow off my shoulder, and after she ate them, she retook her perch like a tiny, bloodthirsty demon. We even danced to the gramophone, Tilda and I swaying together while Teimei observed with interest but didn't join, explaining that unless she was conjuring an illusion, the only dance she was versed in was the *jiuta mai*.

Toward the end of the evening, I decided to demonstrate Muscadine's gift by altering the strength of various drinks on the fly. The women were thoroughly impressed, especially Tilda.

We parted well past midnight. The ladies staggered off, supporting each other, while I retreated to my study and summoned Arseny.

"Congratulations, sir!" my loyal servant said with a smile. "The whole city is buzzing about you! Your improvisation was a triumph!"

"Thank you, Arseny. But only the polite half of the city buzzes. I need a connection to the less polite half — specifically Nikolai Vorobey."

For the first time in memory, Arseny took a long pause to think.

"Your grandfather dealt with him personally.

All I know is that he furnished us with several individuals intended for sacrifice."

"Good to know. Arseny, do we have an unmarked carriage?"

"Of course, sir. It's used for errands and grocery runs."

"Bring it to the back entrance. I need to step out."

After changing into semi-military attire, I decided to visit Madam Ju-Ju. Who better than the owner of a brothel to link me to the city's shadowy underworld?

I arrived at her establishment near two in the morning but was admitted without delay.

"You..." She hesitated, appraising my new persona with an intrigued glance. "The outfit suits you. You're nothing like your grandfather in appearance, but your demeanor is a perfect match. How can I help the hero and savior of the princess?"

I smirked, appreciating how quickly rumors spread.

"I need to speak with Nikolai Vorobey."

The madam paused, deep in thought.

"Introducing you won't be a problem. But he won't do business with you. Especially now, with every dog in the alley recognizing you by that ring and earring," Madam Ju-Ju remarked dryly.

Removing the ring and earring wasn't an option. My arsenal was vast, but most tools required time to activate. And there was always the danger of a random encounter.

"Where does he usually go? Does he have any personal passions?"

"He's big cat lover," the madam replied after a brief pause. "He even runs a small shelter for strays by the Obvodny Canal. He's often there on Sundays."

"Perfect. Tomorrow, we'll go find a friend — or companion — for my Memeow."

The madam didn't seem to understand but wrote down the shelter's address. In return, I handed her a generous stack of cash.

* * *

Memeow was ecstatic when I explained where we were going and why. I did, however, have to caution her about the animals' troubled pasts and the possibility that they might not be friendly.

"And they don't speak like we do," I tried to clarify the difference between a sentient being and a domestic pet.

"That's because you don't know how to meow properly or use your eyes to communicate. I'll have no trouble understanding them," Memeow declared confidently.

The fluffy troublemaker scurried from one shoulder to the other, sticking her head out the carriage window and mentally commenting on everything she saw.

The unmarked carriage pulled up to a nondescript alley littered with old newspapers and trash. The air smelled faintly of wood and fire, but there were no rats in sight.

"Master, we've had street urchins tailing us for about two blocks now," my driver informed me via the blood link.

"That's fine; we're here with good intentions. If they make a move, call for help."

The carriage stopped in front of a rusty metal door leading to a courtyard. My swarm of mosquitoes had already scouted the area, bringing back blood samples from five men. Another dozen loitered in nearby buildings, peering out at us through grimy, cracked windows.

I stepped out with Memeow, who tucked herself under my coat, leaving only her curious whiskers visible. After knocking politely on the door a few times, we entered.

The courtyard had been repurposed into spacious enclosures where cats played and fed at ease. A few pens housed dogs, but cats were the majority residents here.

"Come on out, my little queen," I called to Memeow, allowing her to roam free. "Choose someone you'll be comfortable with and willing to obey."

Memeow emerged from under my coat, sauntering regally toward the enclosures. Her bold meow echoed between the walls. The cats stopped their antics and turned their attention to her. One by one, they approached the mesh, sniffed her, exchanged a few meows and eye-blinks, and moved on.

The ritual repeated until Memeow stopped and shifted her tone from commanding to pleading.

She began coaxing someone to approach the fence but received no response.

The little one dashed back to me, circling my feet anxiously.

"She's hurting! Help her! Heal her quickly!" Memeow urged, nudging me toward a specific pen.

I approached and saw, in the corner, a large, spotted cat with one eye crusted with blood, a torn ear, and what seemed to be broken hind legs. The cat gazed at the world with indifference, resigned to her fate. The other cats paraded in front of us, vying for attention, but Memeow was insistent about the spotted one.

"And how am I supposed to heal her? I'm no healer."

"Take her into the family," Aedes interjected.

"Are you serious? An animal?" My disbelief was palpable.

"Sure, why not? She'll make a good nanny for your little one. There's no restriction on animals — they're under our divine patronage as much as plants are, and only afterward do we extend our patronage to humans. You can register her as Maura Prokomarina if you like. Besides, she's no ordinary stray; she's a purebred Bengal."

"A what?" The term meant nothing to me. "Sounds like a nationality."

"Oh, you country bumpkin," Aedes scoffed. "Just take her with you and you'll understand later."

I asked the visibly nervous Memeow to see if the cat would agree to serve me in exchange for healing.

The little one let out a high-pitched squeak, and the injured cat began dragging herself toward the fence. She clawed pitifully at the wooden floorboards with her front paws, pulling her battered body forward in agonizing movements. Inch by inch, she approached, hissing in pain, until she was right in front of me.

I cut my palm open with my earring, drawing blood. Crimson drops fell onto the cat's infected wounds, absorbing into her flesh without a trace.

Repeating the Komarin oath of loyalty, I spoke the words while Memeow translated them into feline speech. The Bengal murmured something back, her soft purring interwoven with a lingering echo of pain.

"Who did this to you?" I asked.

"I was protecting a child from his sadistic father," came her deep, feminine reply.

"Well, Aedes, looks like I can understand animals now?" I was astonished.

"Blood ties convert her mental speech into something you can comprehend — and vice versa," Aedes explained with a sigh, as though stating the obvious to a slow learner.

Focusing on our blood connection, I attempted to diagnose her injuries in broad strokes. I wasn't a healer, much less a veterinarian. But as the head of my family and a blood mage, I could siphon strength from others and channel it into the one in need. If we had a healer in the family, I could have amplified their magic and transferred it into

Maura. But we didn't — and that was my failing. Thankfully, we had Zhiva.

"Zhiva, could you heal a cat?" I asked through the blood link.

A wave of confusion and disbelief met me.

"How? Where's this cat? Where are you?" came her bewildered response.

"Doesn't matter. I'll describe her injuries as best I can. You'll conjure a healing spell and the blood link will communicate and release it here," I explained my idea. "Just make the spell strong — there'll be mana loss during the transfer."

"Let's try," Zhiva agreed hesitantly, still unsure if it was possible. I shared her doubts. After all, no one had attempted something like this before. But just because it hadn't been done didn't mean it was impossible.

I tried my best to describe all of Maura's injuries in detail, down to the smallest cuts, infections and fractures. Zhiva, like a thorough healer, asked clarifying questions as though she were examining the patient in person. Five minutes later, she produced an impressively large life-magic impulse. It seemed powerful enough to revive a human on-site, though we weren't sure if it would retain enough potency to heal the cat across more than a hundred kilometers.

The mana coursed through the blood link, losing some of its intensity and focus along the way. I tracked its approach, placing my open palms over Maura's most severe injuries. For half a minute, nothing happened. Then my palms began to grow hot and a soft white glow emanated from them.

The cat twitched but didn't struggle, enduring the experiment stoically. Out of the corner of my eye, I noticed some of the cloaked thugs taking advantage of my distraction and moving to encircle me from behind. Memeow leapt into action, hissing menacingly to guard my back.

After a minute, Zhiva's magic faded, and Maura stood up shakily on her legs. Her eye wound had healed, though it left an unsightly scar. The torn ear hadn't grown back, but the infections and bone fractures were now gone.

"Thank you!" came a reverent voice from Maura. She tentatively touched my hand with her paw, then nuzzled her head against my palm.

Behind me, Memeow kept hissing until I heard a raspy voice cut through the tense silence that had surrounded us:

"Who are you? And what did you do to Maura?"

Chapter 20

Well, at least they hadn't put a knife to my throat — small relief that. I rose slowly and turned toward the voice, careful not to make any sudden movements.

The speaker was a man of average height, dressed in gray work clothes and a cap pulled low over his forehead. A cigarette dangled from his lips, its rich scent suggesting it wasn't the cheapest brand. Everything about him screamed petty crime boss. Behind him, four burly men in similar attire stood casually with their eyes focused on me, watching me closely.

Memeow climbed up onto my shoulder, her fur bristling as she hissed menacingly at the man.

"Gavrila Petrovich Vinogradov, at your service," I replied. "I'd like to adopt Maura here into my family."

"And what's a nobleman doing in the slums by

the Obvodny Canal?" the shelter's owner asked, squinting slightly.

"This lovely little lady brought me here," I replied, stroking Memeow's scruff. "It seems she's found herself a friend and asked me to bring her home."

The cat arched her back and purred languidly, her eyes half-closed in bliss as her tail fluffed out behind her.

"She's a beauty, all right," the boss's tone softened a fraction. "And she's chosen a good friend. How'd you manage to help her? I called in a healer, but he couldn't do much. Said his magic only works on humans."

I was surprised. So a healer here wouldn't have helped me anyway? I'd thought, after seeing Sveta's treatments, that nothing was beyond their reach — ergs excluded.

"I dabble in life magic," I improvised quickly. "It seems to have been enough to heal hear most critical injuries. Though, to be honest, I feel like my hands have been scalded with boiling water."

That part, at least, was true. My palms burned fiercely, so that even petting the cat was excruciatingly painful.

"You're a man of many talents, Gavrila Petrovich," the stranger chuckled. "Winemaking, cat breeding, life magic..."

"And you are...?" I said, trailing off, inviting him to introduce himself.

"I'm the one you must've been looking for when you wandered into this backwater," the local boss bared his teeth in a grin that didn't faze me. "You're not easily intimidated, are you?"

"Well, everyone and their uncle knows about me after the incident with the princess," I said casually, continuing to stroke Memeow. "So, if there's any trouble, it wouldn't be too hard for me to perform a repeat act. Especially since there are fewer than twenty of you here, not counting the kids. And I wouldn't harm the kids. As you can see, I've got no reason to worry."

Nikolai Vorobey looked at me thoughtfully, then glanced at Memeow and Maura. Somehow, the latter had already slipped out of her enclosure and was sitting beside me, watching the thugs around us warily.

"Why are all you young people so audacious these days?" he muttered under his breath before continuing louder, "What do you want from me? Forgive me, but a charming cat like that doesn't warrant you visiting this place. Plus, I can see you came well prepared."

Ah, now this was a different conversation. I smiled amiably and began, "Quite by accident, just under a week ago, a contract passed through your hands. A hit job on a group of mages — a very lucrative and unique job, I'm sure you know exactly what I'm talking about." Vorobey raised an eyebrow at how much I knew and stubbed out his cigarette. I went on: "The contract was fulfilled, payment was made, but now the hitmen are being taken out one by one by a death mage."

That caught Nikolai's attention. His eyes

darted nervously.

"Judging by your reaction," I continued, "the contract to eliminate the hitmen didn't go through you. Which means you, as the intermediary, could also become a target in the course of the house-cleaning under way."

Vorobey inhaled deeply, preparing to object, but I raised a hand to stop him.

"Your reputation might protect you, but given the kind of money involved — and there are millions in play — it won't matter. And I haven't even mentioned the risk to your reputation itself."

"My reputation is untouchable," Vorobey snarled, his tone growing more aggressive. "You think you can come here and try and bluff me?"

"Bluff?" I feigned indignation. "Hardly. It's just that sooner or later, word will get out that the hitmen you hired were taken out. Someone leaked all this to me already, so it stands to reason that smarter people will conclude it's unsafe to work with you. In the end, we circle back to the same outcome: your elimination. After all, resources that stop being useful get discarded."

Now it seemed Vorobey fully grasped the precariousness of his position. I wasn't threatening him, merely pointing out the facts. The shadow world would've come to the same conclusion soon enough. Reputation is hard-earned but it can be lost in an instant too.

"You didn't come to save my soul," he observed. "What do you want?"

"A name."

Nikolai shook his head, lit another cigarette, and dismissed his meatheads with a wave of his hand. He walked over to the cat enclosures, unlocking their nondescript latches to release the animals. Surprisingly, the cats didn't scatter. Instead, they waited patiently while Saint Petersburg's shadow kingpin squatted down onto the cobblestones.

The fluffy creatures surrounded him, purring, rubbing against him, and offering their backs, ears and bellies for his affection. He stroked each one, his lips curling into a faint smile, his look distant as though he were far away from here. I didn't rush him. The fact that he'd sent away his thugs gave me hope.

"Cats, Gavrila Petrovich, are smart creatures," he said finally. "They won't pick a losing fight unless it's to protect their young. Isn't that right, Maura?" His gaze lingered affectionately on the patched-up cat, one of the few who hadn't approached him. "Humans, unfortunately, lack such caution.

"That's to say, you're no match for him. And neither am I. He's on a level where even our Ministry of Defense failed to take him down. Imperial patronage doesn't come cheap."

This was at least intriguing. I had assumed the clients were from the upper echelons of the defense bureaucracy, but it seemed there were other interested parties involved. Meanwhile, Vorobey continued:

"A mouse and a rat will always find common

ground, while birds who fly higher up don't even notice the rodents scurrying beneath them."

We understood each other.

"May I make a voluntary donation to the shelter?" I asked him.

"No need. I can take care of my girls myself," the boss replied, puffing on his next cigarette. "But thank you for taking care of Maura! I'm glad she's found her home and family."

"May I say goodbye?" came a shy question through the blood link.

"Of course," I replied to Maura and then added aloud to Vorobey, "About the death mage… I'm trying to save what's left of the squad, and maybe I can deflect some of the questions aimed at you."

The cat approached the shelter's owner and purred something softly, nuzzling her head against his side. He gently scratched her behind the ear and let her go. A few minutes later, we left the shelter by the Obvodny Canal.

* * *

In Count Orlov's office, a flawless young woman materialized from the shadows. Porcelain skin, ash-blond curls, a high bosom, a narrow waist, and a dress that clung to every curve — her appearance would make even the most jaded connoisseur of feminine charms, like the count, feel his pulse quicken and his trousers tighten.

Sensing the effect she'd had, the woman smirked and transformed, becoming an unremarkable wallflower no one would notice.

"Forgive me, Your Excellency. I didn't have time to change my appearance after the mission," her lifeless, dull voice bore no trace of her true age. To be fair, the count didn't know her age and didn't care to.

"What news do you bring?"

"Your suspicions were entirely correct. This was a systematic land grab planned for personal enrichment."

"That rat!" the minister hissed, his anger rising slowly. "Behind my back! Against the will of the Emperor himself!" The desk groaned under the blow of Orlov's mighty hands. "I'll destroy him! I'll turn him inside out! I'll have the scum executed!"

"I wouldn't recommend that," came a completely neutral suggestion from the Shadow.

"What?" The count nearly choked on air. "Why not?"

"For ten years, unspeakable things have been happening right under your nose. Counterintelligence won't let that slide — they'll launch an investigation. Do you really want that?" The Shadow examined her nails, alternately lengthening and shortening them. "Let the boy handle it. That way, the mess stays internal, and the youngster gets a taste of blood."

Orlov fell silent, digesting the Shadow's reasoning. Her suggestion was acceptable for a man of power like him, but the soldier within him resisted fiercely. Deep down, the part of him that still believed in the ideals of honor, loyalty, and camaraderie balked at leaving an eighteen-year-old boy to face a seasoned schemer who'd deceived the Minister of Defense for a decade.

"I can't tell whether this is all your deep hate for the Komarin family or merely an unusual form of love for your grandson," Orlov said, scrutinizing the Shadow's utterly indifferent face.

"There's a fine line between love and hate, and the old baron crossed it," the Shadow said with a predatory grin. "He bound me with an oath so harsh that I had to starve, age alongside him, and raise this brat. But judging by what I see, the last of the Komarins might amount to something. That is why I think you should let him resolve the problem you both share."

* * *

My outing had turned out unexpectedly productive and gave me much to think about. The level of backroom dealings was so high I had no business being there. My grandfather hadn't even hinted at such developments.

If the mice and rats symbolized family totems, and the high-flying birds referred to the Falcon and the Eagle, the picture became even grimmer. The Ministry of Internal Affairs, represented by Myshkin (whose family totem was the Mouse god), had brazenly involved itself in defense matters and was thriving. Quite clearly, the imperial bureaucracy had become infested with all kinds of rodents.

But that was all at the higher echelons of power. I needed to sort things out on a more manageable level. My opponents there were no less formidable — the death mage alone was a nightmare. I wore my protective amulets constantly, but my girls needed similar or better protection. My cadets, too, required safeguarding. I made a mental note to discuss the matter with Arseny and Spider.

During the ride home, I overheard Maura and Memeow's conversation. They talked about their families, powers and working together. It seemed we'd found an excellent nanny for the kitten. As if sensing my thoughts, Maura asked,

"May I occasionally step away for personal matters, leaving the little one in the care of another adult?"

I nearly whistled in surprise. What a sense of responsibility! What instincts!

"Of course! You're not a servant — you're a full-fledged member of our family. I'd like you to help look after Memeow, nurture her hunting instincts and instill discipline, in so far as that's possible," I laughed, as the kitten licked my cheek with her raspy tongue. "And monitor her condition. She's a unique being with a power of her own. Using it is dangerous for now — she's too young and the mana costs are too great. She nearly died of magical exhaustion the last time she used it."

Maura nodded thoughtfully, listening to my explanation.

"What replenishes her energy? Meat, or...?" Ye gods, even this cat was sentient!

"We're priestesses of the goddess; we've always been more intelligent," the Bengal replied with a touch of self-satisfaction. "So, you're lucky. But you haven't answered my question."

"Do you know what macros are?" I asked in response. The cat nodded. "Feed her those. Meat might work for a while, but it won't replenish her mana reserves."

We rode in silence for some time before I decided to ask, "Now since I was honest with you, could you be honest with me in turn? Whom is it that you plan on visiting?"

Maura hesitated, clearly debating whether to tell me the truth, but her indecision didn't last long.

"A boy, nine years old. He lives in the slums. A bastard of some nobleman, for which he's been beaten repeatedly by his cuckolded father. His mother died at the end of summer from the abuse, and now the scoundrel's violence has gone unchecked. The last time I tried to intervene, it didn't go well. The difference in strength was too great."

"When was this?"

"Just under a week ago."

"Show me where they live."

Maura sent me the image through our blood link — a filthy shack in the workers' quarter at the edge of the Sparrow gang's territory, near the shipyards.

I shared the image with the coachman, asking if he could find the place. He said no, but we decided to start at the shipyards and let Maura guide us from there.

Sunday in the workers' quarter was a time of drunken revelry. Laborers, soused on cheap beer, roamed the streets harassing everyone in sight, celebrating their only day off. The air was thick with the stench of sweat, booze and stale tobacco. In the seedy taverns, women of questionable virtue flaunted their dubious charms.

I sent the mosquitoes to search for children, specifying the age, gender, and possible injuries we were looking for.

Maura, still unsteady on her feet, looked around, trying to recognize any familiar landmarks. She sneezed repeatedly, overwhelmed by the tobacco smoke, as she attempted to catch the trail. For fifteen minutes, we pushed through the narrow streets, squeezing past gawkers, petty thieves and idlers. The coachman cursed endlessly having to maneuver carefully to avoid running anyone over.

The crooked alleys grew quieter the closer we got to the outskirts. My mosquitoes brought grim news: there were at least two dozen boys in the area who matched the description, half of whom had been beaten. Three of them were in the direction we were heading, and one was being beaten at that very moment. Even if it wasn't the boy we were looking for, I couldn't just pass by.

Maura tried to call me in a different direction as I leapt from the carriage, dashed into a filthy alley and burst into a nearby house. The flimsy door, hanging from a single hinge, offered no resistance. From deeper inside, I heard the drunken roars of a brute beating a child who no longer screamed, only whimpered.

"You little bastard! Talking back again, huh? I'll kill you! Just like your whore of a mother!" bellowed a bloated pig of a man in a greasy undershirt and torn trousers. Spittle flew as he yelled, and the heavy belt with its officer's buckle whistled down again and again on a thin, blond boy. The child, curled up in a corner, tried to shield his head with his arms, crying softly in a single, pitiful note.

Without a moment's hesitation, I swung a stool at the brute's head, before the belt could fall again. The overwhelming urge to beat him senseless surged within me, and I barely managed to restrain myself. Instead, I knelt in front of the boy to assess his injuries.

That was a mistake. Seeing the lacerated arms, broken, swollen fingers, and dried blood in his straw-blond hair sent a wave of rage coursing through me. I was on the verge of losing control when Maura's voice broke through the bloody haze:

"It's him. He's mine. We made it! He's safe!"

The cat hobbled toward the boy, swaying slightly, meowing softly.

The boy went silent when he saw her. Then, tears welled up in his eyes and he began to cry quietly. He gently stroked Maura and kissed her fur. Through his sobs, I heard him whisper:

"I was scared. I thought you were dead. I looked for you. Two days. I was so hungry, so I came back home. And then he began hitting me again. But you came back for me! You survived! You didn't forget me!"

Tears streamed down his face, carving clean paths through the grime. Carefully, I tried to wipe the blood from his face with a handkerchief — and froze. Looking up at me were pale, icy-blue eyes that were eerily familiar. The blood crusted on his skin revealed a faint, nearly imperceptible sprout of healing magic in his aura. Sitting before me, smearing tears and blood across his face, was in illegitimate child of the Hawthorn family.

Chapter 21

I understood that if you combed through the slums carefully enough, you could find members of every noble family. But to see their totem traits emerge? That was something else entirely. The boy probably had some kind of gift — how else could he have survived such severe beatings? It seemed he had unconsciously been healing himself.

I stared at the brute, unable to leave things as they were. This scum had killed his wife and tormented her child. He'd even managed to maim the pet cat. But first, I needed to get the boy out of here. It was too early for him to see how a sadist soon becomes the victim.

Lifting the boy in my arms, along with Maura, I noted how light he was. His torn clothes couldn't hide the bruises and scrapes and I even noticed round scars on him that looked like cigarette burns. Rage simmered beneath my skin. The boy, curled up like a frightened animal, stared at me with wide, wary eyes.

"Don't be afraid. No one will hurt you again. You and Maura — and another little furry friend — will wait for me in my carriage. I'll come back soon and take you to a beautiful house with plenty of food, where no one will ever harm you."

He nodded silently, clutching the cat tighter.

"What are you going to do, sir?" Maura asked.

"Have a heart-to-heart with that pig there," I growled mentally, opening the carriage door and placing the boy inside. "Watch over him; I won't be long," I instructed the coachman, who nodded silently. Then I headed back for my "conversation."

I'm not a fan of torture. But experience has shown that you can learn much more with kind words and torture than with kind words alone.

Not liking torture and not knowing how to do it are entirely different things. And right now, my sense of humanity was on an indefinite leave of absence.

I returned to the house and, while the brute was still unconscious, used my own blood to draw a very special rune on the back of his neck. Healers used it to immobilize patients during amputations. For this "father," I made a small adjustment: He wouldn't be able to move anything below his neck, but he'd feel everything perfectly.

I didn't bother with formalities like tying him to a chair. The floor was more fitting for a creature like him. The first slap brought him to consciousness; the second made him curse.

"What the...! Who the hell are you?" His blood-shot eyes widened as anger and fear fought for dominance within him. "Do you even know who you're messing with?"

"And who might that be?" My grin was toothy enough to unnerve the condemned, but it didn't faze him — a pity. "A murderer? A sadist? An animal abuser? A bastard?"

I twirled a thin needle from my earring before his eyes, ensuring he caught sight of the family ring on my hand.

"The fact that you're an aristocrat doesn't give you the right to assault a servant of another house," he stammered, switching to a more formal tone upon noticing my signet ring. "What do you want? You barged into my home, abducted my son and now you're laying hands on me!"

"Servant, you say? Let's see about that."

I pricked his relatively clean cheek with the needle, drawing a bead of blood. The droplet soaked into my fingers, replaying the last half hour of his life in my mind.

Beyond the child's beating, there was something else.

The brute had been searching the house frantically, tearing through cabinets, drawers and under the bed, even rummaging through the grain sacks. Then the boy had walked through the door, and the man immediately attacked him with fists and shouts:

"Where's the money? I'm asking you, where is it? Where did that bitch hide it?" Then came more blows. "You'll pay for everything, you little bas-tard!"

The questions gave way to more blows. The boy tried to protest that he didn't know anything but it did no good. Snapping back to the present, I picked up the man's belt, wrapping one end around my fist.

The first strike made him squeal, a sound so high-pitched he truly sounded like a pig.

"What were you looking for before you started beating the boy?" My voice was calm, though the fury within me seethed dangerously close to the surface.

"I — I don't know what you mean! Please, stop!" The coward whined, unused to being on the receiving end.

"Liar!" The next blow landed squarely on his backside.

"I wasn't looking for anything! Please, stop!" wailed the sadist.

More strikes reduced him to tears and ragged panting. Finally, he broke, and his words spilled out in a desperate torrent:

"She was a maid to some young aristocrat when her lordling took her! They offered me good money to marry her and look after the brat. And I agreed, fool that I was. She was a fine girl and had the tits and ass to match. I thought she'd be grate-ful that I covered her shame. But she avoided me like I was diseased! And I'm no saint. I needed a woman! I put up with her until she had the brat, but after that, I stopped tolerating it. I took what I wanted — and I paid her back for avoiding me!" At the recollection, his voice even grew husky with lecherous excitement, causing a wave of nausea in me. "She'd sneak out every month and come back with money. Must've been running to spread her legs for that aristocrat again. But then I overdid it once, and she died. And now — now where's the money? Where do I get it? I beat the boy to find out where to go, who to ask for the payments!"

A thin, trembling voice piped up behind me. "He's lying." I turned to see the boy staring at his stepfather with an expression so cold it froze the blood in my veins. "He raped and beat my mother," the boy said, his voice steady despite the horrors he recounted. "She tried to get protection, but it didn't work. The money she brought home came from the bank, given to her when she showed a ring and passed a blood verification. He decided to kill me when he realized he wouldn't get any more money."

"You're lying, you little bastard! That's not how it happened! Not at all!" the brute shrieked, his voice dripping with hatred as he glared at the boy.

Ignoring the outburst, the boy disappeared deeper into the house and returned with a small wooden box, no larger than his tiny fist. On his finger, I noticed a child-sized silver ring adorned with the Hawthorn emblem.

"You little bastard! I should've strangled you in the cradle!" bellowed the stepfather, thrashing as the boy approached him with a stony expression. The boy's small hand reached out, gently resting on the brute's forehead, as if offering a final moment of forgiveness.

"Mother said one day I'd be able to save people from monsters like you," the boy whispered. "She said life and death are always in balance within me. For her, I always gave life. I couldn't save her, but for you…"

From his palm, a tiny green orb emerged, sinking into the man's forehead. The brute gasped, his body convulsing as his eyes filled with blood. His face twisted in a grotesque spasm, saliva dripping from the corner of his mouth. Within seconds, he fell silent.

I had deliberately chosen not to intervene. The boy needed to face his fear, to exact justice for the years of pain, humiliation, and the loss of his mother. And he had done it. At just nine years old, he hadn't broken down. A small, trembling voice snapped me out of my thoughts. "Am I bad now? Will they arrest me?"

I looked at the child — a boy who had just vanquished his worst nightmare yet was now once again just a child. The adaptability of a young mind is truly remarkable. It was time to leave this place, but first, I knelt before him.

"What's your name?" I asked, leveling with him.

"Andrey."

"And mine — " I hesitated, unsure which name to use. "I have two. At home, I'm Mikhail Yurievich, but here, I'm Gavrila Petrovich."

"Like a spy?" The boy's eyes lit up. "A real

one?"

"Almost," I said with a smile, relieved to see a spark of emotion return to his face. "Remember, you're not bad or good. You are you," I explained. "You avenged yourself and your mother. That was the right thing to do. You had every reason."

The boy had faced too much: his first kill, his first conscious use of power. If I coddled him now, if I showed weakness, he might break. So I spoke to him as an equal. There would be time for grieving later.

"Your power is meant for healing and saving people," I continued. "But if someone comes into your home and tries to hurt you or your family, you can use your gift to defend yourself, just like today. And that will be right — not bad, not good, just right. Do you understand?"

The boy nodded hesitantly.

"Protecting the weak is right, like Maura protected me," he said, placing his small, ringed hand trustingly in mine. Together, without looking back, we left behind the horrors of his past.

I ordered my mosquitoes to drain the corpse completely while the opportunity remained. Their gratitude filtered back to me through the blood link.

We climbed into the carriage in silence. The coachman's eyes widened like saucers at the sight of us. Maura lowered her head, crawling into the boy's lap.

"Forgive me — I disobeyed your orders," came the Bengal's repentant voice. "But he needed this.

Desperately."

"I'm not angry," I admitted, recognizing the truth of her words. "But warn me next time. Did you distract the coachman, too?"

The cat nodded meekly. I accepted the coachman's apologies while silently acknowledging that Andrey, Maura, and Memeow would likely be the cause of many future headaches.

On the way home, I contacted Arseny through the blood link, asking him to prepare a room and clothes for our new guest. I also requested a meeting with Count Boris Sergeyevich Hawthorn, chief physician to the imperial family and Sveta's father. Lastly, I made a note to speak with Teimei — her gift for illusions might help shield Andrey from the nightmares I was certain would come. When life itself is a nightmare, it's hard to separate dreams from reality.

* * *

The meeting was scheduled for early morning and when I arrived, Boris Sergeyevich greeted me personally. Tall, lean, with blond hair and gray eyes, he radiated composure and seriousness.

"Please, follow me, Gavrila Petrovich. Since I've pulled you out of your bed at such an ungodly hour, we should have some green tea to perk us up."

"If you don't mind, I'd prefer coffee," I replied.

"As a healer, I must point out that coffee is less healthy than tea and provides a weaker energizing effect," my host said with a smile. "Professional bias, you understand."

"Life itself is unhealthy as it is — one way or another, it ends up killing you," I quipped. "I prefer to live with enjoyment."

With this light banter, we made our way to the greenhouse. Rows of medicinal plants and exotic flowers grew alongside ordinary trees and small fountains. Hidden in the depths of the greenhouse, behind a strange vine with purple leaves, was a secluded gazebo with a pair of chairs and a tea table.

As soon as we sat down, a servant appeared with a tray bearing our chosen drinks, along with a selection of pastries, chocolates, and crepes with various fillings.

"I must once again apologize for arranging such an early meeting," said Boris Sergeyevich Hawthorn in a measured tone, "but my schedule isn't entirely my own and I cannot always adjust it to my liking."

It was understandable. Being the guardian of the Emperor's health could not be an easy task.

We sipped our morning drinks, easing into a leisurely discussion of current events, including the condition of Akira Inari.

"The lord is still in a magical coma," Boris Sergeyevich said with a resigned shrug. "The Japanese imperial family is demanding that the culprits be punished — or at the very least, that the heir of one of their most influential clans be returned."

"And let me guess, they want the Kuril Islands as a parting gift?" I smirked at the audacity of the Japanese demands.

"Gavrila Petrovich," Boris Sergeyevich's voice shifted to one of professional curiosity, "since we're having this private conversation, tell me — what exactly did you do to him? Maria and Andrey have forbidden me from disturbing you, but I need some way to bring him back to consciousness."

"I didn't do anything," I deflected quickly, quelling any suspicions of supernatural factors. "When the vines attempted to breach his shield, they released a toxin from their systems. In other words, Akira Inari is currently suffering from the very poison he intended for his victim."

Boris Sergeyevich's expression darkened, his demeanor suddenly serious.

"Why didn't you ask for help? You should be dead... the concentration, the dosage..." His gray eyes scrutinized me, noting my generally healthy appearance save for a slight tiredness. "I simply don't understand."

"I've already explained this to Their Highnesses, but I will tell you too: I was wearing a divine artifact. It burned away the toxin, returning it all to Akira," I said, carefully setting aside my empty cup. It was time to broach the topic I had come for. "Boris Sergeyevich, while Akira Inari's fate is undoubtedly intriguing, I requested this meeting for a personal matter."

The healer visibly relaxed, a fatherly smile spreading across his face.

"Of course, Gavrila Petrovich. My daughter warned me about this, but I didn't expect her suitor to be such a notable figure."

It was a good thing I had already finished my coffee — otherwise, I would've sputtered it all over the tea table. So, Svetlana not only had her eye on me but had already dropped hints about it to her father? I had considered settling down eventually, and having a healer in the family would certainly be advantageous, but to have it all handed to me on a silver platter like this? That was unexpected indeed.

"Boris Sergeyevich, Svetlana would be an invaluable addition to any family," I began, testing the waters. "But we wouldn't want to rush things, so I now formally request your permission to court her. I see this union not as a political alliance but as a personal bond. I wouldn't want her to regret any hasty decisions."

Did I just see a flicker of respect in Count Hawthorn's gaze?

"You know, Gavrila Petrovich, I'm glad we see eye to eye on this. Svetlana..." He hesitated, searching for the right words. "She's strong-willed, I won't deny it. But I want her to be happy in her marriage."

"I couldn't agree more," I replied sincerely. "It would be a shame to squander such a rare individual by forcing her into an unhappy union."

My eyes lingered on the ring on the healer's hand. Made of adamantine like mine, it would have been plain if not for the intricate emerald carving of their family's patron deity.

"Does my status trouble you?" Hawthorn asked directly, catching my glance.

"Not at all. If anything, it's my status that should trouble you."

"Happiness doesn't depend on status, Gavrila Petrovich, believe me — I know." Boris Sergeyevich sighed. "I love my children more than life itself, but I couldn't give them a warm family environment. When my wife passed..." He trailed off, lost in thought.

Something didn't quite add up. Boris Sergeyevich was clearly a devoted father, willing to prioritize his daughter's happiness over political gain. It seemed unthinkable that he would abandon a son or grandson to the slums. The family signet ring only deepened the mystery — it wasn't given to just anyone.

"Boris Sergeyevich," I ventured cautiously, "forgive my boldness, but why doesn't Svetlana wear a ring signifying her lineage?"

"Why should she?" he replied with a smile, eager to share their family traditions. "In our line of work, it's a sign of magical immaturity — a symbol of childhood, so to speak. We have silver rings for those of the main family line with healing powers and copper ones for the cadet branches. All are worn until the first initiation, usually around twelve years old. Svetlana, of course, was ahead of the curve, showing her gift at just ten. After initiation, the ring becomes optional, appearing or disappearing at the wearer's will."

I mentally whistled, estimating the strength of the boy I'd taken in, who at his young age was already showing his powers. Perhaps his initiation had occurred spontaneously under stress. Then again, Svetlana herself was no weakling.

"Then how do you explain missing a mage in your family who completed initiation at nine years old?" I asked bluntly. I expected embarrassment — or at least indignation — but Boris Sergeyevich only laughed.

"Impossible, Gavrila Petrovich. The main family line currently has just three members: myself, my twenty-four-year-old son Slava and Svetlana, who just turned eighteen last year. I can guarantee I didn't father another child elsewhere, and my son certainly wouldn't have made me a grandfather at..." He calculated, adding pregnancy to the boy's age, "...under fourteen years old. Don't you think?"

He was smiling, but I found nothing amusing. I wasn't opposed to taking the boy into my family, but once the truth came out, I didn't need additional complications with my future father-in-law. Time to play dumb.

"Boris Sergeyevich, you're probably right," I said, feigning nonchalance. "How many silver rings should there be in your treasury?"

"Five," he replied with a paternal smile.

"Then how do you explain this?" I asked, placing a small wooden box on the table. Inside was the child's ring that Andrey had given me only two hours earlier.

Chapter 22

For the first time during our conversation Count Hawthorn betrayed a reaction. His trembling hands lifted the small box, his gaze locked on the ring inside. A thin stream of greenish light connected the ring to him — a phenomenon I had seen before when Svetlana and Andrey used their hereditary healing powers.

"Incredible, the ring is genuine!" Boris Sergeyevich murmured, dazed, as he returned the ring to the box. His face hardened, his features sharpening. His storm-gray eyes glinted with a cold fury. "Would you care to explain yourself, Gavrila Petrovich?"

"Calm down," I snapped, cutting through his rising anger. The cordial air reigning in the room previously had gone in a flash. "I'm here to determine whether you're even fit to take custody of the child."

"How dare you?" The porcelain teacup in the count's hands shattered with a pitiful crack. "He's part of our family! He doesn't belong in some backwater house with an upstart lordling who lacks connections, money and proper tutors!"

Had I been eighteen, I might have snapped, lashed out or even started a fight. But instead, I simply smirked at the incensed patriarch, and took a bite of a crepe topped with red caviar.

"I dare," I said calmly. "Since when is a princely house with assets exceeding a hundred million in gold considered a 'backwater'?" It was a bluff, of course. I had no real connection to the Vinogradovs, but a good bluff is worth more than its weight in gold. "As for custody of the boy, we do have an emperor with a rather compelling gift. I fear, once the evidence is presented, the trial would not end well for you. Not due to any crime of course, but the overwhelming guilt you'd feel." I wiped my fingers with my napkin, having first dipped them in a bowl with rose water. "And you are sure to feel this guilt once you see the following..."

From the inside pocket of my jacket, I pulled out a small macro and placed it on the table. Unlike the red macros used to nurture Memeow, this one was black — likely due to the emotions I had poured into it while recording my memories.

"That's an unusual macro. Where did you get it?" Count Hawthorn eyed the dark macro warily.

"Trust me, you're better off not knowing," I chuckled, recalling the grim process of its creation.

"How does it work?"

"Like any other macro, though this one is quite weak and contains only memories."

"Memories? Is that even possible?" His eyes widened in disbelief.

"It's a family secret," I said with a sly wink. "Go on — don't be shy."

Hesitantly, he clasped the macro in his hand. His expression went blank as he absorbed its contents. Five minutes later, Boris Sergeyevich stared at me with wild eyes, frozen like a statue.

I poured a generous measure of cognac from the crystal decanter served with our coffee, offering it to my prospective father-in-law.

"Drink this. It'll help."

Wordlessly, he downed the glass without flinching. A second quickly followed, eliciting only a small cough. Healer or not, there's no cure for a man's nerves like a stiff drink.

"It's not every day you find out you've become a grandfather," he said softly. His face cycled through a kaleidoscope of emotions: disbelief, joy, sorrow, shame and even revulsion. Guilt was certainly among them.

I shrugged indifferently, suggesting that stranger things have happened.

"Forgive me," he said, struggling to process the revelations. "I'm trying to understand how this happened. Did my son know? Or was it my late wife's doing? At the time, I was accompanying the Emperor during yet another border skirmish with

the Japanese. I wasn't seeing to household matters. Slava left for the cadet corps at fourteen —
my wife insisted. Less than a year later, she was
gone. Svetlana went to her grandmother. I never
reviewed my wife's accounts. I knew she supported
the poor and sick through her foundation. Dona-
tions flowed regularly in her memory. I drowned
my grief in work, avoiding the empty house. If a
girl sought help then, no one would've been able to
provide it. I didn't know. None of us knew."

I studied the stunned man and, despite everything, believed him. My belief wasn't blind; my
mosquito scouts had already brought me a taste
of his blood. Sharing in his memories, I saw the
truth.

Hawthorn had left family responsibilities to his
wife, missing not only his children's upbringing
but also the birth of his grandson. His wife, however, had been decisive: arranging a marriage for
the girl, giving the grandson a ring, and sending
their son to the cadet corps to instill discipline. Yet
she hadn't foreseen her own death.

"Your story is tragic, but it doesn't change Andrey's current situation," I said, steering the conversation back to my purpose. "In my opinion, he
needs psychological support, education, and medical care. For now, I recommend focusing on building trust and forging a connection with him before
taking him in."

Hawthorn nodded slowly, agreeing. "You're
right. I can only imagine what he thinks of our
family now," he said, clutching his head. "May I at

least meet him and provide treatment? From what I saw in the memories... he needs help."

"That's precisely why I am here today."

Boris Sergeyevich made a few calls on his commulet. One of them surprised me — it wasn't every day a healer defied the emperor's schedule.

"Peter, I need a day off for urgent family matters," Hawthorn said, his voice almost pleading.

"Have you lost your mind, Boris? A day off, with half an hour until the meeting with those mongrels... I'm not sitting down at the table with the Nipponites without your presence! Can't you reschedule?"

"I can't. I've become a grandfather," Hawthorn interrupted, his tone leaving no room for argument.

"What? Was it Slava or Svetlana? No, Svetlana wouldn't... Masha would've known. Slava just left for his posting — how? Young love, I suppose. Congratulations, Boris, but the Nipponites won't care."

"My grandson has multiple injuries — fractures, burns and more. I'm taking the day off, Peter, and the Nipponites can shove Mount Fuji where the sun doesn't rise. We'll deal with them later."

There was silence on the line for a moment.

"Fine. Let the Nipponites meditate for a bit. Go tend to your grandson. You can explain it to me later."

* * *

This is how one discovers the human side of royalty. Both Princess Maria and Prince Andrey, as well as the Emperor Peter Alexeyevich himself, had the capacity for friendship outside the throne room, even if they often struggled to balance personal and state matters.

During the ride to my estate, Hawthorn couldn't sit still. He peppered me with questions about his grandson but abruptly fell silent, his brows furrowing deeply.

"It doesn't add up," he muttered.

I waited quietly, letting him work through his thoughts.

"It doesn't make sense at all," he added, as if for emphasis.

"Gavrila Petrovich," he finally said, fixing me with a sharp, frosty gaze, "you could have taken a uniquely gifted healer into your family, potentially even stronger than me, yet you came to me and told me everything. Why?"

I shrugged noncommittally. Sometimes silence is golden.

"We'd also like to know what's behind this sudden generosity," chimed in Muscadine and Aedes in unison.

"Why don't you argue it out among yourselves?" I teased the gods. "It'll be ten years before the boy grows up and masters his abilities, yet if I present him to Hawthorn now, I can benefit from his family's resources right away. And let's not forget, I plan to bring Svetlana into my family eventually."

No answer followed. Perhaps they'd have laughed if I'd told them the truth — or failed to understand entirely. Svetlana, though willful, had grown up kind and selfless. She healed me without hesitation and even tried to assist me during my interrogation. Someone like her could only have been raised with love and care, not in a tyrannical household. There had to be a good reason for the boy's abandonment, and yet they'd still given him the family ring. It all felt too complex to judge too hastily. It seemed most likely that the boy had simply been... lost. That was what I was thinking on my way to meet Hawthorn that morning, and it turned out to be close to the truth.

Lost in my reflections, I didn't say anything and it fell to Hawthorn to break the silence again.

"I don't understand. Are you truly so indifferent to power, status and wealth? You could have demanded anything from me in exchange for the boy."

"You have all those things," I replied simply. "Did they help save your wife?"

Hawthorn grimaced painedly and averted his gaze. The conversation ended there. I turned to watch the city blocks flash by. The blow to his pride had been necessary, though I sympathized with him. I, too, had once possessed power and resources, yet I hadn't been able to save someone close to me. I had learned from it — apparently, Boris Sergeyevich had not.

* * *

Agatha ran through the forest, barely touching the ground. The sheer joy of feeling strength surging within her, of feeling young and light — alive — was intoxicating.

Twenty-five years. Great Tick! She had waited a quarter century for this moment. She had been one of the most powerful blood mages in her land, only to fall because of her feelings.

She clicked her fangs in irritation.

It was one thing to voluntarily grow old alongside the man she loved, experiencing a life of quiet adventures and intimacy. She'd done that before, taking an indefinite leave from service, changing her appearance and living as an ordinary woman. It was entirely another thing to be bound by a blood oath, shackled on a short leash that tightened at every step. It was suffocating — far worse than any physical torment.

The baron, it seemed, had known something she hadn't foreseen. He had subjugated her, binding her to his family like some familiar.

Blood Almighty! She would have preferred being raped, beaten or tortured to the bondage he forced on her. Anything but the endless days of existing without independence, without freedom. He had made her a puppet with a caged soul, forced to teach, care for and protect his progeny until death.

She had loved the baron madly but she had come to hate him just as fiercely in the end.

When the soul of the last Komarin passed, the leash slackened. One by one, the seals that subjugated her faded away, freeing her abilities, her thirst and her vengeance. The rest was a blur of blood-soaked exhilaration, a kingdom of carnage in which she reigned like a bloody queen.

Memories pierced through the haze: the resurrection of the youngest Komarin, the ring, the sparring — even the explosion. May the Great Tick bless the inventors of instant teleportation scrolls. Without them, she'd have been nothing more than mincemeat beneath the ruins of Hmarevo. It wouldn't have killed her, oh no, but recovering her physical form would have taken eons.

For a month, she indulged in every reckless whim, visiting her sisters to dispel the seals that remained on her. She had succeeded in removing all but one — the blood seal. Though the soul of the last Komarin was gone, the body remained alive. Her ultimate freedom required either the boy's physical death or, less likely, a voluntary release from the family.

If only the old baron had been wiser, like he was in the early years of their acquaintance. Had he not betrayed her, she might have revealed the identity of the one orchestrating their family's downfall. Instead, he had made his choice and his betrayal had bred further betrayal.

She laughed bitterly at the irony. She knew who was behind it all, but she would never tell. The sooner the Komarin line was extinguished completely, the sooner she would be free.

* * *

Tilda greeted us at our manor. This time, she had chosen a formal look — a white pantsuit that accentuated her violet hair and amethyst eyes, as well as her figure. The erg played the role of hostess like a virtuoso, serving tea, coffee and a light breakfast while keeping the conversation light and engaging.

Count Hawthorn was impressed. His expression showed not lust but genuine admiration for what he saw as a work of art. If only he'd witnessed her first appearance at the Vydrin estate — that had been truly jaw-dropping.

We weren't allowed to see Andrey immediately as Teimei was still treating him.

"May I join you?" Hawthorn asked softly. "He's my grandson, after all, and I have more experience as a healer."

"And he hates your entire family," Tilda replied with a sweet smile. "Are you sure your presence won't undo three hours of work by another therapist?"

He had no reply to that. The fear of doing more harm than good won out over familial instincts. Tilda stayed to keep Count Hawthorn company while I left to attend to family matters. I instructed Arseny to commission modern amulets for protection against death mages. In light of recent events, I also contacted Elena to verify that I hadn't fathered any other Komarin heirs. Her reaction was not what I expected.

"Your Grace, it's been some twenty years since anything like this happened, ever since that incident involving your father. But even then, the child was stillborn. Since that time, all young women have been given a special reagent to avoid accidents. But if you want this... well, do you realize how long the line of willing participants would be?"

I matched up the dates and was taken aback. So, what does this mean? Mikhail's father had fathered a bastard while already officially married? Sure, no one would bat an eye at polygamy here, but still, Mikhail's grandfather had married as a widower, and his father and uncles each had only one wife. It seemed everything, as always, came down to personal choice.

I hadn't yet decided which path I'd take. The practical approach would be to form several unions to build alliances and expand my spheres of influence — ideally in the areas of medicine, trade, banking and transportation. After studying my grandfather's records, I was confident I could financially support as many as five wives. But emotionally? Each wife came with a mother-in-law attached. That alone was enough to give me pause. At least they wouldn't be dropping by unannounced, thanks to Hmarevo being on restricted territory. That at least was one small mercy.

Lost in thought, I didn't realize I'd reached Teimei's room. The door swung open silently, and I peeked inside. The young woman was sitting cross-legged on a plush light rug, not far from the fireplace where we'd had the bridal shower just a couple of weeks earlier. She was gently stroking Andrey's golden curls as he slept soundly in her lap. My two fluffy companions, Maura and Memeow, were curled up around the boy. The scene was so tender and domestic that it felt utterly out of place in the chaos of the past month.

Teimei was quietly singing in her native language, and I noticed a smoky tapestry of dreams emanating from her fingers, swaddling the child in their illusion. Andrey smiled in his sleep, a bright, joyful expression on his face. I didn't know what dreams Teimei was spinning for him, but they were clearly the happiest ones he'd known in his bleak life.

As she sang I melted into her voice, which rippled like forest birdsong. It carried me far away, to the Neva River embankment, where a little boy walked hand in hand with a young, beautiful woman. He was eating ice cream, his laughter ringing pure and bright. The river sparkled with countless reflections, a gentle breeze brought coolness to its shores, refreshing the small, happy family in its stroll. Watching them filled me with peace and tranquility — a feeling of serenity that shattered into a thousand shards when, through the blood link, the Mosquito school's perimeter defense system sent me an alert.

A moment later Spider's voice came in through the blood link:

"Baron, the death mage is here!"

Chapter 23

I IMMEDIATELY TOOK OFF, sprinting back to Hawthorn's room. If there was anyone who knew how to handle a death mage, it would have to be the imperial healer.

Bursting into the room, I hit him with two questions right off the bat:

"Boris Sergeyevich, how do we fight death mages?" I unbuttoned my shirt to reveal the chain holding three oak talismans. "And how much time will this artifact's protection buy us?"

Count Hawthorn gave me a condescending smile and, unfortunately, a response I didn't want to hear.

"Gavrila Petrovich, all death mages are registered. Each has a unique mana signature. If one of them starts a clan war, it'll be their death sentence."

"If I wanted a lecture, I would've asked for one!"

I barked at the healer, unable to contain my frustration. "My people are in danger! How much time do they have?"

At last, it seemed the gravity of the situation dawned on him.

"That combination should withstand either one area of effect spell, three group spells or nine individually targeted attacks," he explained hesitantly.

"What do you mean by 'area of effect' and 'group spells'?" I pressed, unsure what these terms entailed in this plane.

"An area of effect or AoE spell covers two soccer fields and about one soccer field for the latter."

"May Aedes and the Blood Spirit save us," I muttered in horror. "What's the cooldown period between those spells?"

"Ten minutes," he stammered, blushing as his gaze fell on Tilda, who had started removing her clothing with mechanical precision.

"Three of those minutes are already gone," I snapped my fingers in front of his face to pull him out of his daze. "Weapons? What works against them?"

"Anything can kill them, but they usually strike from a distance while staying out of sight."

Finally, some good news. I pulled out the portal scrolls from my inner pocket. My people wouldn't be left defenseless — not while my heart still beat.

"I'm going with you!" Tilda and Hawthorn said at once.

"What?" Tilda bristled, her eyes flashing with defiance. "I missed the orgy. I'm not missing the fight."

As my friend's skin shimmered with camouflage scales, the healer couldn't take his eyes off her.

"I can identify the mage's signature and treat the injured, but only a life mage can bring someone back from the dead," Hawthorn explained.

"We've got one," I murmured, handing out the transfer scrolls to my allies. "We just need to make it in time."

Thank Aedes, the scrolls worked flawlessly this time. Two transfers later, we'd lost more precious minutes, but we arrived at Little Quagmire.

"Damn it all!" Of the litany of curses I uttered as we arrived, this was the only printable phrase. Up to three hundred civilians could be caught in this crossfire and I hadn't even considered them! Damn it! I'd gotten too used to living alone, out on the edge of nowhere, all by my great and terrible self. But here things were different!

Wait. The edge... Of course!

"Spider, tell me we've got boats, rafts, anything, and that you've started evacuating the civilians to the open waters of Lake Ladoga!" I prayed silently to Aedes and the Blood Spirit, awaiting the answer.

"Yes, Your Grace!" came the reply from the commander of my bloodbound. "We've set up a temporary base on Valaam. Little Quagmire is being evacuated, and cadets are being transported here. Portal scrolls don't work on school grounds, though," he added, his voice tinged with apology. "Still, we've used most of our scroll reserves. Almost three and a half hundred souls..."

I exhaled in relief. Better to pay with gold than with lives.

"Where was the mage spotted? How much time do we have?"

"He's coming from Lakhdenpokhya, following the same route that Marcus's defectors took. Estimated time until he is in position to attack is thirty minutes."

Hawthorn shifted nervously from foot to foot, confused as to why we'd suddenly stopped in the middle of the forest near an unfamiliar village despite my urgency.

"How did you manage to detect the death mage?" I pressed for details.

"Our men out in the field were attacked with a death vortex three times but couldn't figure out where the attack came from. They had to use portal scrolls to retreat back to the school."

That was the right decision. I didn't have enough clan members to waste on suicidal heroics. A tactical retreat in order to regroup was the smartest move — especially since it would be easier for me to defend everyone in one place. I had an idea, but first, I needed to get everyone else to safety.

"Gavrila Petrovich, what are we waiting for? Time is running out!" Count Hawthorn interjected, drawing my attention.

"I'm receiving situational updates," I replied while continuing my blood link conversation with Spider. "When will the cadets arrive?"

"In ten minutes. They think it's just another drill."

I turned to Hawthorn and asked what was probably one of the stupidest questions of my life:

"Boris Sergeyevich, what's your security clearance level?"

"Top secret, of course," the imperial healer answered cautiously. "Why do you ask?"

"Because you're standing on a classified facility belonging to a covert subdivision of the Ministry of Defense, deeded to the Komarin family by direct decree of Emperor Alexei Krechet. Everything you see and learn here is strictly confidential." I paused to let him absorb the information. "Now, I must ask you to swear an oath of non-disclosure regarding any of my family's powers or techniques that you witness here. For clarity's sake, this oath will be mutual."

Hawthorn's eyebrows slowly climbed upward. His expression clearly said, "What could you possibly show me that outdoes the hybrid magic you used to defend the princess?" But the truth was that we were capable of far more than that.

However, Boris Sergeyevich wouldn't have been the imperial family's healer if he didn't know how to keep secrets. No sooner did he take the oath of secrecy, than the faint rumble of engines came from behind us. On the outskirts of Little Quagmire, pairs of bloodbound and cadets rode in on strange three-wheeled ATVs. Although light-weight and maneuverable, they were loud and had limited carrying capacity.

The instructors cut the engines and began herding the chaotic crowd into a semblance of order with brisk commands. Instructions were given on the move: conduct reconnaissance, set up a fortified camp, coordinate civilians, and ensure their protection. Each cadet received a portal scroll, broke its seal and vanished into the portals.

A light touch on my shoulder told me who it was before I turned. Behind me stood four cadets who had joined the rescue effort during the breach. Their faces were tense and they had scrolls clutched tightly in their hands, but they hadn't used them yet.

"This isn't a drill, is it?" Sveta said, looking into my eyes searchingly. "Let us stay. We can help."

"No, it isn't," I admitted, choosing honesty to prevent reckless heroics. "A rogue death mage is waging war on us. You're going to Valaam where you'll be out of harm's way."

Did I imagine it, or did even Medvedev flinch at the news? For her part, Sveta only raised her chin defiantly. I shook my head. There was a time for bravery and a time for following orders. I leaned close to her ear and whispered firmly, "Don't even think about it. Not now. If you stay, both your father and I will be too focused on keeping you safe to fight properly. Don't make our job harder — I'm begging you."

I was shamelessly manipulating her, using a

heated tone, appealing to her sense of responsibility, and even bringing up her father all to make a heartfelt plea. And it worked. Her shoulders slumped in reluctant resignation. Taking her hands in mine, I gave them a reassuring squeeze, not expecting her to pull me in toward her for a sudden, forceful kiss.

Pulling back, she hissed angrily, "You'd better not die here, or I'll come and drag you back from the afterlife myself! You still owe me!" Her fingers found the seal on her scroll, but her voice softened as she added, "And tell my father I love him."

I nodded, and she vanished.

Tilda and Hawthorn stared at me with unreadable expressions. I'd figure things out with Tilda later, but Boris Sergeyevich would need a very different explanation for a kiss with a strange girl while supposedly courting his daughter.

"Your daughter sends her regards," I said, deliberately breezy. "Said she's planning on preparing us some barbecue in Valaam in time for our return and that we should hurry."

The look on Hawthorn's face was priceless. He opened and closed his mouth like a fish out of water before regaining his composure.

"Well, Sveta, you've really outdone yourself this time... So this is Madam Duplessis' finishing school..." he muttered, shaking his head to clear it. "What's our next move?"

"We return to the school and prepare to defend it. I've got a couple of surprises ready for that bastard."

* * *

Strangely enough, the situation had reached a stalemate. The mage couldn't reach us, holed up like rats in a burrow, and we couldn't locate him out in the vast forest. Blindly striking out wasn't an option — my bloodbound's spells lacked the range of the death mage's. For the past half hour, we'd been putting on more of a show of resistance than actually fighting back.

And yet, my men had earned their keep. Without their prayers to Aedes, our shield wouldn't have lasted this long. For the first hour, the spell held on sheer power and skillful control. And still, the damned death mage showed no signs of exhaustion.

At the start of the second hour, I contacted Beetle, who was overseeing the civilians and cadets. I quickly outlined the situation and asked him to organize a prayer circle or something similar in honor of Aedes. Within fifteen minutes, I could see the stream of prayers replenishing the mana pool in the basement.

"What's going on here?" Aedes' voice rang out five minutes later.

"They're trying to kill us," I said flatly. "A death mage — level five or six, with macro-enhancements. He's been hammering us non-stop for two hours now."

"Son of a — " muttered our patron deity. Apparently, even gods could curse colorfully. "Draw as much power as you can from the mana pool, then bring in the Hmarevo villagers. I'll transfer everything to you. And listen..." he hesitated. "Don't die yet. I'll figure something out."

The voice faded, but I kept the shield up — a feat that, given my current level of magic and the restrictive seals on my arm, was nothing short of heroic.

By the third hour, I contacted Elena and asked her, by any means necessary, to get the Hmarevo villagers praying to Aedes. I don't know what she told them, but fifteen minutes later, I was functioning as a conduit in two directions. Aedes channeled mana into me from the faithful and I diverted part of it into the mana pool while using the rest to sustain the shield.

Hawthorn had his hands full too. Magical exhaustion was a condition that caused damage to the body's weakest organs and systems, tearing up whichever was most vulnerable. For the past two hours, he'd been patching up those injuries in both me and the elemental mages.

As bizarre as it sounds, I found myself contemplating how valuable a death mage could be to my family. A mage of this caliber was a rare prize for any bloodline. But how could I possibly recruit one?

It wasn't the oath that worried me. Even our patron deity couldn't locate the death mage on his territory. The more immediate problem was not getting annihilated in the process.

The clue — and unexpected help — came from an unlikely source. At the edge of my blood sense,

I suddenly felt the presence of another family member, though the link was... strange, almost servile. Imagine my shock when I realized it was the dowager baroness herself, Agatha Petrovna Komarin.

* * *

Agatha was ready for everything and anything, except being contacted directly by the Komarin family's patron god. By birth, she was a Kleshcheva, whose patron god was the Great Tick, but through an oath and wedlock, she had become a Komarin. The gods, however, were no fools — they didn't meddle with those who didn't believe in them.

Her relationship with Aedes had always been a sort of armed standoff. He didn't require worship from her, but he didn't tolerate any invocation of the Great Tick either.

"Well, hello there, baroness," came a mocking voice in her head. "I see you've been busy — you've nearly dispelled all your binding seals."

"Hello... to you too," Agatha managed to stammer, forcing politeness toward what was, essentially, a foreign god. "Well, I'm not the only one who cheats, but at least I don't announce it to the whole world," she said, apparently alluding to Aedes summoning my soul from another plane.

"And you're right not to," the god replied. "You've always been a clever woman. It's a shame things didn't work out with the baron."

"Didn't work out? What business is that of yours?" she sounded like she wanted to snap, but held her tongue out of common sense.

"You see? Clever," Aedes chuckled, evidently reading her thoughts. "I can release you from your oath to my family, freeing you without any loss of power or accompanying curses."

"And who am I supposed to kill for you to do that? The Emperor?" she retorted sarcastically, unable to believe her ears.

Such offers didn't exist — gods never willingly let go of their believers. It would be like giving up free faith, prestige and reputation. No — a freebie like that could only be cheese in a mouse trap.

"Maybe you won't have to kill anyone," the god mused with some hesitation. "But knowing you, killing wouldn't be a problem. Help the Komarins at the school, and I'll set you free. You have my divine word!"

For a brief moment, a shadow of an enormous mosquito appeared before Agatha, blotting out the sun. It was enough to send chills down her spine. Whatever was happening at the school, it must be serious if such a unique reward was on the table.

"I accept," the baroness agreed, pulling a portal scroll from her cloak. She would've used her reusable teleportation ring, but the youngest Komarin still had it. She wondered if he'd learned how to use it yet.

Arriving outside Little Quagmire, the last thing Agatha expected was to hear the thunder of a ferocious magical battle. The closer she got to the school, the clearer it became — this wasn't some scrap; it was an outright brawl of life and death.

On one side was a death mage of considerable strength, and on the other… She wished she knew who was holding the defense for the Komarins.

To avoid being caught in the crossfire, Agatha used a hereditary ability that had once made her one of the best spies in the land: *Death Feint*. This ability mimicked the complete cessation of vital processes, rendering her neither alive nor dead. Life and death magic had no effect on her — she was simply a shadow, observing and analyzing.

The death mage wasn't holding back, unleashing spell after spell at the school, none of them weaker than mid-tier. Yet he remained hidden. Out of curiosity, the shadow slipped closer to observe him. He was strong, undoubtedly a Level 5 or 6, but no mage could sustain such an unrelenting barrage of magic for long.

She noted how he clenched another macro in his fist to replenish his strength.

"You're a suicidal fool, darling!" the shadow thought. "If you're this reliant on macros, addiction must be right around the corner. Or maybe you've got nothing left to lose," she added to herself, noting the savage, almost possessed expression on the mage's face.

The surrounding forest had long since been reduced to dust, grass and shrubs had crumbled to powder, and the ground beneath death mage's feet had turned to ash. Even the stone buildings near the school were cracking, yet those inside were still alive. Spells of water, wind and earth periodically lashed out from within, vainly trying to strike the enemy. The elemental mages wouldn't have lasted more than a few hits if not for the strange, flickering crimson dome over the school. The death mage's spells simply slid off it, dispersing into the surroundings.

Ever the scholar of sorcery, Agatha was captivated by the dome's origins and energy source. In her studies of ancient texts, she had encountered something similar — a personal blood magic shield crafted on battlefields from literal rivers of blood. But that was enough to protect only one mage, and here was a shield covering an entire building! "Who *are* you?" she thought.

"Why do you hesitate, Agatha Petrovna?" came a familiar voice in her head. "Standing there on the threshold, afraid to check in on your grandson? What if he's been missing you?"

CHAPTER 24

"Why do you hesitate, Agatha Petrovna?" I addressed my grandmother through the blood link. "Standing there on the threshold, afraid to check in on your grandson? What if he's been missing you?"

Her response was dead silence. I'd always known my sense of humor left something to be desired. And in situations like this, my tongue was my worst enemy.

"Jokes aside, Agatha Petrovna, we've got a death mage holed up somewhere nearby, slinging mid-tier spells like he's got a magical machine gun," I warned her quickly. She had saved me from an explosion that destroyed our entire manor and I considered it polite to return the favor. "Be careful and don't get hit. These days, us Komarins are worth our weight in gold."

"Well, hello, grandson! I've got some questions

for you," she replied, sounding somewhat flustered. "I know about the mage. But who's casting that intriguing blood shield of yours?"

"Do you like it?"

"Of course! But I don't see rivers of blood fueling it," she remarked uncertainly.

"Blood's only needed at the base level. After that, you can use raw mana," I explained, sharing the principle behind the upgraded blood shield protecting us. Judging by her colorful curse (in a language I didn't recognize) Nan was impressed indeed.

"Impressive," was her concise verdict.

"You impress me too," I replied, with no hint of flattery. "Bloodbound keys are one thing, but backup defensive circuits in armored vehicles powered by mage blood? I nearly tore myself in half trying to transport eleven people through one portal scroll — and those tightwads brought two armored vehicles with them!"

"Nonsense!" she shot back, a mix of disbelief and admiration in her voice. "Everyone knows one scroll equals one person!"

"Ask Spider later — he'll confirm it!" I laughed.

She didn't say anything, and I didn't rush her. She'd come here for a reason, fully aware of the risks. Aedes might have promised her something tempting, but I wouldn't boss her around or give orders. What worked better than any command was the servile bond tied to the baroness. Treating one of our own like that didn't sit right with me. To me, she was a Komarin, and her forced bondage was a stain on my family's reputation. That would have to change.

"You're a curious one, grandson," Agatha said at last. "But it remains to see just how curious. Let's get to work. I can kill the death mage and end your siege," she offered casually, as if it were the simplest thing in the world.

What kind of enhancements did she have at her disposal to be so confident that she could wade into a storm of death magic? Yet her tone left no doubt — Agatha seemed absolutely sure of her abilities.

"Killing him would be too easy," I admitted honestly. "And I'd hate to waste a magical machine gun like that. Can you at least pinpoint his location first?"

Oddly, there was no need for further explanation. Instead of replying, Agatha shared her memory of watching the death mage consuming the macros.

"You're incredible, Nan," I said, unable to hide my admiration. She'd been close enough to breathe down his neck, and he hadn't noticed a thing. "Can you just knock him out for now? We'll send him to a corrective labor camp. He'll come back a changed mage."

"Misha, did you fall down the stairs? Are you suffering from exhaustion? What corrective labor camp?" Agatha snapped. "This is an unregistered death mage who's gone rogue! He needs to be eliminated, end of story! The crown will thank you — and in cash, no less."

"Listen here, granny," I snapped, "This family has more money than it knows what to do with. What we don't have is a death mage of our own. Are you catching my drift or do you have more questions to pester me with?"

My reply came out sharper and more overbearing than I intended, yet while we sat their arguing, my blood boiled painfully in my veins. Divine grace wasn't endless, and I didn't want to consume macros by the dozen like that suicidal fool. The last thing I needed was to become an addict.

"Understood, Your Excellence," Agatha replied in an utterly neutral tone.

Great. I'd let my emotions get the better of me and had probably forced her compliance with sheer authority. Ugh. This had to be fixed.

"How long will it take to neutralize the threat?"

"Five minutes," came her equally emotionless reply.

"Understood. Keep an eye on him, if you'd be so kind," I asked, trying to smooth over the awkwardness of my earlier outburst.

"As you wish, Your Grace," she replied.

* * *

Boris Sergeyevich Hawthorn had been watching Gavrila Petrovich with growing unease for hours. The young man had been holding the line against a death mage entirely on his own.

Nestled deep in the Karelian forest and surrounded by swamps, the stone keep they were in commanded respect. But its purpose was unclear. The complete absence of family magic in this location suggested it was no ordinary place. Count Hawthorn was no weak mage himself and had a significant magical reserve. Yet he couldn't remember the last time he'd had to dig so deep to summon so much magical resistance. Normally, he worked with his hereditary magic and here, that wasn't an option. What astonished him even more was how Gavrila Petrovich had managed to sustain the battle for four straight hours. The other fighters, clad in black military uniforms with no insignia aside from the mosquito emblem, weren't idle either. They took turns casting complex AoE spells, trying to locate the hidden enemy, though so far, their efforts had been fruitless.

What stood out most was the seamless coordination between Vinogradov and his soldiers. They obeyed him without question. Often, it seemed they communicated telepathically, only vocalizing commands or requests when addressing Boris Sergeyevich. No, that wasn't entirely accurate. Everyone else here coordinated openly, but Gavrila Petrovich didn't need to. The more the healer observed him, the more amazed he was. What kind of reserves must he have? And what kind of magic was this, anyway? Boris suspected blood magic as, before the shield appeared over the fortress, Vinogradov had painted strange runes on the basement floor with his own blood.

Telepathy had nothing to do with this — at least, not directly. Then there were the partially sentient vines and roses, which, with great difficulty, could be tied to the Vinogradov family magic. Plant breeders were always coming up with the strangest creations and then marveling at what they'd wrought. Count Hawthorn had his share of similar experiences, though on a smaller scale. Still, he vividly remembered the spitting hawthorn plant from his botany classes — it left an impression that lingered for years.

Vinogradov's warning about state secrets and the oath he'd forced him to take to protect family secrets flashed in his mind. Alongside this came memories of mentions of the Komarin family and their ownership of the land. The mosquito emblems on the soldiers' uniforms clearly hinted at who ruled these parts.

What wasn't clear was why the Komarin family's servants obeyed Vinogradov — or what all these young people were doing here.

Boris Sergeyevich worked hard to push away the thought that his daughter might be nearby. As a father, it was easier to accept that her future fiancé had been caught kissing someone else right before his eyes than to believe that Svetlana had traded Madam Duplessis' finishing school for some experimental military testing ground in the remote wilderness of Karelia.

"Oh, Svetlana, did you meet your unusual beau here?" he wondered. All signs seemed to point to that, and now the doctor had questions — not just for Vinogradov but for his daughter as well.

Suddenly, Gavrila Petrovich, who had been sitting with his eyes closed, stood up, swaying and leaning against the wall. Tilda immediately steadied him, offering her shoulder for support.

"Grid coordinates 6-6. We've got fifteen minutes to slap suppression spells on him before he comes to," Vinogradov rasped. "Oh, and Agatha Petrovna sends her regards to everyone."

Some of the soldiers broke into smiles, even cheering, "She's back, that old bloodsucker!" Others whistled. A few looked puzzled but asked no questions.

"Tilda, your task is to pack up our gift and take it home for some... corrective work," Vinogradov instructed his companion, his smile tinged with venom.

"You mean all the way home?" Tilda emphasized the word, her tone dubious.

"All the way."

"And can I discipline him however I see fit?" The gleam of anticipation in the violet-haired beauty's eyes was impossible to miss.

"Go for it!" Vinogradov replied wearily, only to be nearly bowled over as Tilda threw her arms around him, exclaiming:

"Thank you, thank you, thank you! This is the best gift ever!" She gave Gavrila Petrovich a quick kiss on the cheek and darted off.

"I still need him alive for the family, Tilda!" Vinogradov called after her, shaking his head with a bemused smile. "Women," he muttered to the doctor. "Sergey Borisovich, do me a favor — patch me up. One more step, and I might crumble like an old rotten stump. And we've still got a young troublemaker to catch."

The relationship between Vinogradov and Tilda raised even more questions. Were they friends? Siblings? Something more?

Scanning Vinogradov's body and magical channels, Hawthorn was surprised. His mana reserves weren't completely depleted, but the wear on his channels was severe. The doctor couldn't explain such damage in just four hours. After patching him up as best he could, Hawthorn finally admitted:

"Gavrila Petrovich, you're raising more questions than I'm allowed to have, given the classified nature of this facility. But as the father of the girl you've expressed interest in courting, I'm finding your background very curious."

"Trust me, Sergey Borisovich, you're not the only one," Vinogradov replied as they followed the soldiers out of the dank basement and climbed onto the ATVs. "But until I eliminate the threat to my family, you won't be getting any answers. Sorry."

*　*　*

Arkady Ivanovich Krysin instinctively hunched his shoulders. His companion's voice was quiet and calm, but the weight of his words made them all the more terrifying.

"Arkasha, you've disappointed me. Thirty years ago, I pulled you out of a sewer and gave you a chance to improve your station in life. A good position, the status of family head and a successful match didn't all fall into your lap by accident, you know."

Krysin couldn't see his companion. His keen sense of smell caught traces of cigar smoke, a hint of alcohol, and, predictably, the scent of a man who'd just indulged himself. Exotic women usually put his patron deity in a good mood, but not today.

"You know better than anyone what I do with nonperforming assets," the patron said. Krysin shuddered as the next words came. "I can't hear your answer!"

"You feed them to the rats," Krysin stammered.

"Exactly, Arkasha! But for every rat, I've got a cat. Here, kitty, kitty!"

A black panther sauntered past Krysin. In the dimly lit room, the firelight from the hearth cast shadows as the deadly predator stretched out at the patron's feet, still licking her lips contentedly. Krysin had once witnessed her hunt — watching as a man, bound by suppression spells, was cornered and torn to shreds by this "kitty."

The message was clear. Arkady Ivanovich had gone from managing minor pawns, those who fed the rats, to becoming a liability himself — one step away from being fed to something far worse.

"I'll take care of everything," Krysin mumbled submissively.

"Arkasha, our enemies are digging beneath you and they're digging deep. The hole's as big as the Kremlin tower! But they haven't touched you yet, which means either you've been exceptionally thorough in covering your tracks, or Orlov is giving the Komarin family room to deal with you themselves and keep this entire mess private."

A pause filled the room, broken only by wet, slurping sounds interspersed with feminine moans. Krysin's gaze fixated on the shadow of a girl moving rhythmically between the patron's legs.

"Good girl — just as we agreed," he thought.

Minutes later, the sounds ceased, punctuated by the sharp slap of a hand on bare skin.

"Arkasha," the patron said, his voice relaxed but commanding, "make sure not even the Emperor can take this land from us."

"It shall be done!" Krysin vowed. "In the family struggle to come, our rats will devour them all!"

END OF BOOK ONE

Want to be the first to know about our latest LitRPG, sci fi and fantasy titles from your favorite authors?

Subscribe to our **New Releases** newsletter:
http://eepurl.com/b7niIL

Thank you for reading *The Blood Code!*

If you like what you've read, check out other LitRPG novels published by Magic Dome Books:

NEW RELEASES!

The Hunter's Code
A Portal Progression Fantasy Series
by Oleg Sapphire & Yuri Vinokuroff

The One Who Changes the Future
A Dystopian Portal Progression Fantasy Series
by Boris Romanovsky

How I Built a Magic Empire
A Portal Progression Fantasy Series
by Konstantin Zubov

The Afflicted
A LitRPG Apocalypse Adventure Series
by Konstantin Zubov

Banned
A LitRPG Adventure Series
By Michael Atamanov

An Ideal World for a Sociopath
A LitRPG Apocalypse Adventure Series
by Oleg Sapphire

The Healer's Way
A Portal Progression Fantasy Series
by Oleg Sapphire & Alexey Kovtunov

The Selected
A LitRPG Action Adventure Series
by Vasily Mahanenko & Yuri Vinokuroff

The Last Portal Jumper
A LitRPG Progression Fantasy Series
by Konstantin Zubov

The Dark Healer
A Historical Progression Fantasy Series
by Alex Toxic & Nadya Lee

The Strongest Student
A Portal Progression Action Fantasy Series
by Andrei Tkachev

A Shelter in Spacetime
A LitRPG Apocalypse Series
by Dmitry Dornichev

The Coming of God of Death
A Portal Progression Fantasy Series
by Dmitry Dornichev

The Village
A LitRPG Progression Fantasy Series
by Dmitry Dornichev & Alexey Kovtunov

Law of the Jungle
A Wuxia Progression Fantasy Adventure Series
by Vasily Mahanenko

Condemned (Lord Valevsky: Last of the Line)
A Progression Fantasy LitRPG Series
by Vasily Mahanenko

Living Ice
A Portal Progression Fantasy Series
by Dmitry Sheleg

Ghost in the System
An Apocalypse LitRPG Series
by Alexey Kovtunov

Crossroads of Oblivion
A Portal Progression Fantasy Adventure Series
by Dem Mikhailov

More books and series are coming out soon!

In order to have new books of the series translated faster, we need your help and support! Please consider leaving a review or spread the word by recommending *The Blood Code* to your friends and posting the link on social media. The more people buy the book, the sooner we'll be able to make new translations available.

Thank you!

Till next time!